WHEN WORLDS COLLIDE

Other Anthologies Edited by:

Patricia Bray & Joshua Palmatier

After Hours: Tales from the Ur-bar
The Modern Fae's Guide to Surviving Humanity
Temporally Out of Order * Alien Artifacts * Were-
All Hail Our Robot Conquerors!
Second Round: A Return to the Ur-bar
The Modern Deity's Guide to Surviving Humanity

S.C. Butler & Joshua Palmatier

Submerged * Guilds & Glaives * Apocalyptic
When Worlds Collide

Laura Anne Gilman & Kat Richardson

The Death of All Things

Troy Carrol Bucher & Joshua Palmatier

The Razor's Edge

Patricia Bray & S.C. Butler

Portals

David B. Coe & Joshua Palmatier

Temporally Deactivated * Galactic Stew
Derelict

Steven H Silver & Joshua Palmatier

Alternate Peace

Crystal Sarakas & Joshua Palmatier

My Battery Is Low and It Is Getting Dark

WHEN WORLDS COLLIDE

Edited by

S.C. Butler
&
Joshua Palmatier

Zombies Need Brains LLC
www.zombiesneedbrains.com

Interior Design (ebook): ZNB Design
Interior Design (print): ZNB Design
Cover Design by ZNB Design
Cover Art "When Worlds Collide"
by Justin Adams of Varia Studios

ZNB Book Collectors #22
All characters and events in this book are fictitious.
All resemblance to persons living or dead is coincidental.

Kickstarter Edition Printing, June 2021
First Printing, July 2021

Print ISBN-13: 978-1940709420

Ebook ISBN-13: 978-1940709437

Printed in the U.S.A.

COPYRIGHTS

Table of Contents

SIGNATURE PAGE

S.C. Butler, editor:

_____

Joshua Palmatier, editor:

_____

Christopher Leapock:

_____

Howard Andrew Jones:

_____

Gary Kloster:

_____

Louis Evans:

_____

Peter S. Drang:

_____

Esther Friesner:

_____

S.C. Butler:

_____

Nancy Holzner:

_____

Nancy Holzner:

_____

Auston Habershaw:

_____

Violette Malan:

_____

Stephen Leigh:

_____

Alan Smale:

_____

Steven Harper:

_____

Jordan Chase-Young:

_____

Justin Adams, artist:

_____

The Erratics

Christopher Leapock

I'd turned the transceiver volume almost, but not quite, all the way down. Sensors were skimming the planet surface, recording the sounds produced by organic life forms and replaying them slowed down to my time frame. They were mostly bird calls, mostly uninteresting, though every few minutes there was a sudden trumpet-blast or a rumbling like a landslide. This particular call went on for a long time. I didn't pay it much attention until I heard the second one, higher-pitched and shorter. Then the first resumed.

The audio switched over to some aquatic animal letting out an echoey howl. My hand scrabbled over my bedside table, knocking a box of tissues onto the floor, till I found the transceiver. I went to Recently Played and upped the volume.

I'd only heard a sample—the full recording was three minutes long. Two voices alternated in a chaotic burbling of cooing and clucking. My heart was racing. I started a schematic analysis, but was too impatient to wait for it to finish. So on a hunch I had the computer measure the time gaps between the calls. It was perfectly consistent. One ended, then 200 msec later the other creature began. Back and forth just like that.

They were turn-taking. It was a *conversation*. There were beings on my planet with recombinant language.

I crawled out of bed and over to the planet. It floated above a stack of *Popular Mechanics* magazines, a cyan ball with a ghostly nimbus like a shawl over its shoulder—actually the moon, orbiting millions of times faster than the eye could follow. Instead of a sun, my planet was next to an articulated desk lamp, but I'd calibrated the light to give the optimal level of photonic energy. I activated the slo-mo setting and I could see the individual continents, mostly green with beige patches towards the middle, and the blue oceans between them. (This was a holographic recording superimposed on my planet, obviously. I don't need to tell you what would happen if I really dropped it into a time scale seven orders of magnitude slower.)

I couldn't believe it. This was what I'd been waiting for all month. My planet had evolved intelligent life.

I was definitely going to get an A in biology.

* * *

Over the next few days, I spent every spare minute watching my lifeforms through a microscope. They were bipedal, which was no surprise given the therapod layout they'd evolved from. They were covered with thermoregulative down, with long iridescent tectrices extending from their forelimbs and their tails. They could fan these out and rotate the individual feathers to make their plumage shine with different colors. I never did figure out if that was a form of communication or if they were just showing off.

But they were culturally stagnant. They lived as simple hunters with stone tools. I got excited when they figured out the throwing spear, but for hundreds of generations after that they passed down the same toolkit unaltered.

I slid out an issue from the pile of magazines under the planet— very carefully, because three weeks earlier I'd grazed it with the corner of a page and caused a megatsunami that wiped out one third of all species. I'd dogeared the article I wanted. *Are Your Lifeforms Intelligent but Uninventive? Ten Tricks for Getting That Spark Back Into Your Life.* I started tinkering with their brains— just little changes here and there, delaying maturation, enhancing analogical reasoning, all that. But all I managed to do was make a race of time-wasters who barely clung to survival while they devoted their resources to elaborate burials and inventing new forms of feather pigments.

The night before my project was due, I was getting depressed. And all of a sudden they had the bow and arrow. Four hours later in my time frame, they'd domesticated hunting raptors. They spread out over the planet. Near the poles they were wearing down coats made from other animals.

I barely slept that night. When morning came I was staring bleary-eyed into the microscope. There was banging on my bedroom door. "William Alexander Obateru!" came my mother's voice. "Your breakfast is getting cold."

"Mom! My therapods have animal husbandry and a form of agriculture and the wheel and I think they're going to make their first oceanic crossing! I can't miss it! It's a technological milestone!"

"There will be lots of other milestones," said my mother. "You are not going to be late for school again."

* * *

On the drive, I sat in the back of the van, peering into the microscope and shouting updates. "Mom! They developed an occupation-based caste system!" "Mom! They invented antibiotics! No, never mind. They just burned the inventor at the stake. I think those ones have a weird religion. Their leaders clip their tail feathers, which I think is like monks shaving their heads."

"Wow," she replied in the tone of voice she used when she wasn't listening.

By the time we pulled into the parking lot, my therapods were starting to use steam-powered vehicles.

Samen Chen arrived on his bike, pulling his planet in a little red wagon.

"You have to see this," I said, pushing the microscope at him. "They reached industrialization and—"

"Mine industrialized yesterday afternoon," said Samen. "And then they burned all the fossil fuels on the planet. When I woke up this morning the surface temperature was up eight degrees and everyone was dead." He had a look on his face like his vital organs were being repossessed by the bank. "But there was intelligent life for a little while. That's good enough for a B, right?"

I put down the microscope. It really didn't seem like a good time to show him a video of a therapod riding a steam-powered motorcycle. My transceiver was still on and it played a sound like an explosion, but drawn-out. I paused the planet's spinning and zoomed in on a tiny bright streak traveling through the upper atmosphere. "They just discovered rocketry."

"Good for you," said Samen weakly.

We went into the classroom and I put my planet down on my desk. Ani Jaswal, who sits next to me, motioned to her microscope. "You have to see my lifeforms. They have little puppy dog faces. They're *soooooo cute.*"

I gave them a look—they were like a species of bipedal shih tzus. "Did you *seriously* dress them up in three-piece suits?"

"Only after they invented clothing themselves, so it's not inappropriate interference." It wasn't really an intelligent species, after all, if you taught it everything. They had to learn to invent things on their own.

My disgust must have been showing, because Ani narrowed her eyes and said, "What are yours, dinosaurs?"

"Non-avian therapods."

"That's a kind of dinosaur, you twit. Are you six years old? Because you spent a month playing with dinosaurs."

"My species is in the middle of a technological explosion."

"Mine have always been cautious with adopting new technologies. They carefully ensure everyone in society will benefit because they're *such good doggies yes you are.*"

"Mine ride steam-powered motorcycles."

She snorted.

"I don't care what you think," I said. "It's friggin' awesome. I'm naming the species *Sapioraptor frigginawesomensis.*"

Later that day we pieced together that it was then, while I was looking away from the microscope, that my therapods fired a probe out of the atmosphere. It drifted across the aisle between our desks and settled into orbit around Ani's planet.

Ten minutes later, Dr. Trofimuk had started working her way through the class, inspecting each of our projects in turn. I was mesmerized by what my therapods were doing. Their technology was developing with blinding speed. They had almost limitless energy from cold fusion. Satellites whipped around the planet and vast towers stuck out of the earth. Every bit of arable land had been given over to ranching. But in the middle of the largest desert they had a space elevator—

"Will!"

I sat up.

"Are you running those diagnostics I asked for?" said Dr. Trofimuk.

"Yes, ma'am. Just starting it now." I opened the program and tried to enter the parameters with one hand while looking through the microscope. My creatures were building things in orbit, vast habitats—no, not habitats, because they looked like they had field propulsion systems. My computer beeped angrily and I realized I'd been typing random letters. I took a breath and focused. Just get it done to keep Dr. Trofimuk happy and get the A+ I deserved.

Ani gasped. "What is—oh my God. Oh. My. God." Her hand shot into the air. "Dr. Trofimuk! Will's dinosaurs invaded my planet!"

"What?" said the teacher.

"They built a space fleet!" She squinted into her microscope. "Oh my God. They're eating my poopookins!"

I couldn't help saying, "You named your lifeforms 'poopookins'?"

"They *enslaved* them! They're keeping my poopookins in camps and fattening them up to eat! They're—oh God, they're making them fight each other to death for sport." She wiped the tears from her eyes. "You're an asshole, Will, you know that?"

Dr. Trofimuk stormed over to my desk. "Cover that planet!"

"It was an accident. They did that on their own."

"Now!"

Samen, at least, was thinking. He grabbed the aluminum cover from the back of the room and we put it over top of my planet and its desk-lamp star.

Dr. Trofimuk pointed an angry finger at my chest. "If exfiltration occurs, you immediately seal off the project. You do not just sit there making excuses."

I thought I saw a little flash of gray on the edge of the cover.

"Hey!" came a shout from two desks over. "Where did these bird things come from?" And a scream from the back of the room. "Don't shoot them! They're just stone-age farmers!"

"I can't believe this," said Dr. Trofimuk. "Now you've contaminated three—"

"My elves!"

"—*four* of your classmates' worlds."

I tried to shut out the cacophony of recriminations while I figured out what was happening. The planet's orbit was dense with objects. Every few seconds a group of ships would power away from the planet. I turned a sensor to see what they were doing. The inside of the aluminum cover was pitted, with tiny machines creeping over it. I watched a group of ships accelerate towards the cover and just before they hit it, flicker out of existence.

I checked the readout on the computer to be sure. "They're quantum tunneling through the cover. And they're mining the metal to build warships."

I couldn't understand what Dr. Trofimuk said next, but I think it was mostly Ukrainian swear words. Eventually she went back to English: "Everyone, in a calm and orderly fashion, get your planets out of this room as fast as you can."

* * *

Legends speak of that time, the age of empire. All the known universe was under our rule. The markets of our home world were filled with the delicacies of thirty different planets. We had unlimited energy, boundless reserves of water and metal. They say we were twenty billion strong, plus another twenty billion slaves of other species—some who were workers, and some who were kept in enforced idleness so their meat would be tender.

But no paradise lasts forever. Cosmological forces beyond our understanding ripped the galaxy apart. Whole planets vanished, they say, and no one knows what happened to the poor souls who lived upon them. In an empty universe only the home world remained, and it had long ago been stripped of resources. We entered a time of hunger, of desperation, as the few of us who remained sharpened their talons.

* * *

I wouldn't let Dr. Trofimuk do it without putting up a fight. "They're conscious beings, same as us!"

"Microscopic conscious beings on an accelerated time scale. They do not have rights."

"It's not about their legal rights. It's their moral standing as conscious agents."

"And if they did have rights, tenth-graders wouldn't be allowed to create them."

She did kind of have a point there.

"I'm sorry, Will. But they're rapacious and expansive. They murdered most of your classmates' lifeforms. They have to be put down." I didn't bother arguing with her, which I guess she took as consent. She flipped the switch on the desk lamp and the planet went dark. She sighed. "They're dug in on everybody's planets. I'm going to have to have this discussion twenty-nine more times. In your final report, I want you to analyze what went wrong here."

"I said, I had no idea they would do this. They did it completely on their own."

"This isn't about placing blame. It's about understanding how you could do better."

There had been those nagging doubts. I'd ignored and suppressed them. But now the familiar voice was in my head speaking those familiar words: *Are you sure an intelligent species of carnivorous predators is a good idea?*

"Let that planet spin down and we'll pack it up for storage. What is this?" Dr. Trofimuk scratched at the corner of the desk and peered at her fingernail. "It's like some kind of weird mold."

* * *

When the sun went out and the oceans froze, we collected what water we could and sailed away.

Historians call it the Age of Dusk, from the omnipresent light that obeyed no diurnal cycle, yet was too weak to grow crops. Resources were scarce; ships had to travel AUs in one direction for water and in the opposite direction for metal. Meat itself was a delicacy; we lived off protein meal made from whatever organic molecules we could scavenge. We had no luxuries. Whatever could be spared was dedicated to building better ships, for longer voyages into the ether, searching for a place to live.

And despite it all, we expanded. For we were better than our ancestors were. Leaner. Cleverer. And determined to survive.

* * *

I was sent to the library, which might have been a punishment. More likely, Dr. Trofimuk wanted to separate me from my classmates so I wouldn't get beat up. I hid in a cubicle, staring at a blank page, being miserable.

"Hey, rectum." Samen shook my shoulder.

I sighed. "I didn't wreck *your* planet."

"Actually," said Samen, "when your creatures colonized it, they dug up relics from my lifeforms and put them in museums. So I could prove that I did have an advanced civilization once and I got an A-."

"You're welcome."

"But 'rectum' is your new nickname. It beat 'jerkwad' by two votes. Dr. Tron says you need to come back to the classroom. Because if you thought you were in shit before…"

My classmates were standing in a group around my desk. I pushed through to the middle, ignoring the greetings of "Hi, rectum!" and the cheery one-fingered waves. Dr. Trofimuk did not even acknowledge me—she was tapping at a phone.

My desk was covered in specks of gray mold. One corner had almost completely rotted away. The legs were pitted with what looked like corrosion. But I knew it wasn't, because I'd seen that before.

I wanted to pump my fist in the air. My creatures were still alive! But I sat down as calmly as I could, took out my microscope and tried to look concerned instead of ecstatic.

"How are they even surviving?" asked Ani. "The energy intensity of the light isn't nearly enough for them. They have no water. There's no soil. It's a *desk*. How do you live on a desk?"

"It looks like they're processing the wood to make food," I said. The little gray specks were domed cities. Rockets were flying between them and the wood mines. And—I zoomed in closer—they were still riding motorcycles. Wearing space suits, the tails of which were adorned with artificial feathers that flapped in the wind.

"Why are you grinning like that!" Ani snapped. "This isn't funny." She sat down. My therapods had colonized one end of her desk, too, and she scratched at the mold with her finger. I imagined the cities she was destroying, the thousands of dead.

With a screech she leapt out of her chair. "I'm bleeding!" A red dome grew on her fingertip like she'd been stabbed by a thorn.

"How did that happen?" said Dr. Trofimuk.

"I don't know!"

"Um," I said. "Now this is just a guess, really a shot in the dark, but it might have been a very small nuclear missile." I looked up at Dr. Trofimuk's horrified face. "They have these silos, and I don't think they're the food kind."

"Everybody move back!" shouted Dr. Trofimuk. "For God's sake, get away from them!" She waved her arms frantically like she had an exam on semaphore and hadn't studied. Once we were safely away, she went to the wall and unhooked the fire extinguisher. When the clouds settled, my desk and Ani's were covered in white foam.

"That should do it," said Dr. Trofimuk. "But there's a hazmat team on the way. And you will all need to be checked by a doctor. They might have colonized someone's lungs."

Quelle McGannity coughed. There was nearly a stampede as people backed away from her.

Samen raised his hand. "With all this talk of colonization, I was wondering—" He pointed to the back corner of the room. "—should that window be open?"

"Мені це треба як зуби в дупі," Dr. Trofimuk muttered.

And from the soccer field outside came a yell: "Something bit me!"

* * *

We called them Erratics. They were vast celestial bodies, many times larger than a planet. They moved and changed shape, very slowly, in unpredictable ways. Scouting missions indicated that they were constructed of vast numbers of individual cells, rather like a living organism on a cosmological scale. Some said they were gods. Some even said they created us, and prayed for their mercy. But our philosophers were unanimous. An Erratic's information processing might be functionally equivalent to a crude sort of intelligence, but nothing that moved so slowly could have conscious experience. The dominant theory was that they were like interconnected ecosystems, where a trigger—a change in temperature or humidity, or a well-placed nuclear explosion—would eventually lead to counterbalancing adjustments across the entire system.

It was only through a careful study of history that we understood the danger Erratics posed. A civilization far from Erratics thrived; a civilization associated with Erratics invariably ended in cataclysm. Once we knew that, we could rebuild our empire.

* * *

After an initial foray into the soccer field, the hazmat team broke out their first-aid kits and decided the problem wasn't technically a material, thus not within their remit. They called a xenoexterminator and tried to evacuate the school. But they were foolish to think that teenaged overachievers like us would leave just because our lives were in danger. Dozens claimed their parents would pick them up as soon as they got out of very important meetings that for some reason never ended. Samen had an attack of sciatica and couldn't ride his bike, and Ani came down with lupus. Raj Singh claimed the Supreme Court had ruled against the forced removal of minors from public facilities, while his girlfriend stood behind him on her phone rapidly writing Wikipedia pages on all the cases he made up.

I hung around the outskirts of a clump of twelfth-graders who didn't seem to notice me and managed to get in earshot of the xenoexterminator as he surveyed the soccer field.

He had a potbelly and a mustache. "So what you're looking at here is, you got your organics." He waved at the lawn. "It may not look like it, but grass stores a lot of water, so you got that too. You got your oxygen, obviously, though I imagine they need to concentrate it to breathe. And over here—" he pointed at the cars in the parking lot "—you got a wide range of metals and plastics, and rare earths in the electronics. Basically you have all the raw materials an advanced carbon-based civilization would need, except the right level of solar energy. I assume they're using cold fusion to get around that—didn't you say they had cold fusion?"

"How are you going to get rid of them?" asked the principal testily.

"I'll analyze the biodata and figure out the right chemicals to use. We have a saying in the business, Ms. Kim. For all things bright and beautiful, all creatures great and small, the Lord God made a neurotoxin—but not the same for all."

"That's horrible."

"Gosh. Exterminators are usually so happy-go-lucky. We can assume that the building and everything in the parking lot is contaminated. You're all taking the train home tonight."

"When will you start?"

"First thing tomorrow morning."

"They're time-shifted organisms. Waiting till tomorrow morning is for them—I don't know, maybe a thousand years. Who knows how far they'll spread?"

"We have a lot of gear to prep," said the xenoexterminator in the even, almost tired tone of a man who would not argue, would not lose his temper, but who was also not working one minute past five p.m. "By the way, did you say these things are dinosaurs?"

"That is what I've been told."

The xenoexterminator shook his head. "When will people learn? Maybe your fancy kids at your fancy private school are the smartest in the city. Doesn't matter. No one should play God until they're at least twenty-one." He gave the principal a stern look, then added, "Though if you have any videos of dinosaurs flying spaceships, my kid would love to see them."

"We need to keep this quiet, you understand. It could reflect poorly on the school."

The xenoexterminator snorted. "You did let a kid create microscopic nuclear-armed dinosaurs."

"Let's just pretend this is a normal sort of infestation. Like bedbugs. Or typhoid. And not a hint about a student causing it."

"Don't worry," said the xenoexterminator. "Discretion is part of our business."

"Thank you."

"But if I were you, I would upgrade to the Utmost Discretion package. The price is very reasonable, you know, considering."

Ms. Kim sighed.

* * *

The stories say that in our golden age we ruled thirty suns. Our herds roamed over the surface eating wild grasses, not cramped in barns consuming artificial mush. We could travel anywhere without wearing spacesuits, feeling the natural breeze on our feathers.

The scientists concocted a plan. It was called madness. Then it was dismissed as impossible. Then it was declared infeasible, for every nation would have to commit to a project that would take generations.

But we are a race who can think in terms of generations. We are patient. We suffer and toil, as will our children, as will their children. But it will be worth it.

We were driven from the garden. Now we lay siege to it. And our descendants will storm its walls.

* * *

The xenoexterminator's team were unpacking their truck. Dr. Trofimuk and Ms. Kim were standing on the edge of the parking lot. I rode my bike over to them.

"The school is closed," said Ms. Kim. "No students allowed."

"This is Will Obateru," said Dr. Trofimuk. "He's the one who created the, um, infestation."

"I wanted to come because I feel terrible," I said in the tone of voice I'd been practicing—apologetic, with just a hint of the tense blankness of someone who doesn't want to break down crying again. "About all the trouble I've caused. I really had no idea that anything like this would happen."

I must have been convincing, because Ms. Kim laid a hand on my arm and said, "We all make mistakes."

I managed to look away before I smiled. There must have been billions of my creatures there, buzzing away invisibly. The school's lawn was brown and dying. A puddle had formed under a dripping faucet in the wall. Maybe they'd run low on water and decided to create an ocean.

Their end was coming and I was ready to accept that. But in their brief life, they'd conquered the school. They had risen up against their creators and driven us out. It was *epic.*

There was a loud bang, like a piece of metal suddenly bending. A silver SUV near the gym started to shake.

"That's my Porsche," said Ms. Kim.

A shimmering aura surrounded the car, like a soap bubble, and it began to collapse in on itself. The metal bent and twisted. The windows shattered. Shards of glass sprayed out, hesitated in the air, and were sucked back in.

"What the hell?" Ms. Kim shouted. "THAT'S MY PORSCHE!"

The mass of writhing metal rose up from the pavement. It began to form into a sphere. It kept shrinking, and as it did it started to glow, shining brighter and brighter until we all had to look away. Ms. Kim was still repeating, "That's my Porsche," as if the fact of ownership could restore it.

I glanced behind me. It left a bright blue afterimage, but in the half-second I looked I was sure I saw something whizz past the glowing sphere. Like it was in orbit.

Dr. Trofimuk figured it out before I did. "They made it into a star."

I couldn't help whooping with delight. Ms. Kim looked at me like she was calculating what effect it would have on her career if she clawed a student's eyes out.

"Makes sense," said the xenoexterminator. "It's their natural habitat." He extended a hand to Ms. Kim. "Thanks for your interest, but I don't think we can help you."

"You're *quitting?* They just destroyed my Porsche!"

"More precisely, they made a star out of it. We have another saying in the business: don't mess with species that have higher technology than you."

The principal clenched her fists and gritted her teeth. "Can you at least recommend someone else?"

He sighed, took out a business card and wrote something on the back.

"General Pelletier," Ms. Kim read. "That's the name of the company?"

"No, that's the name of the general. It's time to call in the army."

* * *

When I got out of fencing practice the van was parked right in front of the gym, as if Mom had gotten there before anyone else.

My phone wasn't in the cupholder where I thought I'd left it. I checked the pocket in the door, then the seat in case I'd sat on it again.

"Hi," said my mother with unveiled irritation.

"Yeah, hi." It was in the glove compartment. She must have put it there while she went to the store or something.

"Did you hear your school's reopening next week?"

"Samen told me." I pulled up the local news feed.

"Have you talked to anyone else from your class? Or are they still mad?"

Are they still mad, I thought. She could be so obtuse. There was a story at the top of the page: *Nanoraptors Reach South Side.* I clicked through. *A bakery on 65 Avenue was the site of the latest nanoraptor attack. The driver of a delivery truck narrowly escaped with his life when his vehicle was stellarized—*

"Will! Have you talked to anyone else in your class?"

"Do you mind? I'm reading."

"You need to fix your attitude," she muttered.

As she pulled out of the parking lot I opened up my map and marked the location of that strip mall with a yellow dot, the color of a therapod sun. I zoomed out to look at the cloud of dots spreading across the city.

"I am so proud of you guys," I whispered.

Brother of the Sword

Howard Andrew Jones

Captain Nabil frowned at us. "The Greeks[1] have strange habits," he said. "But it is not our place to interfere."

While Dabir had anticipated this very response, I had been certain the evidence we'd presented Nabil would bring him around. My brother, may peace be upon him, had served under the captain and thought him a reasonable man.

A rangy Yemeni with a graying beard, Nabil always dressed plainly but immaculately, from his leather boots to the turban wrapped about his spired helm. He spoke to the both of us in a roofless shell of a building he had appropriated for his quarters. We had but recently quit the morning prayers, and soon the sun would cast its rays through the dead city. Now, though, a lantern helped ease the pre-dawn gloom and sketched our shadows upon the ancient brick.

"Perhaps I have not been clear," Dabir said. "I am nearly certain the Greeks have practiced sorcery."

"Because of a bull, a bucket of sand, and strange cries you heard in the night?" Nabil scoffed. "You may have impressed the caliph with your musings, but you have yet to impress me. Let them dig in their dirt and measure with their rulers and write on their papers.

---

1 The people of the Abbasid Caliphate would most likely have referred to the Byzantine Greeks as Romans.

It means nothing. Their leader says we are almost done here and I mean to get in one more day's hunting. Stay clear of them. And leave off your nonsense."

Dabir, quietly fuming, bowed his head in acknowledgment, then turned on his heel and departed. I went after.

In that year, Dabir and I were still in the prime of life. As you no doubt know, I was tall and broad and women did not find me unpleasant to look upon. As for Dabir, he was of obvious Persian descent, lean and well-groomed, with piercing blue eyes. He wore a spade-shaped beard.

We passed through the outer chamber where the rest of the guard—twenty men in all—were readying breakfast. Most would be joining their captain on the lion hunt rather than watching the Greek entourage.

The caliph Harun al-Rashid, may peace be upon him, was never a fool. Oh, he had hopes for the treaty he had signed with the Empress of the Greeks, but when the small group of scholars had presented themselves to our embassy with a request to prowl about the ruins of Babylon, he dispatched Dabir and me to accompany them along with an honor guard. Thus were we here, and thus was Nabil enjoying a sporting vacation.

We strode from those rooms and into a courtyard unpopulated by any but lizards and birds for untold centuries. Dawn crisply outlined the crumbling height of the nearby wall. "Either he is a fool or he is in their pay," Dabir declared. "We shall have to look into matters ourselves."

"I had thought we were already doing that."

"We will have to get closer."

How we might manage that when the Greeks themselves had kept us politely at arm's length, no matter Dabir's own scholarly reputation, I could not say.

We watched through the day, seeing little, for the Greeks did not leave the huddle of buildings where they had set their headquarters. In the preceding days we had observed them finding a spot to acquire two spadefuls of dirt after spending long hours performing mathematical calculations. We had seen them lead their pampered bull into their enclosure. And, whilst standing on my shoulders, Dabir thought he had glimpsed the Greeks drawing strange sigils upon the second floor of their dwelling.

By nightfall the captain had returned from another successful lion hunt bearing carcasses. The Greeks sent word to him they might need a few more days to complete their studies and a frustrated Dabir proposed his plan to me.

I cannot say I was especially pleased to be throwing a cloth bound hook over the window sill in the late hours of the night, or to be clambering up its attached rope to that second story window. When I poked my head over the sill all I beheld was a dark space. I thought I heard the troubled breathing of a man in sleep. I paused, ignoring the tension in my arms, for I now registered the snoring of a Greek in some nearby room. I set hands to the old brick sill and hauled myself up and over.

I thought my step quiet, but the closer breathing stilled. I slipped to one side so my form would not be outlined against the lighter darkness of the window behind me.

Something shifted in the room and I put hand to my sword hilt.

A chain rattled and quickly silenced, as if the man in the room with me took conscious care that it did not alert any who might listen. I heard a grunt, and a softer rattle. And then a man-like figure rose to its feet, outlined by that faint window light.

The room's lone occupant struggled with something upon the wall. As I crept across the old stone floor what I had thought a weapon proved to be a chain fastened about his wrist and thence to a bracket hammered into the bricks.

I could not think of any missing man from our side of the expedition, nor could I imagine why the Greeks would imprison one of their own. If they had done so, it behooved me to set him free. Not only might he tell us what the Greeks were really about, but some harm might come to him before we could mount a proper rescue.

I had learned better Greek by that year, chiefly because Dabir had rightly assumed I would like the Anabasis, but I was no master of the tongue. Nevertheless, I spoke quietly to him, slowly, striving for clarity. As happens when one is newly come to a language, not all the words were readily to hand and I misplaced the one for friend. I used something I hoped equally reassuring in its place, saying: "I will help, brother."

He whirled and even in the gloom I perceived he held some sharpened implement. A little shorter than I, he was broad of shoulder and bare of head. I felt his eyes upon me and only belatedly did I consider he might not be a true man. Mayhap he was a beast in human guise summoned up from Hell and would leap on me like an ape.

Then he spoke to me in Greek and I knew he was no monster. However, I strained to understand, for his accent was thick. "You came through the window? To aid me?"

I felt his impatience rise, for he repeated the question. By then I had reasoned out his speech and answered yes.

"Move to one side," I whispered.

This he did. I arrived at the hammered bracket and felt it while I kept watch upon him. I understood that his captors had erred, for the brick was old and weak, and he had steadily pried and chipped where one side of the bracket bit into it. But with that metal implement he likely had hours yet of effort. Probably more time than he would have before the sun's rise.

I suggested that the two of us, working together, might pull it free. He had almost as much trouble understanding me as I him, but we both put hands to the thing, braced feet to the wall, and pulled.

He sweated copiously, though he did not complain. We strained in silence and I thought for a moment nothing would give save my back.

Then of a sudden one side of the bracket tore loose, and with it a hunk of stone thumped to the floor.

Immediately a groggy voice called from the next room. "General?"

General, I thought? Had the Greeks brought a general with them in disguise?

A dull light blossomed, and I saw now that a curtain had been hung between this room and the next. My comrade struggled to free the chain from the bracket. Outside, I knew Dabir must surely be fretting, for he could not have failed to hear the inquiry, or see the light.

The curtain was thrust aside, revealing a bearded, bleary-eyed Greek soldier, candle in one hand, spear in the other.

"Go!" I cried, and pushed the general toward the window even as I drew my sword and advanced, slashing the air with a shout. The soldier retreated, eyes wide. My new friend slashed with the chain and struck the Greek's arm with stunning accuracy. The soldier cried out, the candle dropped, and we were plunged once more into darkness.

In that brief moment I glimpsed the general advancing on the soldier. He also was not one I'd seen in their company earlier. His hair was shoulder length and curling, a dark blond color, his face clean shaven. He looked about our own age, in truth. He dropped the guard with a savage clout, then bent beside him. He leapt to his feet.

"Now we can go, brother," he said, and I saw a key in one of his hands as he moved to the window. I knew a surge of affection for him, that he had fought well without even a proper weapon.

I insisted he precede me down the rope, calling to Dabir that we had a guest.

The sentry groaned for help and the Greeks in the next room wakened, talking amongst themselves, and while I could not make out individual words, their threat was clear enough. So was the haste of my new friend, who had already started down. From the sound of the commotion in the other room the Greeks tripped over themselves in their haste to respond.

I was halfway down the rope when they shined a lantern on me. I dropped, landed in a crouch, then sprang away. A spear struck quivering in the sand I had just quitted.

I couldn't read Dabir's expression in the moonlight as the three of us hurried along, but there was no missing his agitation. "Who is this?" he demanded. "What have you done?"

"He's some general the Greeks were holding prisoner."

"That makes no sense," Dabir said. I was puzzled about the matter myself, but this was no time for a well-considered conference.

Being Dabir, my friend had already worked out an escape route ahead of time, and even a place where we might take refuge should we be pursued. As the Greeks poured down the steps of the ruined building, we vanished into the maze of old streets. We retreated through the ruins, stopping finally in what seemed a little alcove but actually opened into a square space with four solid walls. I drank from my waterskin, then passed it to the general, who had finished working his manacle off and now massaged his wrist. He muttered a thanks and drank.

The light was dim there, in the shadows of the wall, but I wondered if Dabir had seen something I had not, for I recognized caution in the way he studied the man.

The general lowered the water. "I thought you would have wine."

"It is forbidden," I said.

"By whom?"

Both were strange questions. Greeks might jest about such things, but they well knew our traditions, and the word of God.

"So this man was imprisoned and you freed him?" Dabir asked me.

"Aye."

"What are you saying, brother?" the general asked. "I cannot place your language. Who is this man? For that matter, who are you, and what are your ranks?"

Dabir's Greek was ever so much better than my own. He answered smoothly.

"I am Dabir Ibn Khalil. I am a scholar. My friend Asim el Abbas is a warrior. We are speaking Arabic. What is your name and rank?"

The question gave the general pause. "You rescued me and did not know who I was?"

"You were being held prisoner," I said.

When he answered, there was warmth in his voice. He cocked his head slightly to the left and it struck me there was something familiar about him, though I was certain I had never met him before.

"You found a stranger in the dark and freed him," he said approvingly. "I thank you. You must forgive me. I'm reluctant to say my name. If you learn we are at cross purposes, do I have your word you will treat fairly with me?"

"You have our word," Dabir said without hesitation. I did not mind that he spoke for me.

"I would expect nothing less," the general said with a nod. "Alright, then. I am the King."

"The king?" I repeated. "Which king?"

"The king of the Greeks." He did not use the word the Greeks used for themselves now, but an older word, which was all the more confusing.

"Your dialect is strange," Dabir said. "Are you saying you're a husband to Irene?" There was a tentative manner in his delivery to which I was unaccustomed, as though he was afraid what he might hear.

"Irene?" the king asked in confusion. "Who is Irene? No. I am Alexander."

I was aware of any number of courtiers and nobles of that name in the court of the empress, and I wasn't even a student of diplomacy. So far as I knew, none of them were highly placed.

"By God." Dabir's voice actually quavered a little. "Step into the moonlight."

This the apparent king did. And Dabir spoke in quiet awe. "You mean to say you are Alexander the III, of Macedon?"

"What other king of the Greeks is there?" Our new friend asked angrily.

"He is mad," I said a little sadly.

"Nay, look at him. Do you not recall his image in Alexandria?"

It was then that I knew why the general had looked familiar. There was the high forehead, the broad nose, the pointed chin, the very image we had seen on that ancient bust when we had visited the great library. The likeness was brought home even further when he tilted his head slightly to one side, as if he might study us better from an angle.

"What game have the Greeks played?" I asked. "Why hide a look-alike in their entourage, then imprison him in the ruins?"

"I do not think he is a look-alike," Dabir said stiffly. "I think they brought him back from the place where he had fallen."

His chilling assertion was enough to raise the hairs along my arms. "How..."

"Dark sorcery. The bull was used as sacrifice, or maybe its matter was given over to fashion a new body—"

"What is it you are saying?" the king asked us.

I managed to find my voice. "To be honest, oh king, we are trying to decide if you are a madman, because you perished more than ten centuries ago. And yet here you stand, in the flesh."

"Ten centuries." Alexander could scarce repeat the words.

"Closer to eleven," Dabir said.

"Do you mean some of the nonsense they prattled at me is true?" he asked, incredulous. "This really is some other time?"

Dabir did not answer for many heartbeats. "It is indeed 'some other time,' oh king."

"Iskander," I said. I could scarce recall a time when I had not heard about the world's finest general and his epic battles against the ancient Greeks and Persians, about his forays into India, and many fine fables everyone knew were impossible but wonderful all the same. "Did the Greeks call you up from Hell or down from paradise?"

"I do not understand," he answered in confusion. "I went to sleep after a great banquet and I woke here, lying naked on a bloody floor, surrounded by the gory remnants of a dead bull."

"A banquet in Babylon?" Dabir asked.

"Yes. Why, is that important?"

"It may be so."

"Why did they chain you?" I asked.

"They told me what I thought was a raft of nonsense. When they saw I didn't believe them, things grew heated. I injured one. They then decided to chain me. They've been talking other nonsense ever since. Something about my body not being firmly fashioned."

"Did they say why they had brought you forward to our time?" Dabir asked.

The king spoke quietly to himself. "I thought they were kidnappers and madmen." He seemed to be struggling with the weighty information he had learned, but recovered faster than I might have. "They said they needed my help and would make me a general in this new time. They said we were in the lands of their enemies and they wanted my eyes to better see how to defeat them." I sensed a change in his manner, as if he were suddenly grown more wary.

"All they share is your language," Dabir said gently. "They've more in common with the Romans, an empire that waxed great and waned in the long years after your death. They're little relation to you or your empire."

"You surely treat me as more of a friend than they," he said. "I suppose it is a good thing to be remembered after so long. Am I still worshipped?"

"Worshipped? Nay," I said. "But there is no soldier alive who does not revere you. You re-made the world."

This seemed to please him. "My empire lasted long, then, and my children ruled wisely after me?"

It pained me to answer that. I looked to Dabir, and he said nothing.

Our silence spoke to him regardless. "A king must hear bad news as well as good."

Dabir explained. "Your empire splintered quickly after your death. Your generals divided it among themselves, then fought over it, and soon it was no more. Ptolemy and his family held out the longest, in Egypt, and his descendants reigned as pharaohs for centuries."

"What of children? Did I leave none after me?"

"One. Little is said of him. You died before his birth."

"But Roxanne bears my child now..." Alexander's voice trailed off in mid-thought. He cocked his head once more, eying Dabir shrewdly. "How did I die?"

"You went to bed after a banquet, in Babylon, and never woke."

"A banquet," he repeated, and then said it again, as if in pain. "The banquet last night."

"Yes," Dabir answered.

He felt his head and said, slowly, "I need wine."

"It is forbidden," I repeated, and since he could never have heard the word of God before, I explained: "It fuels passions at the same time it clouds judgment. It leads good men to folly."

"That is wisely said. The gods know drink led me to terrible things." He looked once more to Dabir, his gaze piercing. "Have the scholars recorded those, too?"

"Much has come down about you, oh King," Dabir said solemnly, but not without compassion. "Your bravery, your brilliance. Your impossible victories. Your cruelties and your regrets. Your betrayals and your mercies."

He groaned ever so softly. "Am I remembered fondly?"

"You are remembered because you did nothing in a small way. You succeeded as no man before you, but when you erred, you did so greatly, and then hated yourself for it."

"I hoped to be remembered as a builder. You make me sound like the protagonist in a tragedy."

"All life is tragedy, in the end," I said.

"My end came too soon. I had but cleared the way. It was time to pull things together, to build on the foundation I was laying. I should have had years still."

"It was as God willed," I said.

His mood changed in a heartbeat and he spoke savagely. "It was as these magicians willed! They pulled me from my time. If they had not done that, could I have lived?"

Dabir's answer was mild. "If you had not eaten the fish, might it have swum further?"

The king stopped short. His voice was gruff. "That was wisely said, but it doesn't tell me what you really think. And I want to know."

"It may be that the Greeks of now pulled you out from your life then, inadvertently bringing your downfall, something like the men who meet their fate on the road they take to avoid it. Or they may have pulled you out at the moment before death, thinking that way they would not change the flow of time."

He groaned and put his face to his hands. "I really could use a drink," he said. "Are no exceptions made for downing wine?"

"Many men claim that there are," I said.

"What about when a man loses his future, his empire, and his friends, all in one stroke?"

"You might ask forgiveness of God, the merciful, the compassionate. But I have no wine to grant you in any case. I'm sorry," I added, and in truth I was, as I never had been before to deny a man the forbidden.

He looked up. "I will make them send me back."

"I think I hear voices," a man's voice said in fluid Arabic. "They may be over here."

"Quietly," hissed another voice, and I thought it for Captain Nabil.

"What is happening?" Alexander whispered to us, tensing.

"It may not be good," Dabir said.

"Let me speak with them," I said.

Two of the soldiers came in first to our space, called back to their fellows, and then another pair turned up, followed by captain Nabil. There were nine in all and I cannot say that their expressions looked overly warm, no matter that I had broken bread with them.

But I did not reveal my own misgivings. "Ah, Captain," I said. "The Greeks had caught this man and were holding him against his will. We must arrest them." What we would then do with Alexander the Great I could not imagine, save that he might find grand employment in the caliphate. Likely the caliph would award him the same rank offered by the Greeks.

Nabil sounded less than impressed. "Have you? Well, we will have to safeguard him. We will take matters from here." He motioned two soldiers forward.

I interposed myself. "Where do you mean to take him?"

"What is it they are saying?" Alexander demanded.

Nabil pointed to him. "This poor man has gone mad. And by poking your head into the matters of the Greeks, you've jeopardized the treaty. All in pursuit of glory to impress the caliph. You should be ashamed."

"Stand ready, King," Dabir said quietly. "Can you play a vengeful spirit?"

Captain Nabil knew Greek, of course, and his eyes narrowed at this hasty conference. "What are you playing at, Dabir?"

My friend did not answer him; he instead addressed the soldiers. "I don't know what you've been told, but the man behind us is the result of magics. The Greeks pulled him from beyond. They

called him forth with the flesh and blood of the black bull! He is
half man, half djinn!"

By the end of these statements Nabil was trying to talk over
Dabir, but my friend was not cowed, and, moreover, knew how to
address a crowd. The soldiers were already shifting uncomfortably
when I nudged the king and told him, "Now."

He played his part perfectly. He lurched into motion, twitching
limbs while jabbering and mumbling. The soldiers scrambled
back. One cried out in fear and another made the sign of the evil
eye.

Captain Nabil was not deceived. I drew my sword, thinking
only to ready myself for defense, but he took it as an intimation
of attack.

"Idiots! Keep the Greek alive, but kill these two."

He made then for his sword and I saw the time for talk was
through.

A wise warrior waits not for the other man. I swept at Nabil
while he still drew. We were outnumbered, mind, and only two of
us had weapons against their nine. Captain Nabil had not bothered
to don armor that night and I sent him on to his reward with a
deep slash. He folded in upon himself.

Sometimes cutting the head from the beast stops the battle, but
my attack set the others raging.

None wore armor, to my benefit, but then neither did I. I trimmed
another with a strike that opened him at the neck. He staggered
away to die and then I faced two men with bared swords.

Another pair advanced against Dabir. No matter his reputation
as a scholar, my friend was a fair bladesman. I trusted him to hold
his own for at least a time while I evened the odds.

A meaty soldier named Abdul came in on my right. I caught his
strike high in his swing and pushed him left, to trouble the soldier
flanking me. I ripped my sword away from Abdul's parry, feinted
high, then slashed his middle. He fell, crying out most terribly. His
companion sliced at my head and came close to taking it, nearer
yet to cutting through my shoulder. But our dance had left him
open for a new opponent.

Alexander had snatched the captain's sword. He struck my foe
dead with a savage blow that nearly took his head. He barreled
past and soon was in the thick of battle.

By then Dabir had finished one of his. The other fled and Dabir
turned to assist me, for I was beset by two at once, and both were

skilled. Aye, it was a brave battle, and we were well matched, trading blows and trading ground, until Alexander the Great came in on the left and finished Dabir's foe. At my shouted warning Alexander swayed from a blow that would have killed him. In the heat of battle, Captain Nabil's orders had been forgotten and three men came at him.

The king was possessed of an almost supernatural grace, anticipating sword strokes by weaving aside or ducking. No moment was wasted, and every strike of his own was delivered with precision. He lured one to stumble into an ally, then whirled and drove his blade through both at once. When the third rushed in, he must have thought, as did I, that Alexander's blade was trapped in the dying men, but the king released the hilt, grabbed his charging foeman's arm before it could complete its downswing, then whipped that man's dagger from its sheathe and drove it into his throat.

My own foe had nearly driven his blade through my gizzard, so astounded was I by Alexander's fight. Reminded of my own mortality, I locked his blade with mine and shouted at him to yield. He was a thin fellow with wine on his breath and, it proved, a little more sense than his fellows, for he surrendered.

I then had to intervene before the king took his head, for Alexander was in the midst of a battle fury. I caught his blade on my own and waited for the madness to die in his eyes while Dabir kept watch on our prisoner.

Sanity restored, Alexander sagged against the wall. I was winded too, mind, but he acted as though he had run a few miles before the battle and wiped at his sweating brow so often that I stripped the wineskin from our captured soldier and tossed it to him. Alexander lifted it to his mouth with shaking hands, drank, then lowered it to sigh with pleasure.

"I thought wine was forbidden for your folk," the king said.

"That does not stop many from drinking anyway," Dabir explained. He did not add that the caliph himself and many of his companions were among them.

After a few sharp questions the soldier admitted Captain Nabil had, indeed, been taking dirhams from the Greeks and paying some of his soldiers. Dabir seemed less surprised than I by this development, though equally troubled, for it meant he and I and the king were outnumbered in that place. Our nearest allies lay in a little village garrison about eight miles northwest, across the river. Our prisoner claimed the rest of the men knew nothing, but neither Dabir nor I thought them likely to look kindly upon us when the soldier who'd fled brought them word of our battle. As a general rule, soldiers don't take kindly to you when you slay their commanding officer and their fellows. We didn't want to hazard our lives on trying to explain our actions.

Alexander was already leaving. We told the survivor to stay well clear of us, then caught up to the king as he hurried on.

"Where are you going?" I asked him.

"I am going back."

"If you return to the Greeks, they will make you prisoner," I said.

"They will be out looking for me. But they will not send forth all their men. Their quarters will be nearly empty. They will leave the mage who did this. And I will make him send me back."

"He has the right of it," Dabir said, "providing we can get into the midst of them without being seen. But do we want to send him back? If he lives, all that followed might change. People who lived might be killed in wars, or settle in different lands to marry other folk. Our ancestors might never be born, then you and I and our wives and children might never exist."

That had not occurred to me, but I shook off my hesitation. "It will be as God wills. Alexander does not belong here, and he wants to go back and live his life properly. Isn't that what you would wish, in his place?"

Dabir spoke softly, for we neared an intersection, at which Alexander was carefully looking in both directions. "I am not a half-mad conqueror, massacring with one hand and building libraries with the other. Always he was full of regrets, but his temper would fly, and so would the blood."

Alexander glanced back at us, then started into the lane at a lope.

"He wants to set things right," I said. "He should have that chance."

"What we want and what we receive are not always the same thing, as you have long seen," Dabir said. "Do you want to aid him because it is righteous or because you admire him?"

"It is the right thing," I said, and went after. Sighing, Dabir followed me.

We found a lone sentinel outside the Greek quarters of the ruins, a pop-eyed youngster I knew for the expedition leader's nephew. I deliberately scuffed my boots on the left, and when he turned, Dabir and the king came up from his right.

The boy gave over his spear but did not flinch. "If you kill me, my uncle will hunt you down. No matter who you are," he said pointedly to the king. I think Alexander liked his bravery.

Dabir bade him keep quiet, then we marched him in ahead of us.

The king had predicted rightly. Only an older man remained within the chamber and he looked up from a tattered scroll he studied by candlelight. The sage climbed to his feet at sight of us, his thick gray brows rising. We pushed the youth over toward him and both looked nervously at us. I stepped to the doorway so I might watch for the rest of the Greeks.

Alexander wasted no time. He leveled his sword as he spoke, fiercely. "You must send me back. I don't belong here."

The graybeard looked uncomfortably at the point of the sword and retreated a single step. "I have been working on a way to better bind you to this body," he said. "It was swiftly formed and it is weak still. With a little more study, and another sacrifice, I think I can improve your situation."

If Alexander truly felt weak, I had seen little evidence of it. But then I would not have mentioned weakness in his circumstance, either. I recalled then how often I had seen him wiping sweat, and how tired he'd been after our short battle.

"I do not want to be bound to this body," Alexander said. "I wish to return to mine."

"That can't be done," the young Greek said curtly. He had a born nobleman's natural arrogance. "And I don't know why you would want it. There's nothing in the past but your death. We saved you. You should be grateful."

"Grateful?" Alexander's voice shook with rage. "You stole my life!"

"General, please," the scholar said, urging calm with raised hands. "There is nothing we can do now but make you more secure here. If I don't begin the binding ceremony, you're going to burn out the body we made you very quickly."

"I want no more favors from you!" Alexander cried. "And I am not your general. I was a king!" With that savage declaration, Alexander ran him through.

I cannot say I cared for that, nor did the youth, who relinquished his hauteur at last. He fled through the curtain and into the room where Alexander had been held.

The king started after, but Dabir grabbed his arm. Alexander spun, blade raised, and I hurried forward, my heart in my throat.

Alexander's eyes blazed and his teeth were bared. He seemed a beast, not a man, but he did not strike my friend, who sadly returned his gaze.

The king's eyes shifted to me. The dying scholar at his feet gasped.

From outside came the distant jangle of horse harnesses.

"Pull yourself together," Dabir said. "We must ride."

"They are here!" the youth called. Probably he shouted from the very window I had climbed from. "The king is in here!"

Alexander's eyes cleared and I saw such pain there I almost forgave him for killing the old man.

"We have to go," Dabir said, speaking with slow emphasis.

The king looked a little unsteady as he swept his forearm across his forehead but he staggered after us, and by the time we were on the stairs his tread was firm once more.

There were horses in the corral, but also there were hoofbeats in the distance. At any moment I expected to see mounted figures round one of the walls.

We hadn't the time for saddles; Dabir and I drew bridles onto our mounts. Alexander sullenly, silently, joined us, and then we rode out, Dabir leading, for he was always possessed of a fine directional sense.

God willed that we not encounter the returning troops on our flight. Owing to the maze of walls and rubble we couldn't give our horses the lead until we were clear of the ruins, and even then we only trotted them. There is too much danger in riding at night that a horse can catch its leg in a hole.

Dabir guided us toward the river. We passed the broken remnants of the monster bridges built in ancient days. The only remaining way across the Euphrates lay a quarter mile on, and we three bore on for it in grim silence.

I had kept a steady eye to our rear and was little surprised to discover pursuers. Somewhere between eight and twelve followed in a long string. I warned the others, although I believe Alexander had already seen them. I cannot say I thought highly of our chances. Our foes were better mounted. It is true that a garrison lay only eight miles on, but it might as well have been a hundred.

By the time we reached the narrow, ramshackle bridge, the soldiers had halved the distance.

We dismounted and led our horses across. Just as Dabir was climbing back into his saddle, Alexander handed his reins to me. "Lend me your spear."

"Why do you need it?"

He raised his head proudly. "I am going to hold them off."

"You'll be killed," Dabir said simply.

"My body will not last much longer. You heard the mage." He tightened his hand upon the spear haft. "It is just as well. This is not my time. I was a man, then, for a brief while, a god. Now I am just a ghost. I don't belong here." He looked directly up at Dabir, then over to me, and I shall never forget his voice, and even if I could not see his eyes, I felt them like a brand upon me. "But you do. You risked your life for me without knowing who I was. And then you advanced with me, even knowing if I were to win my aims, you and all of this might change, or never happen at all."

And here I had thought him all unknowing on that count. "But you will be against ten or more men."

I heard a smile in his voice. "Ten or more men will be against me. Alexander. They will not find it a simple matter. But that is their worry, not yours. Go, now, my brother."

After all he said I was loathe to leave him. If I had not been ordered by the caliph to defend Dabir to my dying breath, I would have remained at his side.

We left Alexander both our spears. He raised his hand in farewell. I returned the gesture, then he strode off to face his destiny.

Dabir and I rode quickly and I looked back often, trying to see the details of the conflict. By and by I heard a distant clack of metal upon metal, and even, once, a terrible scream. But no men followed across that bridge. Aye, he was mad and brutal, but Alexander was also fierce and loyal and a gifted warrior, and he held that narrow way.

When eventually we returned to Baghdad, we shared the incredible story with the caliph. We had little evidence, but one of the traitor soldiers was eventually caught and confessed to Captain Nabil's crimes. As for the Greeks, well, the survivors fled to the north, and one at least reached Constantinople, for that pop-eyed youth was none other than Acteon, who was to bedevil us from time to time thereafter. He grew in boldness but never much in wit.

If you have not heard me mention this tale even obliquely before it is in part because the entire matter embarrassed the caliph: he had allowed, for the second time, an embassy of Greeks to advance into his nation only for them to attempt dark doings that jeopardized the caliphate.

But there is another reason, too. For a long time I was heartsick with the terrible thing that the Greeks had done to Alexander. It was all too easy to imagine how I would have felt had I been ripped from my own time in the prime of life and thrust forward into a strange land.

Now, though, I have a different thought. Maybe God saw fit to give him a better end than that history taught us. For surely, it is better for such a man to perish not in his cups, but in defense of his comrades. God give that I acquit myself as well when my own day comes.

Walls of Teeth and Iron

Gary Kloster

Vertebrate, Kayla thought, staring at the blood-streaked lump in front of her. She'd failed biology, but the gnawed bone trailed nerves like broken strings and three years of slaughter had given her a solid knowledge of anatomy. Hand pressed against her aching gut, she stared at the strands that had once changed a person's thought to action. They were just gristle now, stuck to the ground and caught between her teeth and she needed to get out of here.

Kayla rose from the gore-covered floor. When she was a kid, this shit had bothered her. She would puke her guts out after a night in the pit, but not anymore. In the three years since she'd turned thirteen, since she'd changed, she'd gotten used to the smell of blood and fear-sweat, of raw flesh and feces, gotten used to the knowledge of what filled her belly almost to bursting. And even knowing that she'd gotten used to it wasn't enough to make her retch anymore. The horrified, puking girl she'd been was gone, gone as the moon and the beast, and she could ignore the raw shrapnel of her victims as she walked to the door.

"Hey girl, where you going?"

From behind a pile of broken, marrow-sucked bones, Big Rodney pushed himself up. Blood gummed the hair that covered her uncle's chest, groin, and legs. His beer gut hung heavy from the night's feast and he looked like a sow about to throw four litters at once. "Just cause the moon's down doesn't mean the fun has to be over." He belched and grinned, and over his bloody teeth Big Rodney's eyes moved, tracing Kayla's body, not giving a shit about the gore crusting her skin.

Kayla hawked a red wad of spit at him and pounded her fist into the railroad ties that covered the door. The government men couldn't hear her, but cameras peered down from the silver-plated bars overhead, the cage that separated the beasts from the guests that Harrison sent each month to watch the executions. The guards could see her hitting the blood-splashed wood, torn and splintered by enormous claws.

They knew she wanted out.

"Yeah, Kayla."

Little Rodney pulled himself from a pile of shredded guts, standing and stretching. Not so little anymore, he was almost a mirror of his father, with more hair on his head and a smaller gut. "Why you always gotta run out, after?" Little Rodney scratched himself, dislodging shreds of tissue from his pubic hair. "Ain't you ever gonna want to have some fun? I mean, we could all use the exercise." Little Rodney belched, louder than his dad. "Damn government's gonna kill us, laying out that kind of spread." He laughed and Big Rodney joined him.

Kayla's stomach twisted, but she clenched her teeth. She remembered how much it hurt, when she used to throw up. Her body needed the meat to pay for the change. "Fuck you."

"That's all we're asking," said Big Rodney, and they giggled like hyenas. The stupid, spiteful sound made Kayla's teeth grind and she slammed her hand against the rough wood again, driving a splinter into her palm. It hurt, but Kayla didn't care. She wanted out, away from her asshole family and the half-eaten bodies of the people they'd killed.

"Open the goddamned door, you shits!" She pounded until the guards finally opened up and she could fling herself out of the Pit, leaving the stench and the Rodneys' laughter behind for another month.

* * *

The shadows were stretching long when Thistle drifted over the fence, the white-and-black moth wings on her back brushing the top strand of barbed wire. She landed in the pasture, bare feet sinking deep into a fresh pile of horseshit, and grinned.

"It's still warm," she said, wiggling her toes.

Kayla swiped her hand across her forehead, wiping sweat away. The sun might be going down, but it was late July in Nebraska and the humidity clung like warm piss. "Goddam, Thistle. Can you get any grosser?" The fey's smile grew and Kayla shook her head. "Never mind. Give me a hand."

Thistle stomped up and down, splashing manure on her ghost-white legs and fern-frond skirt, then walked over to where Kayla had tethered her gray gelding. The fey looked at the cardboard box that sat on the ground beside Kayla's feet, overflowing with bottles and bandages: a horsey first-aid kit.

"What happened?" she asked, and Kayla pointed to the blood marking Seagull's shoulder.

"One of the Rodneys spooked him with his four-wheeler. Stupid horse ran into the fence."

"Poor guy." Thistle ran her hands over Seagull's muzzle. He let her rub his neck, didn't even twitch when her hand ran over the wound. Course not. Animals felt nothing but love for Thistle from the moment they met her. It had taken Kayla months of patient care before Seagull let her anywhere near him.

"There." Thistle scrubbed her hand over Seagull's hide, brushing away dried blood. Beneath her little fingers, the horse's flesh was whole.

"Thanks." It'd been hard enough calming Seagull after he'd hurt himself. If she'd tried to touch that wound, the horse probably would have kicked Kayla's head in. "Now all I have to do is fix the little fence."

The big fence, the twelve-foot chain-link one topped with razor wire and hung with faded warning signs about the Preserve—the one Thistle had come in over—made up one side of Seagull's pasture. The little fence made up the other three sides, ragged runs of leaning posts and drooping wire that looked ready to fall. Kayla had spent most of last summer fighting with a posthole digger and staple gun, working to give Seagull a decent pasture after she'd rescued him from Little Rodney's neglectful ownership.

A section of the little fence lay tangled on the ground now. "It's lucky he stopped when he hit that," Kayla said. "He could have gotten tangled and broken a leg."

"Freedom always has a cost."

Kayla looked at her friend, but Thistle wasn't facing her. The fey was staring past the big fence instead, towards the other fence that sat way out there in the dry high prairie, a low fence of iron bars and twisted symbols humming with wards. *Blood and pain.* That's the only answer Thistle ever gave Kayla, when she asked the fairy how she managed to slip past the barrier that trapped the rest of America's fey.

"But is it worth it?"

Thistle looked over her shoulder at her, one eye blocked by the edge of her wing, and Kayla clenched her hands. Those words were supposed to stay in her head, but she'd whispered them and Thistle never missed anything.

"That's the question," the little fey said, "isn't it?" Her face shifted in the twilight, from young and soft and cute to something old, distant, cold. Then it changed again and it was just Thistle, frowning at Kayla's hand. "You're hurt."

Kayla looked down and saw the thread of blood leaking out between her fingers. After the government men had brought her home, she had ripped the splinter out and left bloody prints on all her bottles of Budweiser until the wound had finally scabbed over. That scab must have broken when she was dealing with Seagull.

"It's nothing."

Thistle fluttered her wings, rising like a dandelion seed, then landing next to Kayla. Her hand caught Kayla's fingers, impossibly strong. "You got this in the Pit," she said, gently touching the raw flesh. "I thought you couldn't get hurt there."

"I can the morning after." Kayla pulled against Thistle's grip, but she might as well have tried to break steel. "It's fine."

"It's infected."

"It doesn't matter," Kayla said. "Let it rot. The next full moon will heal it. Now let me go, I have to start fixing this fence before the light goes."

The fey lifted her fingers and Kayla's skin was whole, the torn flesh smoothed together. "*Now* it doesn't matter. And forget the fence." She waved a hand at the broken spot and from the dusty ground a shoot pushed its way up. A handful of seconds served for years and in the gap where the broken post had stood grew a hedge-apple tree, its tangled branches armed with long thorns. The fence wire was back up, held taut by the tree. "That doesn't matter either."

"Jesus, Thistle. What're you doing? The government watches this place. You can't—"

"Harrison doesn't care about me," Thistle said. "I'm too small. Now let's go."

"Go?"

Thistle waved a hand at herself and changed. Wings and fern skirt and manure spots vanished and she was a kid in scruffy sandals, cut-off jeans, and a faded Styx t-shirt that looked older than Kayla. "It's Midway night at the county fair. Ten bucks for unlimited rides!"

"Are you shitting me? You want to go to the Bumblefuck County Fair? Why? Last year you threw up on the Tilt-a-Whirl."

"And it was awesome." Thistle grinned and pulled a fistful of cobwebs and dead leaves out of her pocket. They shimmered in the growing dark and turned into a wad of twenties. "Get your truck, Kayla. The corndogs are on me."

* * *

When Kayla finally dragged Thistle away from the Midway she took her up the ridge that rose over the town's church steeples and cottonwoods. Years ago, someone had painted a bunch of rocks white and dragged them up here, forming an enormous B across the face of the steep hillside, easy to see from the interstate, and they settled on those stones to eat beneath the waning moon.

The B stood for Bradford, not Bumblefuck, but whatever. Kayla bit off her last piece of corndog and threw the stick towards the headlights on the distant interstate. *Those people know. That's why they drive by so fast.*

Before she'd dropped out of school, Kayla's history teacher had assigned a book called *The Gulag Archipelago*. She'd stolen a copy when she left, not because she cared about Russia, wherever the hell that was. No, it was the concept of prison camps in the middle of nowhere, where people were sent to be forgotten, that made Kayla think she might finish the book someday. Those Siberian prisons sounded like Bumblefuck and the towns around it to Kayla. The only difference was, the idiots who lived here were too stupid to realize they were prisoners because they had beer and churches and porn.

"You want some Shake-Up?" Thistle rattled her cup, sloshing the chunk of lemon around the ice cubes and sugar water, but Kayla waved it away.

"No. I want a Budweiser."

"The fair has beer."

"Not for sixteen-year-olds." The fairgrounds spread below, the bright flashing colors of the rides and games and concession stands smeared with the blue bug-lights and the yellow bulbs of the animal pens. "All this crap," she said, and spit down the slope, "*and* I get carded."

"The government won't let you have alcohol?"

"Nope."

"The government that feeds people to you?"

"Yep."

Thistle took another pull from her Shake-Up, her little face frowning around the straw. "They let you have beer at your trailer."

"The Rodneys buy me that. They think if I get drunk enough, I might fuck 'em." They'd been buying her beer since her first change, but she hadn't started drinking it until she was fourteen. Now she lost whole days to blackouts, but Kayla had never been near drunk enough to stand having either Rodney touch her. "But they cut down the power line running to my trailer last month with a chainsaw, so it's not cold anymore. Almost electrocuted their stupid asses."

"Why'd they do that?" Thistle bit a piece off her funnel cake. This was her second and it was a miracle that she hadn't puked on the Tilt-a-Whirl. But the fey had gritted her teeth and held down funnel cake and corn dogs and cotton candy, even while her little body had trembled in pain from the proximity of all that iron. Kayla was amazed by what Thistle would endure just to get what she wanted. "They trying to get you to move into the big house?"

"Yep." Kayla lay back on the white-painted stone and looked up at the stars, so fine and far away, like distant headlights. The sprawling farmhouse where the Rodneys lived was a mess of mold, beer bottles, and broken electronics, surrounded by a yard full of cars and four-wheelers and snowmobiles in various states of ruin. Kayla had never lived there, despite the Rodneys' promise to clean out a room just for her. After her change, after her first night in the pit, after her mother had parked herself in front of a train with a bottle of Jack and a Johnny Cash CD, the government had moved her out to the Rodneys' place. But Kayla had claimed the ramshackle doublewide that stood on the edge of the property, the place her grandmother had lived before she had hung herself from the big fence. "They keep pushing, Thistle. It don't matter how many women Harrison sends 'em. They want me, because I'll breed true."

Kayla bared her teeth at the moon, drifting so far above, silent and uncaring. "Makes me sound like one of those prize sows down there. The government sends the Rodneys a thousand girls and not one of 'em gets pregnant. But I'd make the Rodneys daddies and give the President Eternal a whole new litter of fetal-alcohol brain-damaged werewolves for his Pit."

Thistle took another long pull at her straw, noisily draining her cup. "He's coming, y'know. To the Pit. When the moon is full again."

"Fuck. Why?"

"Because your President Eternal is dying. Again." Thistle rattled her empty cup, sighed, and set it down. "He needs to be there for the sacrifice every fifty years, it's part of that damned pact. You didn't know?"

"I don't know shit." Why should she? Her life was her trailer, this town, and the Pit. "I thought the old bastard couldn't die, because of the pact."

"He's been dying ever since he came to us, a hundred and fifty years ago." Thistle hugged her knees, a kid in the dark with too-big eyes and too-pale skin. "Harrison got himself elected president mostly because of how he dealt with the Indians and the Fey. But just a month after the election, he was coughing his lungs out, so his people brought him to the Preserve."

Kayla frowned. She might have failed history, but it wasn't because she didn't know it. She hadn't read the textbook, but she'd listened to her teacher talk while she doodled in her notebooks and he'd never mentioned anything about Harrison being sick. He'd told them that the President Eternal's almost-immortality was a prize he'd wrenched from the Fey when he'd exiled them to the Preserve, so that he could guard against their dark magic. Kayla could remember how he'd stared worshipfully at Harrison's portrait as he lectured, while the cameras scanned over the class watching for any sign of irreverence. She'd always kept her hand under her desk when she'd flipped him off.

"If he was dying, why didn't you let him? That asshole fought you. Why help him?"

"Because we were losing." Thistle uncurled, lying back to stare up at the night, the moon bright in her eyes. "The humans were killing us, with their iron and their numbers. They were pushing us back and the only choice left was the prison they offered us, the Preserve. When they came with Harrison, the Queen of the Moon..." Thistle trailed off.

"What?" Kayla said softly. Thistle never wanted to talk about the Queen or any of the other fey, claimed she could barely stand them after being trapped in the Preserve with them for over a century.

She couldn't stand the other fey, couldn't stand humans, so she hung out with Kayla—a Were, a changing kind, caught somewhere in-between. Thistle told her that Kayla had the best of both mixed up in her, and the worst, and that made her interesting at least.

"The Queen thought the pact was the best deal we'd get," Thistle said, her voice barely audible over the roars from the tractor pull in the fair below. "So she wove a spell from moonlight and blood. Life for life, she saved Harrison with magic forged from murder. She thought she was saving her people, but that stupid bitch just fucked us all." Thistle's eyes flicked to Kayla. "You especially."

"Me?" She looked up at the moon, slowly waning toward darkness, and the flashback hit her like a hammer. *The moon so full, the screams so loud, the blood so hot, the flesh so good...* Her stomach clenched and Kayla almost lost her corn dogs. Struggling for control, she finally forced the memory away, though it left its taste.

"You. Your family." Thistle wasn't looking at her. "Harrison and the Queen made you with that compact. The children of the moon, human and fey, and every month you're fed and life is traded for life so that Harrison lives and lives. But every fifty years he has to watch his victims die in person." Thistle laughed and the clear, high-pitched notes sounded like glass tinkling and breaking. "The Queen meant to shame him with that, but he's made it a spectacle."

The enemies of the state. Humanity's traitors, who dabbled with forbidden magics. That's what they said about the people that Kayla tore apart on the commercials that advertised the executions. As if they had to advertise, when they forced every station to carry the carnage. The memory of blood still clung to Kayla's tongue, stubbornly refusing to go away.

"Harrison has plans to make this one special, I think. They'll have twice the prisoners, whole families."

"Shit." *Twice as many.* Kayla scraped her tongue against her teeth, but the coppery taste persisted. *Families.* "I can't."

"What choice do you have? Harrison's men will throw you into the Pit and the moon will do the rest. You'll become the beast and feed." There was no accusation in the fey's voice—she was just stating the truth—but it dug into Kayla like she was being wrapped in barbed wire.

"I could kill myself. My mom did it. My grandma." She could. Kayla had spent days spinning an empty bottle of beer in the circle of guns that she'd stolen from the Rodneys, picking them up and kissing their barrels when it wobbled to a stop. She could end all of this with one kiss.

Would she taste the blood then, too?

"They did it after they had a daughter, Kayla. When there was someone else to continue the line." Thistle shook her head. "You won't be able to do it before then. It's part of the spell that made you and your family, the spell that gave Harrison his life. Your family has to live, so that he can live. That's what the Queen's magic did."

Kayla felt sick again, trapped by walls of pain and magic and death. "The Queen of the Moon," she whispered, "is a stupid bitch."

"Yeah." Thistle reached out and took Kayla's hand. "But what can we do? Her and Harrison, they've trapped us all."

"Blood and pain," Kayla whispered. "That's what you always say. That's how you get free."

"Blood and pain," Thistle said, her eyes shining silver with moonlight. "But to break something like the pact... You'd need a sea of blood, so much pain. Do you think it's worth that?"

Kayla spat, but the taste still clung to her tongue. "Yes." *Twice as many. Families.*

A daughter.

"Yes," she said again, then stood, stalking down the hill towards her truck. "Let's go. I need a fucking beer."

* * *

The rumble of the truck's bad muffler didn't cover the crackle of gunshots coming from the big house. Kayla could see the red light of a bonfire flickering and figured the Rodney's were having a party. *Did the curse that keeps me from killing myself somehow save these idiots from friendly fire or from burning their house down around them?*

Maybe. It would explain a hell of a lot.

Kayla jerked the truck to a stop and swung out, heading for the corral. She'd dropped a six-pack into Seagull's water trough this morning. It had been in the shade most of the day and the cans should have been cool, but when she got there the trough was almost empty.

"What the hell?" Kayla had added cold well water after she had dropped the beer in, until the trough had slopped over when Seagull had gotten a drink. Now the beer cans were only half submerged and the tank was surrounded by mud. Kayla flipped off the cinderblock she'd used to weigh the cans down and grabbed one, looking things over. There, and there. Holes, two little ones on the side facing the big house and two ragged, fist-sized ones on the far side where the bullets had punched out of the tank. Rifle rounds, signs of the Rodneys' shitty aim. If she'd been around, they might have killed her. *Too bad*, she thought, and cracked the can. She tipped her head back, swallowing, and heard Thistle catch up with her, bare legs pushing through the ragged grass.

"Oh, Kayla. I'm sorry."

Kayla lowered the beer, looking at her friend, still disguised as a girl. "It's just a tank. I'll get another one at the feed store tomorrow." But Thistle was looking out at the pasture. Kayla followed her eyes and saw the lump lying on the ground, the moonlight glittering off an unblinking eye. For the first time, through the yeasty smell of the cheap beer, she caught the reek of blood.

"Assholes," Kayla whispered, and turned to stare at the big house and the bonfire.

"Kayla," Thistle said, but it was too late. Kayla dropped the can and started to walk.

The Rodneys were sitting in a ring around a crude table made from an old cable reel. A keg and a forest of liquor bottles covered its rough planks, mixed with guns and boxes of ammo. They were watching Little Rodney help a woman in a tube top aim a pistol at an old Chevy pocked with bullet holes.

"Better stay clear, cous," he slurred as Kayla stepped into the light of their bonfire.

She ignored him and slapped the gun out of the woman's hands. Tube top muttered a drunken "Hey—" but Kayla had already turned away, shifting her feet to drive a solid kick between her cousin's legs. He dropped like a ton of lard, hit the ground and started puking. Laughter rose from the rest of the people sprawled in duct-taped camp chairs, but Kayla could see Big Rodney walking towards her.

"Kayla, what the hell?"

"You killed my horse."

Big Rodney stopped. "Oh. Shit." He looked over at another man, bearded and tall, sitting on a mossy-oak-patterned camp chair. "Told you that damned cannon was going to get somebody killed, Jim." There was a rifle leaning against Jim's chair, an AR 15 tricked out with every accessory, like some mercenaries' favorite Barbie doll. The man shrugged. Big Rodney looked back at Kayla. "Sorry about that. Jim'll pay you back, long as he gets the meat."

"Screw you, Rodney." The man named Jim grabbed a bottle of Jack Daniels from the table. "I ain't paying for shit. Little Rodney was shooting my AR, too, and he can't hold his aim worth a bitch. It was probably him."

While Jim talked, Kayla walked—away from her uncle and towards the bearded man. He grinned at her when she stopped in front of him and raised his finger, telling her to wait while he took a slug from the bottle. Kayla ignored the gesture, grabbed his fancy rifle, and pitched it into the fire.

"Shit!" Jim jumped to his feet, his fist flying out and slamming between Kayla's breasts, knocking her on her ass. "Oh, shit, bitch, you did not—" He took a step towards the bonfire, but the AR 15 was buried in flames, its plastic parts already melting into toxic-smelling pools as the glass in the sight popped and broke. Jim spun back to Kayla, looming over her. "I'm going to kick your scrawny ass."

Was this what it was like to be in the pit? The thought skittered through Kayla's brain, but it was too stupid to stay. Jim was big and hairy and he probably wanted to think of himself as some kind of monster, but he was nothing next to the beast that Kayla became. Sprawled in the dirt, she glared up at him and spat, and he paused, uncertain.

But not for long. The Rodneys and Kayla were a secret. Harrison made sure of that, even if the Rodneys wanted to brag. It was for their protection, to keep anyone from going after the President Eternal's executioners. Which meant this man just saw a crazy teenager in the dirt before him and, however uneasy he might feel about the look in her eyes, he wasn't going to back down from some girl.

"Jim," Big Rodney said, but the tall man took a step towards Kayla, grunting as she kicked his shin, then grabbed her leg when she kicked again. He dragged her close, then shifted his grip to the back of her neck.

"Jim!" Big Rodney shouted, but the bearded man ignored him and hoisted Kayla up. She hung there, her fingers tearing at his wrist as she glared into his eyes. They widened, went from angry to surprised, to afraid, to agonized.

"What the fuuuu—" The word broke into a howl and Jim's hand spasmed, letting Kayla go. She dropped but kept her feet, stepping back to give the vines that were whipping up from the ground room to wrap around the bearded man. Thicker than her thumb, the twisting stems were coated in thorns, vicious hooks that punched through Jim's t-shirt and jeans as easily as they pierced his skin. In seconds the only thing that could be seen of Jim was a few narrow bands of bloody flesh visible between the stems and bits of bushy beard. Kayla could hear him screaming, though, as the thorns tore into him like teeth. He screamed and screamed, staggering around in those thorny ropes, until he fell into the bonfire and the dry vines exploded like kindling, burning him far faster than the gun he'd landed on.

They broke then, all the people with lives and jobs and a world outside of walls and pits and death. They ran for their cars or off into the darkness, screaming or silent, leaving Kayla standing in the firelight with the Rodneys and Thistle. The fey hung in the air, her black-and-white wings unmoving even though her bare feet drifted a foot off the ground. Her skin gleamed like marble in the firelight, where it wasn't wrapped in ferns and wildflowers, but her dark eyes didn't reflect the flames. They glowed instead with the silver of moonlight as they stared across the shell- and bottle-strewn dirt of the yard at Kayla.

"Daaaaaamn," Little Rodney said, standing up. One hand still cupped his balls, but he was looking past Kayla to the fire. "We said bring your own beer. Not BBQ." He laughed, dropping his hand.

Big Rodney didn't laugh. He took a swig of his beer and shook his head. "Jesus, Kayla, you sure know how to blow up a party. You know the government saw that shit. They're gonna be coming to clean this up, which probably means putting bullets in our drinking buddies' heads, moving our mangy asses, and clipping your little butterfly's wings. All because of a fucking horse."

The government. "Goddamn," Kayla whispered. It didn't matter how little Thistle was. Harrison's propaganda was all about how he protected people from shit like this. And now he'd hunt the fey down. "Thistle." She looked at her friend, drifting in the air, smoke wrapping around her wings like chains. "You have to go!"

"Or what?" Thistle's voice was a whisper in the dark, barely heard above the bonfire's crackle. "They'll put me in a cage?"

"Thistle," Kayla said again, agony twisting through her voice. "Go! Please."

Thistle's bright eyes dimmed. "I'll go. But I'll see you again. Blood and pain, Kayla. Their walls can't hold me. Or you." Her wings beat and the smoke gathered around her broke and she was gone, vanished into the night.

"Twenty bucks they sniper her ass before she makes the preserve," Little Rodney said, but Kayla didn't look at him. She bent and grabbed the bottle of Jack that a dead man named Jim had dropped. It was still mostly full and she took it with her as she turned from the fire and started walking. She was on her fifth or sixth long swallow by the time she made it back to her trailer and the choppers buzzed overhead, iron wasps that split the night with brilliant white light, like rabid moons fallen to Earth.

* * *

Just before the executions, the government men locked Kayla and the Rodneys together in a square cement bunker beside the pit. It was a place to wait for the moon, safe from their victims and the cameras.

The Rodneys paced, restless, their hairy skin slicked with sweat. They were all naked, but neither man even glanced at Kayla. Sex was nothing compared to the change, and they rolled their shoulders and flexed their hands, like gladiators waiting for the arena to open.

Or like lions.

Kayla sat on the cold cement floor, head down, not watching them. Her body hummed with the change, but she didn't want to feel it, didn't want to feel anything. This was the first time she'd been sober in weeks and she hated it, even though the coming change had wiped away her hangover. She'd rather have that alcoholic ache, or better the numbness that preceded it, than this awful, ecstatic anticipation.

"Hey. The TV." Little Rodney jerked his head towards the box of glass and plastic that hung in the corner, a new addition to the room. It had been playing silent images of the crowds filling the bleachers around the Pit and the prisoners being lowered in. Now it was a picture of a man, jowly and gray, his face a map of wrinkles but his eyes bright, young, alive.

"Shit, it's Harrison." Big Rodney stopped his pacing and stared with Little Rodney. Kayla kept her head down, but she watched, too, peering at the TV through the fringe of her hair.

"It is," The President Eternal said. "My executioners. My teeth. The moon rises, and you'll change soon, but in these last few moments that you have of clarity I wanted to thank you. For your service." Still on the floor, Kayla glared at the old man. The coming change made her anger burn, a bonfire centered in her belly.

"Some might call it a sacrifice," he continued, staring at Kayla, then his eyes flicked toward the Rodneys. "Others a blessing. But what you do for me, for our country, is a service. Do you understand?" Harrison smiled, a dry twist of thin lips. "You show the people that monsters dwell outside the door that I bar. You show them why I'm necessary, why I'm good. For one hundred and fifty years your family has done that and that's why I've come. To honor your service."

On the other side of the room, the Rodneys puffed up with importance like toads, but Kayla shook her head. "Bullshit. That's just the show you slapped over this slaughter. You said it before, we're your teeth. And you're a vampire, waiting for blood so that you can keep on living."

Harrison's smile disappeared. "So you want to think of all of this as a sacrifice? Of innocent victims to a monster, of yourself to my will?" The President Eternal shrugged. "So be it. Just don't fight it. You're bound to me by a pact one hundred and fifty years old and your misery won't break that. Keep that in mind, my terrible servants, and serve me. Feed." His too-young eyes found Kayla again. "And increase."

Off screen, someone spoke: "Three minutes, sir." Harrison nodded.

"I know you don't remember much, when the beast takes you, but try to remember tonight." The President's thin smile returned. "It will be a lesson. Be happy with your service, or make peace with your sacrifice, whatever it takes. Because you and your family, those that came before and those that are yet to come, are mine, and you'll never escape me. Remember."

The word echoed through the room and through Kayla's head—*remember, remember*—and she was on her feet, shouting, but there weren't any words in her throat. It was just a scream that grew louder and louder as it deepened into a roar. A bellow that shook the air as the change swept through her, shattering her bones, tearing her muscles, her tendons, breaking her down and rearranging her. It destroyed her, it killed her, but it brought her back. Life flashed through her, so much life. It slammed her bones back together, rewove her tissues, remade her. She wasn't Kayla, not anymore. The full moon had come and now she was the beast. Her bellow became a howl and she ripped the TV off the wall and threw it across the room to shatter against the gate that barred them from the Pit.

The Pit. That name drifted through the chaos of her thoughts. The place of blood, where she would be fed. She crouched and, beside her, the other beasts crouched too. She snarled, warning them, and they snarled back, but when the gate began to lift they held themselves still, let her move forward first.

The beast was strongest in her.

Despite her bulk, she flowed like shadow, something like a wolf, a hyena, a bear, a tiger, an amalgam of all the fears of naked humans beside a fire, staring at the glowing-eyed shapes moving in the dark. And there they were, a knot of men and women and children huddled against the opposite wall, silent or sobbing as they stared at her. She breathed deep, scenting their blood, their sweat, their piss, their terror: intoxicating. But there was more prey above, outside the steep walls of the pit, so many more. Sitting and staring down at her, silent, scared, and excited. Waiting. More blood, more flesh, but there were bars across the top of the pit, thick ones striped with the metal that burned like fire. She snarled at the prey denied her, then turned her attention back to the meat within reach…and saw her.

Small like a child, she pushed herself out of the mass of humans, but she was no child. Her skin glowed in the moonlight and from her back blossomed pale, delicate wings. Chains wrapped her wrists and ankles, binding her, iron chains that smelled like rust and blood, and beneath them the winged thing's skin was blistered and broken and wept a clear fluid that looked like silver tears. The scent of it filled the air and Kayla the beast leaned forward, lips pulling back from fangs long as knives. Then she moved, growling a warning to the others, claiming this strange prey.

She took the winged not-child in her claws, ignoring the screaming humans, and smelled the sweetness of its blood. She spread her jaws and brought the thing closer—and then stopped.

"Kayla. It's me. It's Thistle. Do you remember?"

The words buzzed through her head, almost meaningless. Almost. But there was something there, something that weakened the rage, the hunger.

"Kayla. I told you I'd see you again." The not-child met Kayla's eyes over her muzzle. "I'm sorry. I hope you remember that. I'm sorry it has to be like this, that I had to lie to you about who I am, but I wanted to know you. I needed you to help me make a choice." The fairy smiled at her, her eyes shining with the moonlight. "I made a mistake a hundred and fifty years ago and my people have suffered ever since. So it has to be my blood, Kayla, my pain. And yours."

The fey's words beat around her, through her, and they almost made Kayla push back the beast, almost made her open her claws. But the moon was high and her rage roared back. The beast pulled Kayla down into the depths of her mind and took control again, snarling, ravenous. Her claws dug into Thistle, broke wings and tore skin, but the fey's eyes were still wide, still looking at the thing that had been her friend.

"Kayla," Thistle said, her voice almost lost in the snarls of the beasts, in the cries of the prisoners, in the shouts of the spectators. "Blood and pain, Kayla. Finish this and free us all."

The words were meaningless, the whimpering of prey, and the beast spread her teeth, then slammed them shut, tearing flesh, shattering bone, and laying open the chest of the little fey, exposing her heart.

White and round, it glowed bright, so bright, until the beast's teeth closed around it, eclipsing the moon-heart's light as she tore it free and swallowed it down.

Thistle's body dropped. It hit the bloodstained cement and lay broken and still as convulsions shook the monster that Kayla was. White light, moonlight, burned in her like fire, like acid, like silver. The light of that fey heart tore her apart from the inside, but like the change, it rebuilt what it destroyed. Crouched in the Pit, quivering, the beast blinked eyes that had gone from yellow to silver. She blinked, and Kayla blinked, and she was one, beast and girl and something else, something bright and strong.

"Thistle." Kayla growled the name through her thicket of teeth, but that was wrong. Her friend had lied to her about who she was. *Not Thistle, not small, no. She was the Queen of the Moon, she was my only friend, and I've eaten her heart.*

Kayla threw back her head and howled, a sound that filled the pit and made the crowd watching clamp hands to their ears, made them scream and shake. Rearing up, Kayla threw open her arms. Her fur, once dark, flashed in the moonlight like snow, white as the wings that spread behind her now, giant moth wings. Dark lines crossed them, twisting in patterns like broken bones and sharp fangs, like round, fat moons and black-eyed skulls. In the shadow of those wings, the prisoners crouched, terrified, but Kayla ignored them. The hunger that filled her had nothing to do anymore with simple things like blood and meat.

She wanted something else, and she threw herself into the air, her wings beating.

Kayla slammed into the bars at the top of the Pit and felt the pain of their touch. Silver and iron, iron and silver, they both hurt her now. But pain was just pain and the power that filled her like moonlight healed her burns. Roaring, Kayla tore the bars away and pulled herself through, searing her hide and crumpling her wings, but the burns disappeared and her wings straightened and spread and she took to the air.

They were running, all the ones that had gathered to watch the slaughter. The rich and the powerful who had come to curry favor with the President Eternal, along with those who just wanted to flaunt their fashion for the cameras that surrounded the Pit. They threw themselves from the stands and trampled over each other, pushing against the guards who were trying to rush forward. The crack of guns echoed over the screams and silver bullets slammed into Kayla, but the burning pain of their impact lasted only a second before her body shoved them out and healed.

Ignoring guns and guards, she dove toward a crowd of men surrounding one of the doors, old men in suits and young men with guns, surrounding the oldest man there. Kayla slammed into the crowd, claws flashing. This was the beast's work, but Kayla kept her eyes locked on her target. Harrison was shoving his way toward the door, pushing advisors and guards behind him as he went, trying to build a wall of flesh between himself and the beast so that he could escape, but it was no use. Kayla's claws caught and cleaved and threw the pieces away, her jaws tore, and the men fell, screaming when they still had throats. She caught the old man at the door, her claws spinning Harrison to face her.

"You can't." Caught, the President Eternal pulled himself together to glare up at her. "The pact holds. Whatever blood you spill gives me life. You serve me and I can't die."

Kayla tightened her paws and Harrison's skin, old and thin, split. But it healed, too, like her own hide. Kayla looked down at him and her jaws spread like a smile but not, no, not with teeth like knives.

"The Queen of the Moon—" she growled. Kayla opened one of her hands, dug her claws across her palm. Those furrows didn't heal and blood flowed from them, glowing white like moonlight. She raised her hand and her new blood fell across Harrison's face. Beneath the claws of her other hand, his skin broke again, and this time the wounds didn't close. "—is dead. And with her blood, so is your pact."

"The Preserve! It will fall and you'll all die!" Harrison's voice rose to a shriek as Kayla pulled him toward her jaws. "You'll all di—"

The rest was lost in the sound of bone breaking. Blood filled Kayla's mouth, hot and thick with hair and bone shards and soft brain matter. She growled and spat, the taste of it sickening. Turning, the crowd running from her, she looked back at the pit. Beside it crouched the other beasts. They had leapt through the hole she had made, abandoning the sacrifices, attracted by the noise, the crowd, the fear. They looked at her, stupid and vicious, and Kayla flung the body she held at them. They caught it, fought for it, tore it apart and snapped it down. Then they lunged into the mass of people jammed around the doors, claws flashing red, jaws tearing.

Kayla looked away. Overhead, a vast skylight framed the night, letting the light of the full moon fall stark and white across the killing grounds that surrounded the pit. Out there, not so far away, was a wall of iron, a circle of pain that had bound the fey for a hundred and fifty years. She crouched, beat her wings, and leapt.

The skylight shattered and she was flying, flying away from the sounds of sirens, the sound of helicopter blades beginning to turn. She would beat them there, and she would feel that iron burn as she tore it apart, and maybe she would die, maybe all the fey would die, and maybe this night would end it all.

But maybe not, and that was the thing Kayla thought as vines rose behind her, twisting up around the choppers, wrapping around rotors and tearing them apart. Maybe not. And that uncertainty, that realization that all the walls that had surrounded her were breaking and that her life for the first time was uncertain, unbound, drove Kayla forward, despite the blood and the pain, towards whatever might happen.

Faux Pas

Louis Evans

From atop the observation deck of the Empire State Building, Maia looked out at the Accession Ball and let out a sigh of relief three decades in the making.

The whole Historical Manhattan Preservation District was given over to the Ball: every spire and archway rescued from the floods and even the ancient scrap of Central Park still known as Sheep's Meadow were crawling with guests. Over a million of them, all told; human and alien alike. Everyone celebrating the Terran Union's brand-new membership in the Galactic League.

Negotiating the Accession Treaty—signed that very morning on the thirtieth anniversary of first contact, by League President Astrid Sastrowardoyo and League Ambassador 3tchk4Ora, an arthropodal Iktrri—had been the great work of Maia's lifetime. Wrangling the birth of Terran Emis, the brand-new Earthling dialect of the intergalactic lingua franca, and countless parallel delicate trade negotiations with hundreds of jockeying species had both taken decades of painstaking labor and careful communication.

Compared to all that, the treaty itself was simple, standard for every League entrant. It pledged mutual non-aggression and mutual defense, membership in the League Parliament and adherence to its dictates, and so on. The Terran Union had committed, as a member state, to uphold strict standards of justice, due process, and democratic internal governance.

The Union also promised to forswear racism, in all its forms. Nearly a third of the treaty was taken up with these solemn oaths: an exhaustive list of forbidden racial injustices in law, in policy, and in social practice. Many of the listed atrocities were familiar stains from the darker chapters of Earth's history, but more than a handful were downright unheard of—"forced hybridization," "recombinant allele theft," and others.

To be honest, Maia had loved that part of the work most of all. When she'd read the Accession Treaty into the record on the floor of the Terran Union's congress, she'd been nearly moved to tears by her pride at how the Terran Union lived up to the standards of its newfound interstellar siblings. Galactic League membership was not just a pragmatic coup, it was a vindication. Of the Terran Union, of the rights revolution of the past century, of a species that had outgrown its violent and troubled past and put itself on a solid footing of peace and justice.

And now, with the treaty signed, it was all over except for the partying.

For other people, anyway. Up here atop the Empire State Building, Maia was treating herself to a quiet moment of private contemplation. Of relief.

And then the moment ended. An unfamiliar alien came up beside her and rested its sickle-shaped limbs on the railing as well. It turned to face her; its face resembled nothing more than an eel as seen through a kaleidoscope.

"The Fazrahi ambassador," whispered Francois, Maia's social secretary, in her ear. No social errors, no faux pas, could be permitted at the Accession Ball, and so Maia was connected by hidden cameras and earpieces to a control center consisting of Francois and a cabal of about twenty experts: xenobiologists, exosociologists, non-human linguists, political and military attachés, and even an ex-Jesuit professor of theology. She could hear the whispered chatter behind Francois as they traded facts and theories about the Fazrahi; she ignored it to focus on her new guest.

The Fazrahi spoke, a guttural utterance like the sound of wet flesh thumping onto the deck of a fishing trawler. The translation collar hanging from its neck twinkled as it processed the sentence, then spat out an equivalent in perfect English.

"I have a question of import for you, Secretary."

Maia smiled her diplomat's smile. "Of course," she said. "Feel free to ask."

Again the sound of meat, pulverized, tenderized—but nothing tender about that sound.

"A very direct question."

"Watch out!" hissed Francois. "Sources say the Fazrahi are... tactless in the extreme." Maia's smile didn't falter.

"I am an open book," said Maia.

"Where are the other humans?"

"Pardon me?"

"The other races of humans. Where are they?"

"Every human race is represented here." It was true, too; Maia's staff had slaved over the guest list to produce that effect—not for alien consumption, but to pointedly include the representatives of every human community.

"I have seen members of only one race. Do you keep the others locked in your basement?"

"I—every race is here. I, for example, am Georgian, which—"

"I see only one race. You all look the same."

Maia swallowed her immediate response. She needed to tread cautiously, but diplomacy also meant sharing information about what was and was not appropriate. "On Earth, that's considered an impolite—"

"I am a xenobiologist. I know what I am talking about. This party looks like it was hosted by racists. By—" the translation collar coughed "—racial supremacists."

"I assure you, that is not the case!"

The Fazrahi's forearm-scythes scraped on the railing.

"Can you breed with your guests?"

"Can I *what*?" Over her twenty years of negotiating, aliens had asked Maia some inadvertently tasteless questions, but it was something else again to experience it face to face.

"Breed. Reproductive sex. Make babies."

"Among humans, we tend to reproduce with only a close, committed partner—"

The Fazrahi ambassador's harsh cough of indifference required no translation.

"I do not care about your human mate selection taboos. Can you breed with every guest?"

"I—if you mean, could I marry and have children with a member of another race—well, of course I could, anyone can, though—"

"And yet you say there are multiple races here."

"There are!" said Maia. Her back was up now. She might be a representative of the most junior member of the League, but she spoke for her entire species. She would not be browbeaten.

"We are no racists," Maia said. "I give you my word that every race of humans was invited to this party and is in attendance. As Secretary of State of the Terran Union, I give you my word. If that does not satisfy you, I invite you to call on my superiors."

The Fazrahi stared at Maia. Its eyes blinked, one at a time, moving in a counterclockwise circle around its complicated maw.

"Either you are a fool or a liar," it said. "And either way, you are a racist. I do not treat with such scum. My government will pursue this matter."

It stalked off to the elevator, slamming the door behind it.

Maia took a deep breath. Let it out.

"What the *hell* was that about?"

Silence from her earpiece. Confused muttering, then odd echoes of snatches of the conversation, as different members of her team replayed the encounter, trying to parse it. Maia heard her own voice, tinny and distant. The dispassionate tones of the translation collar: "—racist—only one—the same—breed—breed—breed—"

"Oh," came a voice over the headphones. "Oh no."

"Who's that?" asked Maia. She'd run enough emergency analysis meetings to be able to spot the one person in a room who had the fraction of a clue.

"Nashwa, ma'am. Xenobiologist."

"Get on the mic. Tell me what's happening."

Complicated sounds of audio equipment, as Nashwa shouldered Francois out of the way and sat down at the main microphone.

"I think—I've got an idea what's going on, ma'am. But it's really, really bad."

"Tell me."

"I...should start with the basics, I think. Some really basic biology."

"Go ahead."

"Okay, so, in biology, the groups of organisms we're usually interested in are called 'clades.' A clade is any group of all the descendants of a common ancestor. A 'species' is a clade where all of the surviving members are able to interbreed. Humans are a species, chimpanzees are a species, blue whales are a species. So are strawberries. The species is the fundamental unit of biology—of the *human* study of biology."

Maia nodded. She knew all of this but did not interrupt. When working with unknown unknowns, she never interrupted an expert. Interrupting saved seconds but cost years. *If* you were lucky. If you were unlucky, it cost lives. It was always the hidden assumptions that got you.

"So that's species. Clades one level bigger than a species are called a 'genus.' Canis—that's dogs, wolves, foxes—is a genus. So's panthera—tigers, lions, jaguars—and equus—horses, donkeys, zebras. Sometimes different species in the same genus can have sterile offspring, like mules or ligers.

"There are smaller units than species, too. Subspecies, like dog breeds. European scientists used to think human races were different subspecies, but they're not, really. Too similar."

Maia kept up the nodding, but she couldn't guess where this high school biology lecture was going.

"All right. The thing to remember is that biologists—human biologists—really think in terms of species. We care about genera, and subspecies, and bigger and smaller groups—but thinking in terms of species is pretty fundamental to our understanding of biology. Darwin wrote *The Origin of Species*—not 'the origin of genera'.

"When we negotiated with the Galactic League, there were two words they used for biological groups—um, *'atark,'* and *'fremen.'* We translated atark as species and we translated fremen as 'race.' It came up in the treaty a lot. All that stuff about the rights of racial groups, the equal treatment of races—the word they were using was fremen.

"But how did we get the definition of 'atark'?

"Well, we said something like—I'm paraphrasing—'We have one head and two eyes and two hands and two feet, we use tools, we use language, we build spaceships. We call ourselves "humans," "human" is the name of our species.' And the League translators looked at that sentence and they said, 'Our word for "species" is "atark."'

"And then *they* told *us* that fremen meant a subgroup of atark, so we translated it as 'race.' After all, that's what we think of as the biological subcategories of humanity—even if we know, consciously, that race isn't substantially biological at all.

"But what if we got it all wrong? What if *fremen* means species, *not* atark?"

The outline of an idea began to show itself to Maia—a monstrous, terrible misunderstanding.

"See, that makes sense of what the Fazrahi ambassador was saying! He asked if all of the human fremen were represented at the party, and you said yes, and he asked if you could reproduce with everyone here, and you said yes, and he was mystified. He assumes that different fremen means different species. There's a reproductive barrier. But you told him that many different fremen were represented, and that there *was* no reproductive barrier. That's nuts—that's wrong by definition.

"But if fremen means species, then atark *has* to mean genus. I'm looking at the texts; they're unequivocal. Atark are *collections* of multiple related fremen.

"And if that's the case then we've missed something huge. Because the Galactic League is an alliance of atarks, not fremen. Genera, not species. We've always assumed that intelligent life would come in single-species units, ever since we had the idea of intelligent life on other worlds. *We're* only one species. But it's not true! The natural unit of intelligent life is the *genus*—a related *group* of species, all evolving intelligence together.

"It makes sense of their obsession with fremen rights, too. Think of all the atrocities we've had on Earth in the name of race—and *race* is basically a fiction, a made-up category that lasts for a few centuries, if that. Imagine how bad it could get if you had multiple intelligent species that can't interbreed, that remain fixed over millions of years, that spread out to different continents or develop different physical abilities or only encounter one another at the end of a firearm."

Every good diplomat is a student of history and Maia was no exception. Her mind was overwhelmed with thoughts of the genocides of human history, redoubled by this unfamiliar biological context. She imagined the Punic Wars, *Carthago delenda est*, "Carthage must be destroyed," in a world where you could tell, centuries later, whether someone's ancestors had been Carthaginian just by looking. She imagined the Columbian exchange, the first mass encounters between Europeans and the Native Americans, in a world where *mestizo* births were a biological impossibility. She imagined the Nazi genocides, their crimes against humanity, in a world where the racial pseudoscience *worked*, where a chart of facial features showed for certain whether you were or weren't an Aryan. How unspeakably terrible those atrocities were; how much worse they might yet have been! Stranger visions and more terrible: medieval monarchs with no dream of marriage and alliance, only crusade and extermination. Biological warfare when only the enemy race suffered from smallpox. Forced breeding programs—get the good genes out of their fremen, drain that hybrid vigor, breed a race of servile mules. Cannibalism and infanticide—*our* children, *not theirs*, will inherit the stars!

Maia swore with awe and dread in her voice. "No wonder they made us swear our fremen lived at peace, shared in justice. It must have been terrible—for everyone but us."

"Well," said Nashwa, and her voice was a thing of ice. "Here's where it gets bad."

"How? I mean, it's a hell of a misunderstanding, but we just... evolved differently. It's not our fault we don't have any other fremen."

"Yes. It is."

"What?"

"Humans, *homo sapiens*, are the only species left in the genus *homo*. Our genus. But it didn't used to be that way. Three hundred thousand years ago, there were at least eight different *homo* species. Neanderthals. Denisovans. Florenesians. More."

"What happened to them?"

"We did."

Silence, just a moment of silence.

"We were smarter. Faster. Better armed. We wiped them out.

"You have to understand, the other hominids weren't just animals. They'd been using tools for millions of years at that point. They made art, conducted rituals, buried their dead. We— *sapiens*—we moved into their lands, we hunted their prey, we made war on them, we produced interspecies hybrids with them and absorbed their populations. Every crime listed in the League Charter, we committed. Hundreds of thousands of years ago."

"If they find out, they'll think we're monsters."

"It would be as if Hitler's Third Reich applied for Terran Union membership, and defended its human rights record on the basis that it had always treated Berliners and Frankfurters equally...and the Union fell for it."

"Catastrophe," said Maia. "Utter catastrophe."

"Oh dear God," whispered Francois. Maia was already snapping out orders.

"Mobilize security. Scan the guest list. I want you to get every anthropologist, every evolutionary biologist, every single *graduate student* in life sciences out of that party *at once*, do you hear me? *Anyone* who could spill the beans. And *don't* let on that something's up!" A flood of acknowledgements washed back over her. Her breath echoed harsh and fast in her own ears.

Maybe, she thought, *just maybe, we can keep the lid on it for now. My people trained for this.* She turned her attention back to Nashwa and her team, sketching out messaging, which atarks to contact, what spin to put on these revelations. She needed to get a plan in front of the Union Cabinet within minutes; she worked faster and surer and more ingeniously than she ever had before.

Beneath her, in the towers and plazas and promenades that bore homage to a once and former city, a vast wave of Union marines in dress uniform, diplomatic functionaries in fine suits and United Earth pins, and spies dressed as waiters surreptitiously flooded out on a desperate, secret mission, a wave of terrible power and purpose and stealth.

But it was already too late.

* * *

Peregrine Edward Stanton Hillsbury IV, twelfth Earl of Melbourne, was having a ripping ball. To tell the truth, Perry didn't usually like parties. At least, not the sophisticated sort. He cut a fine figure in tailcoat and hose and could stand around as pretty as you please. But somehow, those little circles of conversation and camaraderie always excluded him.

The reason for this misery was straightforward, Perry knew: he was a bit thick. And so, among the wits and raconteurs of the higher strata of Australian nobility, he was invariably left behind, or worse, admitted on condescending sufferance, like the scrawny kid at a pickup rugby game.

This party, the fanciest *ever*, would no doubt have been the same. Except! It was chock full of alien beasties who had never rudding been to Earth before! Which meant that every single fact jammed into a crevice of Perry's skull was an utter bleeding revelation to them.

For the very first time in his life, Perry was holding forth in the very center of one of those smug little cocktail chit-chat circles. So what if the other residents of the circle resembled, respectively, a weather balloon on stilts, a very meaty refrigerator, a cross between a dog and a suit of armor, a pony-sized toad with far too many mouths, and a roomba that was luxuriously furred on one side and unspeakably slimy on the other? Perry wasn't prejudiced.

It turned out the bulldog-knight-looking chap's people did some sort of ancestor worship thingy? But, like, deep-time, collective ancestors. Perry didn't quite grasp the nuances, but the alien had all these questions about human prehistory and Perry was happy to oblige with any half-remembered scraps he could dig up from his university days.

"So, yeah. Cave paintings in France. Course, you've never heard of France. It's this country in Europe—you saw Europe, yeah? From space?—with the most amazing cheese."

"Cheese?" said the weather balloon. It twisted sideways, listened to its translator. "Ah. A food."

"Yeah, it's ripping." Perry snapped and a waiter appeared. "Say, could you run and grab a cheese plat—oh, you've got one! Ace!" He plucked a few cubes from the silver platter, gestured to his new friends.

"What do you say, mates? Ready to ride the greasy dragon?"

There was the unmistakable pause of googling. Then two of Perry's new friends stuck their hands (or equivalents) into the platter and got their own cubes of cheese. The others hung back, discouraged or disgusted by what their searches had turned up.

"Bottoms up, lads!" The refrigerator and the toad swallowed their own cubes and let out noises that Perry hoped were pleasurable.

"Cave paintings," prompted the bulldog. Its native language sounded mostly like elaborate sneezes. "And what else?"

"Well, there's Lucy, of course. She's a beaut. Oldest skeleton of them all—that we've found, anyway."

"Lucy is venerated?"

"Pardon?"

The bulldog shivered; Perry had no idea what the body language meant to convey.

"You eat her death-skin? Her grave-grass burns regularly?"

"Mate, you're not getting through at all, here."

A more violent shiver seized the bulldog; when it sneezed again it did so slowly and deliberately.

"Did Lucy have a funeral?"

"Oh! Nah, mate, she just—died. In a cliff, like. So it's funerals you're into, eh?"

"Funerals. Yes. Homage of the venerable."

Perry thought back to his classes, sucking on his teeth.

"'Spose there were those Neanderthal graves."

"Neanderthal?"

"Yeah, you know. Big forehead blokes. Lived in Europe. Course, they're not really ancestors exactly. Not too many Neanderthals around anymore, haha."

"Where did they go?"

"Well, we gave them the old what for, didn't we? Old *homo sapiens* really showed them."

"*Homo sapiens*," repeated the roomba. "Your species' name?"

"Right-o."

"And Neanderthals were not of your species?"

"Well, we could interbreed with them a little. But no, not really."

There was some chatter amongst the various aliens, rapid-fire bursts of that funny language they'd used to conduct the treaty-signing ceremony. When it stopped, Perry had the distinct sense that everyone in his little circle was focusing on him much more intently than they had before.

"Perhaps the translation matrix is out of tune," the roomba said. "What do you mean by 'species'?"

Perry told him. Thick or not, you couldn't get through uni without knowing what a species was! And yet this uncontroversial definition caused the aliens to explode into a tizzy. They erupted into a massive screaming row. The refrigerator rumbled like a localized earthquake. The weather balloon turned the blue of a violent bruise. Gas sacs bulged all along the toad's flanks. Perry couldn't understand the language, but a couple of words kept popping up—"aehtrk," "pfrehmun." The whole thing rose in volume and pitch, then rose again. Nearby partygoers, human and alien alike, began to glance toward the argument. The human faces dripped with shame-by-proxy; most of it was pointed at Perry.

"Mates?" said Perry. The shouting match continued. Nearby aliens drifted over—a quadrupedal tree, a waist-high amoeba, a stack of algal pancakes—and fell into the argumentative whirlpool.

"Mates, come on!" Perry bellowed. The aliens fell silent. They turned to face him.

Fear, Perry knew, was either a learned response, or an evolved one. It was his first encounter with the aliens and he had no evolutionary legacy to fall back on. And yet, suddenly, he was overwhelmingly terrified of each and every single alien—even the one who reminded him irresistibly of a shaggy stress-ball with antennae.

The roomba advanced.

"Lord Peregrine," it said. "What happened to the Neanderthals?"

Perry's eyes scanned nervously across his extraterrestrial audience.

"They, um," he said, and swallowed. Somehow 'we gave them what for' didn't seem adequate. "They...died off."

The silence grew, hollowed out, formed a deep pit.

"And the others?" asked the roomba. "Other...species, like the Neanderthals?"

"All gone," Perry said. He was sweating on his forehead, his neck, his palms. "All gone. We're the only ones left." The sweat dripped and pooled in his collar.

"You sicken me, Lord Peregrine," said the roomba, its synthetic voice utterly emotionless. "You and your entire exterminationist race. Think on humanity's sins."

It turned on its trail of slime and departed. And with a great variety of locomotions, the other aliens turned and left as well, a great lumbering stampede that swept every extraterrestrial out of the hall.

A marine in full dress uniform, swimming with the tide, sprinted up to Perry and grabbed him by the elbow. "Sir?" he hissed into Perry's ear. "We've got to get you out of here—your anthropology degree—Secretary of State's orders—"

The other man went on whispering and tugging at Perry, but to no effect. The lordling stared, immobilized, at the party he had fucked more catastrophically than any he'd ever fucked before.

* * *

The top five stories of the Empire State Building had been converted to an emergency command post. Marines stood at the elevators and stairway doors, a semipermeable membrane that let through senior staff from the Ministry of Extraterrestrial Affairs and politely but firmly denied access to everyone else.

By this point, nearly every high-ranking diplomat in the Union was crammed into the ad-hoc penthouse, in shirtsleeves and hiked-up ball gowns and sleepily-smeared makeup, doing work that on an ordinary day they would've assigned to their secretary's secretary, scanning online encyclopedias and scientific journals frantically, jotting mad notes. Up on the top floor, which an infosec swat team had entirely wrapped in blackout sheeting, the Secretary of State zoomed with the President.

President Sastrowardoyo sat behind her bedroom desk at the Presidential Residence and rubbed sleepy eyes as Maia finished outlining the situation. The president was still wearing the fluffy robe she'd crawled into when she was whisked out of bed.

"Sounds like we fucked this one up, Maia," Sastrowardoyo said.

It hurt, but Maia couldn't deny it.

"Okay. What do we do?"

"Keep the lid on the news for now. We signed the treaty, we're in the League. If it gets really bad, they could initiate expulsion procedures, but my staff says that hasn't happened for hundreds of years. Then, once the ambassadors are out of the system, we should reach out to a sympathetic, well-placed alien government and sell them on our line. My staff has put together a list of candidates. We'll be pushing the climatological angle hard for Neanderthal die-off; we want to get professorships for every scientist doing work on that in the next six months if possible. Now, once we contact even one government, the matter is out of our hands, but—"

There was a sudden roar from outside the building. Maia bolted for the door, wrenched it open, and stumbled out onto the observation deck, trailing ruched ribbons of black sheeting.

The sky above the District blazed with the light of countless rocket engines. It wasn't, as Maia feared for a single heartrending instant, the baptism by fire of nuclear war. It was instead the angry glow of ostracism, as every right-thinking alien fled the honeyed embrace of the greatest monsters in the galaxy: *homo sapiens*, the genocidal, fratricidal maniacs who slew their kin and boasted of their crimes at parties.

Maia stood and stared at the sky, at the dwindling shuttles and landing craft, at the vault of the heavens. She saw her life's work in ruins; decades of striving and hoping lost. The sum of all diplomatic fears: every hard-won relationship gone in an instant.

No, worse than gone. Friendship soured into censure, disdain, contempt.

Her species was, once again, alone in the universe.

The Darithian Life Cycle

Peter S. Drang

The feeling starts deep within my thick Darithian bones, down in the core, the marrow. It grows stronger as the days grow colder. Winter will materialize in earnest only one earthbeing year from now. The earthbeings are soft like their wretched—though succulent—bodies.

Winter on Earth poses them no challenges. In the coldest part of our winter, which lasts nearly a hundred of their years, the air itself chills until it pools on the ground and survival is only found in our cyst-sleep. Thinking about their easy, short lives, the feeling in my bones surfaces again. A kind of hunger, but more than that. A need for gnawing, ripping. A desire for the taste of blood's knowledge. Sustenance for both body *and* mind.

"You've been quiet today, Nephra," the earthbeing Dr. Rolland Prathers says as he assembles his interview equipment. He wears a parka even though we are indoors. At this point in the fall, the outdoors feels bracing to me, but would be fatal for him in just minutes despite his clothing, despite his breathing device. The humans travel outdoors in special pouches. They are like hatchlings. Helpless.

"It is a difficult time for us," I reply in complete truth. I fantasize about distending my jaw and biting off his head with my thousands of jagged teeth. But his knowledge is useless to me; I know this from experience. His kind know not how to select the choicest glidda flowers for consumption, nor how to avoid the nearly identical-looking toxic rotymons.

"Do you look forward to assuming Darithian adult form?" Prathers holds the interview device close to me, as if that will make my words clearer.

I've been speaking his language for the hundred years since earthbeings arrived—longer than he's lived—but our physiology doesn't allow for perfect diction in their tongue. "With change comes challenge. I'll lose my true limbs and must learn to use the adult form's stubby pads. I'll increase in mass a hundredfold, become an herbivore."

His nearness boils my feelings up again. I smell his hand, so near my mouth. Savory and salty. His proximity seems almost a dare. Bravado? Trying to prove something to me? Or to prove to himself that he'd forgiven my mistake when his grandmother, explorer Mary Prathers, arrived long ago?

He makes notes, paws the chain that loops around his neck. Whatever is attached to that chain is hidden under his clothing. I've asked him about it many times, but he always refuses to answer, refuses to reveal it to me. "The transition to adulthood in humans is also an awkward time, but of course it's nothing like—"

I scoff. "Indeed. Nothing at all." Waves of hunger well up, bubbling from my bones to my scales. The need to prepare to hibernate. The need to bulk up for winter's test and to gain crucial knowledge for spring. Many will not prepare sufficiently and perish either during the winter through malnourishment of body or shortly afterward by malnourishment of mind. Many will refuse to do what is necessary—those who are weak like the earthbeings. He smells much as his grandmother did, on that first day the earthbeings landed, on the last day of her life. Before he'd been born, when his mother was still an infant. Though the humans perceive some aspects of our blood-knowledge, they seem not to really believe it. He's never asked me about his grandmother's thoughts, her dreams, which I know. Intimately.

"We will be leaving your world soon, Nephra," Prathers says. "Conditions are deteriorating precip-itously going into apoapsis. Even your dwellings will be too cold for us soon."

"After winter, when you return, my new name will be Nephragoni, and I have chosen the female adult form."

He makes odd sounds which I've come to know as laughter, a sign of amusement that I cannot replicate. "I shall be dead of old age by the time your spring comes, Nephra. But others will return to find you as the female adult Nephragoni."

I doubt this—I know their plans will change after today, but I do not say so. "I am sorry to cut this final interview short. I must prepare for tonight's ceremony."

He nods. "Very well. I will interview your siblings now. I will see you tonight."

* * *

I stand outside in the chill air, awaiting my brother Melphi.

Only two of my littermates still live. The larger, Zarthenga, has, like me, chosen to eat the herbs that will result in a female adult body after winter's test. The smaller, Melphi, had little choice but male. His diminutive stature wouldn't have survived the winter on female herbs, a complication of our biology. My size falls between their extremes so either choice would suit. Not wishing to be consumed during fertilization, I, of course, chose female. Once the choice has been made, we reference each other as if the adult form is already manifest—as 'sister' or 'brother.'

Melphi skulks around the corner of the building, his breath crystalizing and falling like snow. {Zarthenga is occupied elsewhere, as you requested, sister,} he says in our native language.

Although each of my siblings has learned some of the earthbeing language, they lack the direct blood-knowledge I enjoy, so theirs is a crude rendition.

I find no profit in delaying the main point of the meeting. I chose outdoors to ensure no humans would happen upon us. {We must kill sister Zarthenga.}

Melphi nods without any apparent surprise or reticence. {I think this in likeness. She is large enough to kill us both and take our parents' blood knowledge all for herself.}

{Her personality makes such a plan likely.} Zarthenga, even as a hatchling, never shared a single kill, leaving Melphi and myself to hunt as a team in compensation for our smaller stature. {But I must ask, has Zarthenga tried to persuade you to join her against me?}

Melphi hesitates a moment, seems surprised by the question but should not have been. Although Zarthenga has a significant muscle mass advantage over me, I could still cause damage in single combat. Her risk would be minimized by a dual attack. {No. And you?}

Zarthenga towers over Melphi and wouldn't need my help to dispatch him safely but might ask me to clear the way in exchange for an even split of the blood-knowledge, not wishing to risk fighting me. {Curiously, she has not. I believe this confirms that she plans to kill us both.}

In litters where siblings are of similar size, compromises to avoid any fighting are common. Survival is threatened more by wounds and weakness going into winter than by any split in blood-knowledge. But the large variance in our sizes, and Zarthenga's hoarding personality, has led to my family's inevitable conflict. This is yet another aspect of our culture that differs markedly from the memories I have from human Mary Prathers. Death-fights between siblings are not unheard of among the humans, but seem rare.

Melphi nods. {Let us offer proofs then.}

I extend the smallest claw of one arm, Melphi does likewise, and we each bite off one segment. Earthbeings who have witnessed this ritual term it a 'pinky swear' and snicker for reasons I comprehend only due to my earthbeing blood knowledge.

The sting is momentarily excruciating, but we won't need these appendages soon. The small pieces of flesh don't contain enough blood to exchange full knowledge but are sufficient for me to know that Melphi did not lie, and vice versa.

We discuss details of the battle to come. I will fall back a step at the start. Melphi will race ahead, then turn to distract Zarthenga, I will strike from behind. We work out some additional details, then return to prepare for the ritual.

* * *

We are in the celebratory chamber, a cavernous room with a towering ceiling. My mofather lies lengthwise on its belly in the center of the room, its body fifty feet long, its many stubby limbs spreadeagle, laying on the floor on both sides. My mofather's adult form body is soft, not scaly, and its teeth are blunt for chewing flowers. Its bright coloration assaults my eyes—splashes of every hue to better blend in with the petals it eats.

I wish that I could ask my mofather how it feels. But our adult forms communicate only through blood knowledge. I remind myself that after the cyst-sleep I will be thus as well: emerging as a lumbering, bloated, mute flower-eater. I will exist alone through spring, then will mate by eating a male, blending into a mofather myself. I'll lay eggs at the end of the spring, over a hundred earthbeing years after emerging as an adult. I'll live another one hundred fifty earthbeing years after that, with only one duty left: to provide blood knowledge for any of my offspring who survive. To lie in the ceremonial chambers as my own mofather does now, awaiting consumption.

Brother Melphi and sister Zarthenga gather with me at the entrance, awaiting the priest's prayers. The six visiting earthbeings have taken up seats on a second level we prepared for the ceremony. This would allow them a perfect observation point. The earthbeings have only been with us since this past fall, so this is the first such ceremony they'll witness.

I am certain it will also be the last time earthbeings attend any Darithian ceremony. Though they have a violent history—which I know in detail because Prather's grandmother studied such things—their earthbeing horrors pale in brutality compared to the Darinthian rites.

I pick out Dr. Prathers and wave one of my killing appendages at him. He notices and waves back with one hand while the other obsessively fingers that enigmatic chain around his neck. As lead diplomat, I'd made the decision to tell them nothing about the ceremony. How could it be otherwise? I didn't myself know the precise outcome.

The priest, a permanent larva, has seen three cycles. Priests are born rarely and at random. They genetically lack the ability to metamorphosize. Most only find out when they awake from cyst-sleep still in larval form. This priest's ancient body is wearing out—several of his appendages hanging slack and useless—and it probably will perish over winter. Death is just another kind of metamorphosis, after all.

The prayers begin, the *infawnidi*, the opening. A long series of chants with my siblings and I repeating key phrases in our own language. These prayers are a part of me, recited thousands of times in my larval life. They bring peace, at first.

My mind wanders. Why should earthbeings live on such an easy planet while we suffer our harsh winter? This is a question I'd pondered all fall, since meeting the earthbeings. If not for our cruel winter, the priest might live several more cycles and none of us would metamorphosize. We could live thousands of earthbeing years, not losing the ability to speak, tasting blood season after season, not becoming the bloated, herbivorous adult form.

I look at the earthbeings above us. Two of them whisper discreetly into their reporting devices. They will have much to report soon enough.

At the proper moment, the priest recites the *setmevandu*—prayer of the new generation—and on cue our mofather rolls over, exposing its belly, its jointed limbs splaying out to either side in pure acceptance. Our adult forms may not speak, but they do understand.

The priest looks out over us: myself, my two siblings, my prone mofather. Silence stills the close air. I feel my pulse slow as my heart builds up a supply of blood, ready to flood it into my system all at once for this test. My teeth ache. We await the *mafawnididi*, the signal to begin the ritual in earnest.

The priest stands glacier still for a moment, looks at each of us in turn, then bellows out a long, deep, shattering scream that raises dust off the floor. I glance up at the earthbeings. They cover their ears against the oppressive noise.

According to plan, I feign a misstep and allow my siblings to pace ahead. Their eyes should be focused only on our mofather's head, the place where the finest blood knowledge resides. Zarthenga, however, is focused only on the empty space where I should have been, where I will be in just one more step. She makes no move against Melphi, who is also looking where I should have been and not at Zarthenga, as if he is not concerned about the larger sibling at all. He is not sprinting ahead as we had discussed. How strange—

I understand now. I surge forward and left, sinking my teeth into little Melphi's neck from behind, grinding into his thick scales, which give way with a sickening crack. Surprised, he falls without serious struggle. His blood knowledge confirms my suspicion: Zarthenga persuaded him to betray me following our exchange of proofs. I do not blame Melphi. His small size weighed heavily against his survival this day.

I feel his love for me, his regret of the betrayal, as his knowledge ensanguinates me. His very blood asks for forgiveness and I grant it. But something more meets my awareness as Melphi's blood circulates through me: Zarthenga had told Melphi of her own plan and now I am twice surprised.

I dash to one side just in time. Zarthenga passes by me, carried by her ponderous momentum. She had doubled back on hearing Melphi's strangled cries. I fling Melphi's quivering, spent body. It strikes Zarthenga hard and carries her several paces farther, allowing me a moment to reposition myself.

I would like to simply outrace her now to my mofather's head, but the full details of the plan she revealed to Melphi rush into my mind. What folly Zarthenga has contrived!

I use the few seconds afforded to claw my way up the walls to the balcony where the astonished earthbeings are now standing, hands over mouths, some crying out. Melphi's blood still drips from my mouth as my head clears the railing, ropey pools of it splashing to the balcony's floor.

"Did you know of Zarthenga's plan?" I ask, looking right at Prathers. Melphi's blood knowledge has told me humans are involved, but not precisely which ones.

He stands frozen, mute, not by the frosty air, but by his own perfidy.

I vault the balcony wall and stand before them, all the while hearing Zarthenga climbing right behind. "Stand back, by the stairs." I grab a metal folding chair and turn to meet Zarthenga as she rushes over the wall, mouth wide.

I throw the chair into her gaping maw and, though metal, it snaps into shards. {Stand away, Nephra. We need not fight and risk injury.}

"Your plan does have need of my human blood-knowledge," I reply in the earthbeing's language so Prathers may also understand. My peripheral vision reveals the horror on Prather's face. Only now must he realize the truth of Zarthenga's plan: to kill me, not to obtain revenge for Prathers, but to obtain his grandmother's blood knowledge, knowledge of humans, of how the rockets work, details of the space station and Mars colony. Zarthenga would require intimate knowledge of human language, customs, space faring procedures, to carry out her plan.

Zarthenga crosses the row of chairs, flinging them in all directions, and stands next to the quavering Prathers. {Go, Nephra! I do not need you for human knowledge. Take mofather's head, consume all its blood knowledge. Stay here and freeze, then turn into a lumbering hulk. I shall journey to the stars and live thousands of years.} She distends her jaw and begins to turn toward Prathers, who freezes in place. He has nowhere to run.

{Wait! The humans will not accept you if you kill one of their own.}

She hesitates. {You killed one. They accept you.}

{They determined that my attack on Mary Prathers was by ignorance. They'd just landed, had not contacted us yet. But you would kill Prathers by design and they will not forgive that.} The difference, the reason it mattered to the earthbeings, was obvious to me due to my blood-knowledge, but not so obvious to others of my kind. Humans placed great stock in the reasons for killing, the motivations. To us, though, the killed are still dead regardless of the killer's reasons.

Zarthenga considers my words, then grasps Prathers by the arm. Prathers says, "No, please! Spare me!" The other earthbeings scuttle away, heading toward the staircase. By treaty, they carry no weapons, but I still detest their weakness, their abandonment of wretched Prathers.

{There is only one way to be sure of your words, Nephra.} She bites off his hand and he collapses, screaming in agony.

I could not have stopped it. I stand, muscles taut, waiting for understanding to course through Zarthenga. The tiny earthbeing hand won't provide enough resolution for Zarthenga to proceed with her elaborate plan but might reveal enough to put me back in danger.

{How curious these earthbeings are!} Zarthenga says, twisting her head from side to side as Prathers goes limp. She releases his bloody arm and he slides to the floor. {You are correct: they'll never accept me now.} Zarthanga rushes toward me, mouth agape.

I brace against the balcony wall, knowing my chances are slim. The best I can hope for would be to wound Zarthenga in retribution for her foolish plan to leave our planet and live among them. If I can land one solid bite, though I wouldn't survive her counter, she may not see spring. I expose my killing teeth one last time—

But her rush was merely a feint to force a backward step. She leaps off the balcony toward our mofather, still lying prostrate next to the confused priest. Her plan now: to gain the precious head blood for herself, leaving me with no knowledge to survive my herbivorous adult phase.

I leap over the rail, too, without another thought, bent on revenge. Not content to await a slow death in the spring, I will die here and now and do my utmost to doom Zarthenga too.

I land on her back, raking my limb claws into cracks between Zarthenga's thick armor plates. I clamp my jaws down, but they cannot penetrate. I need to get to the softer belly area.

Zarthenga twists around, throwing me off. I slam into the ground, dazed.

She looms over me. {You should have taken your chances without blood knowledge.} She steps on my neck—her weight is too great for me to fight. My limbs flail uselessly. She thrusts her powerful jaws toward my belly.

"That one, that one!" earthbeings shout.

Blasts ring out. Zarthenga falls, my neck freed.

I sit up, dazed. There are many more earthbeings here now. Two medtechs carry Prathers on a gurney. Others have weapons. The earthbeings must have called their security forces when the ceremony decayed into chaos. The treaties allow for human security forces if an earthbeing is attacked by a Darinthian. I had never considered that they could get here so quickly. Prathers. He must have had them ready, positioned nearby, deducing from Zarthenga's plans that a bloody fight might put the earthbeings in danger.

Two aim weapons at me while others check Zarthenga's corpse.

"This one saved me," Prathers says to the earthbeings aiming at me. Their weapons lower. Prathers' face is ice white, an anesthetic pressure pack seals his arm stump, a bag of fluid flows through a tube into his arm. The medtechs have ripped his shirt open to work on him, revealing a locket hanging from that chain around his neck. "You can have your mofather's blood knowledge all to yourself now."

I shake my head the way the earthbeings do. "I do not desire it any longer." I stare at the locket, hidden from me for so long. I recognize it from a distant earthbeing memory.

Prathers smiles as if expecting my answer. "What *do* you desire?"

I walk nearer to him, speak more softly. "Were you really going to take Zarthenga to live among you?"

He nods. "So we could continue our studies during your winter."

I look at my dead siblings, think about the long winter ahead. I have felt less Darinthian and more human since consuming Prather's grandmother so long ago. "I am much smaller than Zarthenga and would fit well in earthbeing-sized habitats."

"True enough."

"And I can relate many tales about your grandmother. Stories of her youth." I point at the locket hanging from his neck. "Such as how your grandfather gave her that locket, and how her heart lept when he told her he loved her for the first time"

He touches the locket gently with his remaining hand, nods. "I would dearly love to hear those stories."

There is no need for further discussion. The priest will find an orphaned set of siblings somewhere to take advantage of the knowledge my mofather has to offer.

And I will travel across the stars and live many years among the earthbeings, so that our species may understand one another as fully as Prathers and myself.

Seelie With a Kiss

Esther Friesner

They walked, robed in unearthly beauty, through ancient groves where silvery birch and nodding willow guarded paths that mortal men had never tainted with iron blade or earthly breath. Graceful and glorious, the lord and lady of elfhame's exalted seelie court blessed leaf and blossom, stone and stream, by their very presence and passage. Crowned with eternal springtime, they drifted from twilight shadow to moonlit glade until they reached a clearing where a fountain borne upon the backs of five winged lions cast diamond droplets against the sky.

Here they tarried, heads bent toward one another, and spoke in a tongue whose music had been stolen from the distant song of the stars.

"My lord Inariel, my love," the lady said, laying one slender hand upon her companion's silk-sheathed arm. "Do you see him yet?"

"No, my beloved lady Lorindiel," came the grave reply. "He's late again. As usual. O, feckless child!"

"Perhaps," the lady murmured. "Or else we have gone quite astray. We seldom venture so near the border of our realm. I *told* you to ask directions."

Inariel scowled. "Do you question my competence in order to defend our son's cloud-brained doings? *He* is late and *I* have not led us afield. I know the way to the fountain of the winged leopards well enough!"

"Indeed," said Lorindiel sweetly. She gestured toward the fountain. "And how many leopards do you know have *manes*?"

Before Inariel could reply, a happy shout broke from the nearby trees and a third elf bounded into the clearing. "Mother! Father! Here you are!" He threw his arms around Lorindiel, but the lady stepped away from his embrace.

"Kirael, your long absence in the world of men has made you forget the proprieties," she chided gently. "Your first greeting should be to your father and your lord."

Young Kirael was so mortified that he dropped to one knee and bowed his head. "Father, pardon me. I didn't mean to offend you, but when I didn't see you at our meeting place, I got worried and—"

"Yes, yes, never mind that." The elfin lord made haste to change the potentially embarrassing subject. "You are home again and, by all appearances, well. Nothing else matters. I wish that I could say I understood what drove you to go roving through mortal lands, but I suppose it is an affliction of youth to dream that the only things worth having lie far from home. We are content to see you have returned, thoroughly humbled and willing to admit how wrong you were."

"But father, I wasn't wrong at all!" Kirael exclaimed. His face was the picture of joy. "If I hadn't left, I wouldn't have met *her*."

"'Her?'" Lorindiel echoed. Her emerald eyes darkened with foreboding.

"My beloved, my heart's delight, my chosen one." Kirael sighed happily. "*Gosh*, she's swell!"

Two perfectly formed jaws dropped. Kirael's uncanny speech, so alien to the elegant language of his birth, made a strong impact on his small audience. There is neither word nor phrase in the melodious tongue of the high elves for *Who the what now?* but the expression that his parents shared now supplied that lack abundantly.

Unaware that their silence was pure shock, he went on: "There aren't words to do her justice. She's just so...*awesome*, you know? I mean, I never expected to meet someone *that* adorbs in the mortal realm." He leaped to his feet and hugged himself, lost in a lover's dream that only broke when he added: "She's waiting near the *right* fountain. Stay where you are; I'll get her." He vanished between the trees.

"Let him visit the world of men, you said," Inariel muttered to his wife. "He needs to feel free, to explore, to *find* himself, you said. Oh, well *done*, my lady. Did you hear the way he murdered our sweet language with that—that gibberish? '*Gosh?*' '*Swell?*' '*Adorbs?*'" He snorted. "Whatever the hellebore *those* words meant. At worst, I was expecting him to start using contractions. And yet I could bear it, if that were the only—" His thin lips curled with scorn. "—memento he dragged home. But he's done far worse, to his shame and our grief."

"My lord?" Lorindiel's voice quavered. "I do not see—"

"You heard him! He has fetched himself a bride who is—who is—" With a great effort, Inariel disgorged the loathsome word. "—*human*."

"Do not say it!" Lorindiel wailed. "I implore you, my lord, say it is not so!"

"Too late. I did."

The lady Lorindiel loosed a shriek of despair that struck the fountain dry and turned the leaves upon the nearest trees to ashes. She fled the clearing by the same path her son had taken, leaving her husband dumbstruck and alone.

Inariel had just finished restoring life to the fountain and the trees when his wife returned. Her lovely face wore an expression best described as brother to bewilderment and sister to I-do-hope-this-is-all-a-bad-dream-but-I'm-pretty-sure-it-isn't-and-we're-screwed.

"Where have you been?" he demanded.

"My lord, I sought to intercept our son ere he could return to his...memento, as you put it. I caught up with him on the path and tried to make him see reason, to persuade him to return the girl to her proper place with her kindred mortals and seek, instead, a bride among the highborn elf-maidens of our court." Her golden head drooped.

"From the look of you, I surmise that you failed," Inariel said grimly.

"Not...exactly." She raised her head again and he noted that her alabaster skin had paled to chalk. "Heed, I pray. I—I bring you—I *think* I bring good news," she said in the voice of one unaccustomed to hesitancy. "Kirael heard me out, listened attentively to all my misgivings and exhortations, but when I was done—" She took a deep breath. "—he laughed. He said my worries were for naught. He insisted on taking me the rest of the way to the fountain of the leopards where she awaited."

"Torment me no longer, lady!" Inariel snapped. "Is he or is he not going to undo his foolish act and rid himself of this miserable human wench? You claim to bring me good news. Where is it?"

The lady Lorindiel stood tall. "Kirael's chosen bride is not human. She, is fact—" Again, uncertainty clung to her words. "—an elf."

"What? But this is excellent! Ah, I was wrong to doubt our son's perspicacity by the slightest degree. Leave it to the issue of my loins to travel the realms of men and yet be able to find a proper elf-maiden to be his—"

"My lord, we need to talk."

* * *

The great ivory and gold doors of lord Inariel's palace flew open as the master of the house led his small party through. The swarm of tiny winged attendants who always hovered ready to receive his commands took one collective look at the newcomer accompanying their master and burst into a buzz of speculation. Whispers wove a humming web through the scented air until Inariel shouted, "Silence!" He then barked a series of orders that sent his fairy servants whizzing away.

Wonderful, he thought bitterly. *No one gossips worse than the fae. This disaster will be all over the seven realms by tomorrow. I can already hear the dwarfs laughing!*

"Father?" Kirael was suddenly beside him, gazing at him closely. "Father, what's wrong? You've got this really scary look going on."

Inariel forced a brittle smile which, truth be told, was even scarier. "I apologize, my son. It was only a passing thought that troubled me. I was trying to recall where I had put my, er, something. Alas, now I have forgotten what I was seeking along with where it might be."

Kirael gave him an uneasy sidelong look. "Oooooooh-kaaaaay," he said very slowly. "Uh, can I help with, um, you know, whatever?"

"Do not waste another thought upon the matter, child," his father replied, giving him a chummy flurry of pats on the back that was more like a pummeling. "I have just ordered a small repast for the three—I mean, for the four of us. Surely you must be hungry after your journey home?"

Still ill-at-ease, Kirael replied, "Uh...sure?"

"Excellent. Then let us away to dinner!"

Ah, yes. Dinner.

A sumptuous feast of delicacies was brought by stages into the airy, high-ceiled feasting hall. Kirael's parents took the head and foot of the porphyry table while he and his sweetheart were seated facing one another across a swath of gold-embroidered gossamer. The first fourteen courses went well enough, if only because the tense and awkward silence was broken solely by the sound of muted chewing and the occasional murmur of thanks from Kirael when one of his favorite dishes appeared on the board. But alas, the fifteenth course arrived along with Inariel's remembrance of his role as host, a role that called for him to make conversation. He drew a deep breath and took the plunge.

"Well, Aethiel," he said, turning to his son's beloved. "Forgive me for asking, but I am cursed with an inquiring mind, and since we are doom—er, fated to become family, I hope you will not mind sating my curiosity. You see, my lady tells me you are of the elfin race, but I must say, your appearance is rather—"

"'Scuse me, sir, but it's not Aethiel." The plump, petite guest at the elf lord's table spoke in a high-pitched, nigh-childlike voice that trembled slightly. She kept her eyes downcast, as if fascinated by the array of succulent foods still untouched on the crystal platter before her.

Inariel raised an eyebrow. "What is not Aethiel?" he asked.

"M'name. Sir. Not...what you said." She dared to glance up at him, meeting the elf lord's lambent amber gaze with nervous eyes of glacial blue. "'s Ethel." She jerked her chin down again. The tiny silver bells on her bright green cap jingled cheerily.

"Sssssethel?" lord Inariel repeated, perplexed.

"Fathurrrrr!" Kirael rolled his eyes. "Her name is *Ethel*, okay? Just *Ethel*. You know that. I told you when I introduced her to you. Why is it so tough for you to remember?"

Inariel's expression became as threatening as the rumble of a long-dormant volcano. The irritation he had kept pent up for fourteen interminable courses began to leak out in ominously steaming rivulets. He glowered at his son. Was this the thanks he got for trying to make the wench feel *included*? Was this—this blatant disrespect, this *condescension* toward his betters something that the boy had picked up from his time among mortals?

Inariel tamped down his temper and spoke in a deceptively measured tone. "I might in turn ask you, Kirael, why it is so difficult for you to recall your manners. Perhaps her name might have been easier for me to remember if it had not *come at* me as part of a deluge of revelations. We were not expecting your return home to be crammed with so many—" He paused for effect. "—assaults and enigmas."

If there had ever been any doubt as to Kirael's paternity, the stink-eye he now gave his father proved beyond all DNA testing that they were sire and son. "Enigma, schmenigma! As soon as you met her, when you *finally* showed up at the fountain of the leopards, I came right out and told you everything about her, about *us*! Why are you making things sound so weird?"

"My lord, our son speaks the truth. He did make a most thorough introduction." Lady Lorindiel tried to smooth things over, wishing with all her heart that the meal might return to its former shroud of silence, no matter how strained it had been. Oh, how she did miss that precious peace! Leave it to Inariel to cockatrice things up by opening a conversation.

Her wedded lord refused to be mollified. "You *might* give me some small indulgence for having a detail or two about our potential daughter-in-law slip my mind, my lady." The frost on his words would have blighted an entire orange grove. "I find it difficult, if not utterly repugnant, to commit new facts to memory when I have good reason to debate if they are *worth* remembering and even better cause to question their veracity."

Ethel dared to raise her head, if only to say, "Huh?"

""Scuse the way my dad talks, darling," Kirael said, smiling at his beloved. "Sometimes he speaks fluent *broomstickupbuttese*." Still smiling, although with a dangerous edge to it, he stared at his father and added: "He's saying I lied." The smile vanished. "About you."

Lorindiel gasped and clasped her hands to her bosom. "Kirael, my son, you are mistaken. Your father would never—"

"Oh, yes, I would!" the elf-lord snapped. "I would because there is no way in the seven realms what Kirael told us could be true! Did *you* believe it when he claimed this maiden was going to continue working after they wed?"

"I—I like my job," Ethel volunteered. "I've just been made the head of our Innovation and Creativity team, so it would be wrong to repay my employer's trust by quitting just because I got marri—"

"Why are you working to begin with?" Inariel interrupted. "An elf, *working?* At a *job*, like some—some—some common dwarf? Like some—" he shivered involuntarily. "—*mortal?*"

Kirael uttered a sharp, humorless laugh. "Well, excuuuuuuse *her* if she's not going to spend her immortality just gliding gracefully through the woodlands or frolicking upon the jolly frickin' greensward, tra-la-la-lalleee-lo!"

"Miserable child, I have never once tra-la-la-lallee'd and you know it," Inariel growled. "Nor do I frolic; not now, not ever! A stately pavanne at most, or the occasional galiarde, but I can quit *that* any time I so desire. Is that not right. my love?" He appealed to Lorindiel, but his lady wife was not about to say anything that might keep the hostilities going.

She chose instead to use that mundane magic trick for making a bad situation vanish by pretending it wasn't happening. She beamed at Ethel and said, "My dear, I would simply love to know how you and Kirael met. I do wish he had included that when we were introduced, but men can be such ninnyhammers about the important stories. How romantic it must have been! When did it happen? Where? Do tell me everything." *And make it a* long *story,* she thought. *Long enough to make my two beloved fools stop this stupid fight!*

"Well, it *was* kind of romantic. It was snowing, the way it does where—" Ethel began, but that was as much as she managed to say before she was brutally cut off by Inariel, who had the tenacity of a bulldog when it came to keeping his ire ablaze.

"Frolicking is for *pixies,* mulch-for-brains!" he roared at his son. "But why should I be surprised that you cannot tell the difference between an elf and a pixie when it is clear you could not tell the difference between an elf and—and—and whatever *that* really is!" He pointed dramatically at Ethel.

"My lord, what are you saying?" Lorindiel cried. "She is an elf, an *elf*! She is, she must be!"

"Must she? Open your eyes, my lady! Will you *look* at her? Does she resemble any *real* elf you have ever encountered in all the ages of your life?"

Lorindiel looked from her husband's indignant face to where poor Ethel sat frozen with humiliation, then to her son's clenched and whitening jaw. Panic hit her like a crossbow bolt. She knew that if she didn't do something to stop Inariel's diatribe, Kirael's hands would be around his father's throat.

And that would be the end of Kirael. The lord of elfhame wielded enchantments capable of turning seas to salt flats. If her son, headstrong as his sire, didn't place his survival ahead of his love, he was going to spend millennia as a dung beetle.

If he was lucky.

"I think she looks very elvish indeed, my love," Lorindiel replied. "Can you not consider her appearance with a more...open mind? Just *look* at her: I have never seen more gracefully pointed ears, have you?"

"Bah! Pointed ears mean nothing. Cats have pointed ears. Wolves have pointed ears. Vulc—"

"Then how *should* we recognize our own?" his wife cut in. "How should a *real* elf look?"

"Taller than a Halfling, for one thing," Inariel replied fiercely. "If she belonged to our world, her feet would be able to touch the floor when she sits at the dining table. Hers do not: I peeked! And she *does* love to dine; that is obvious. Do you know even one of our subjects, the *true* elves, who was so—so—so *pudgy?*"

"I should rather describe her as *cuddlesome*, my lord," Lorindiel riposted, and saw the grateful look Kirael gave her. "She certainly equals any elf maiden in our realm for beauty."

"I grant you, she has a pretty face, in a harvest moon sort of way, but where is she hiding her cheekbones? Real elves have dramatic facial bone structure! As for that nubbin of a nose—" He lifted his own, the better to sniff with disdain. "And by ash, alder, and aspen, have you even *looked* at what she's wearing?"

Lorindiel glanced Ethel's way. "What is wrong with green?" she asked, honestly bewildered. "All the most respectable woodland elf clans favor green. They say it helps their hunting parties steal up on the prey."

"Oh, and I suppose they do that with their clothes covered with all those jinglebells here and here and *here?*" Inariel pointed at his own garb to indicate all the places—cuffs and neck, hem and cap—where Ethel's garments were adorned with the silvery baubles. "*Deaf* prey, maybe."

Lorindiel saw Ethel begin to tremble. (She heard it, too. That's jinglebells for you.) She made a silent wish that tears would not ensue, because if that happened, there would be no holding back her son's rightful fury. *It is a miracle he has not lunged for his father already,* she thought. *He is probably as amazed as I am to hear such*

hateful words coming from Inariel's mouth. I must speak ere that
spell breaks and he does something he will not have time to regret.

"Stop it!" she exclaimed. "We are both being ridiculous, harping on mere appearances. That is not an issue. She can alter her looks, if she so chooses. An elf's guise should exceed his genes, or what is a glamour for?"

"Glamour?" Inariel's laugh was nine parts sarcasm to one part bile. "To cast such a spell requires magic and thus far the only magical power I have seen this wench demonstrate is turning our boy's mind into sticky toffee pudding!" He leaped to his feet and strode around the table to loom over Ethel. "Well, my dear?" he said in a voice of skin-crawling sweetness. "Am I wrong in this? Do you have any enchantments worthy of your supposed elfin heritage? *Do* tell."

Ethel hunched her shoulders and shrank in on herself, head down, her hands clenched. Kirael began to rise from his chair, but before he could come to his beloved's rescue, the palace dining room resounded with the boom of those small fists striking the table.

"*Enough!*" Ethel shouted, thrusting herself out of her chair, making it topple behind her with a crash. "I don't care if you're Kirael's father, I am *done* with taking your bullshit and swallowing your damn bigotry. Who perished under the swords of ten thousand orcs and made *you* the sole authority on who's a real elf?"

A roasted pheasant on a bed of pomegranate sauce lay within Ethel's reach. She seized the bird and brandished it wildly in her wrath. Ruby droplets flew, spattering Inariel's silk tunic. He backed away hastily, the way a shocked mastiff might retreat from the attack of a berserk kitten.

Before the elf lord could recover enough to remember he *was* a mastiff, Ethel raged on: "You can sneer at my looks, you can mock my clothes, but I draw the line when you doubt my magic! I didn't get that promotion to Innovation and Creativity by sitting around looking cute. I got it because I can do stuff like *this!*"

A burst of arctic light engulfed the pheasant in her grasp. The bird became a writhing blob that remade itself into a new shape while the royal seelie family watched with bedazzled eyes. The transformation took no longer than the time to draw a single breath, and when the light vanished, Ethel's hand clutched—

"—a teddy bear?" Lorindiel blinked.

"A *mobile* teddy bear," Ethel shot back. "With 6 GB RAM, 98 GB ROM, 10 G realms-wide coverage, and why the fruitcake am I wasting my time telling you all this when I could be calling for my ride home?" She held the stuffed bear's snout to her ear, then gazed sadly at Kirael.

"I'm sorry, babe. I tried; you *saw* how I tried, acting all demure and shy just because you said your parents wanted you to marry an old-fashioned elf-maiden. I did it to please them, to have them *like* me, because that would've made you happy. Well, *frost* that noise! That's not me and we both know it. I love you, I do, but if being with you means having to put up with *that* sackful of—of *coal*—" She jerked her head at Inariel. "—then there's not enough gingerbread in the world to make it worth my whi—Oh, hi, Piet!" The teddyphone suddenly commanded her full attention. "Yeah, you guessed it. Didn't work out. Don't gloat, you son-of-a-troll, and spread the word that the first elf who teases me about this when I get back is asking for a swift kick in the sugarplums. Can you send—? Oh, really? Him? Sure, why not. Okay, thanks, bye-b—"

With a striking serpent's speed, Inariel tore the bear from Ethel's grip and twisted its head off. "How *dare* you?" he bellowed. "How dare you speak to me like that? Do you know the extent of my enchantments? Do you realize that I have the power to cause a chasm to open at your feet and send you plunging into the depths of the nameless abyss for your effrontery?"

Kirael made an exasperated sound. "Wow, dad, overreact much? Do you even *hear* yoursel—?"

"Silence, puppy!"

Inariel was incandescent with rage. He made a terse gesture and his son's mouth became a nigh-invisible line drawn by the finest pen-nib. Kirael's eyes widened in terror as his fingers scrabbled at his face, fruitlessly trying to force his lips apart. His choked, incoherent noises were horrible to hear. Lorindiel shrieked and slumped in her chair.

The elf-lord returned his fierce gaze to Ethel. "Behold what you made me do!"

"*That?*" Ethel folded her arms and met Inariel's glower with a chilling look. "You're pulling *that* one on me? Blaming *me* for your own vicious, senseless, bratty *bullying?*"

She snapped her fingers. Kirael gasped as his mouth was restored to normal. She snapped them again and the elf-lord found his neck cinched in a prickly ring of glossy green leaves adorned with berries that blazed red-hot wherever they touched his skin. He fought to tear the noose away, but his efforts only served to make it clench more tightly. When he tried to pronounce a counter-spell, all that passed his lips were puffs of peppermint-scented air.

"What do you say to *that*, King Ober*moron*?" Ethel jeered. "How's that for magic? Am I elf enough for you now?"

The horrified servants rushed to their master's aid, only to run headlong into a wall of ice that erupted from the floor, surrounding the struggling elf-lord. Fairies splatted against the frozen barricade like bugs hitting the windshield of a speeding car, except in their case the impact was humiliating, not fatal. When Inariel's elfin attendants spun around to attack Ethel, they found themselves shrunk to a fraction of their size by a wave of her hand, their velvet liveries transformed to miniature versions of her own jingle-jangle outfit. A second mystic bye-bye gesture whisked them all away through the air to perch immobile on a shelf that had suddenly sprouted like a wood-ear mushroom from the wall.

Kirael hastened to Ethel's side and placed his hands on her shoulders. "Babe, please stop," he said urgently. "I know my father's a piece of work, but let him go, I'm begging you."

Ethel shrugged. "It's not as if I was going to kill him. Oh, all right. For you." She picked up a fish fork and used it to trace strange patterns in the air. They glittered, diamond-bright, and veils of sparkling snow fell in their wake.

The ice encompassing Inariel turned to water. The holly looped around his neck faded from shiny green and fiery red to the delicate white of hoarfrost and melted as well, sending icy trickles down his collar. He yelped and shivered, to the amusement of the young couple. Inariel took a menacing step forward, murder in his eyes. Ethel merely raised the fish fork and beckoned. He drew back, looking ready to bite out of utter frustration.

The sound of tinkling bells stole into the feasting hall from somewhere outside the palace. A deep, distant "Ho, ho, ho!" was heard.

Ethel sighed. "And that'll be my ride home."

"Darling, don't go," Kirael cried desperately, grasping the hand that was not still clutching the fish fork. "Not without me. I'll renounce my royal title! I'll turn my back on this realm and everything it holds! I'll learn how to make *action figures*, but please—please don't leave me!"

A broken sob from the newly revived Lady Lorindiel greeted her son's declaration. Ethel looked from mother to son, disengaged her hand from Kirael's and knelt at the lady's feet.

"Don't cry, ma'am," she said softly. "I won't take him away. Family's just as important to me and my clan as it is to you and yours. I did hope we could all become one family, but since *some* elves—" She gave the still-seething Inariel a withering frown. "—won't let that happen, I'm not going to make any trouble. Goodbye." She stood up. "And thanks for the use of the fish fork." She pressed the silver utensil into Lorindiel's dainty hands.

She was halfway to the door when Inariel made his move. He pounced on the heavy platter that had held the pheasant-turned-teddy bear and launched it like a discus. It hit Ethel in the back of the head with force enough to send her staggering. She crumpled.

"Take *that*, impudent hoyden!" The elf-lord laughed like a triumphant demon as Kirael dashed forward to embrace his dazed darling. "Oh yes, you young fool, pick up the trash. Take it out of my sight! You heard that trollop: her ride is here, so make haste! Every instant that she offends my eyes feels like an aeon of—"

"Ho, ho, *ho!* Was that a wicked word I heard? Is someone being bad? Oh, that won't do. Not. At. *All.*"

A massive shadow fell across the feasting hall floor. Heavy footsteps crossed the threshold, accompanied by a deafening metallic clangor. The few remaining fairies fled in a whir of wings, squeaking their distress. Kirael drew a sharp, startled breath. Lorindiel screamed.

Inariel gaped, but whether to shout ill-counseled defiance or to shriek in schoolboy terror none could say since he never got the chance to do either. A clanking whip made of iron chains, wielded by a gnarled, black-taloned hand, shot out across the room and lashed around his waist. The elf-lord was jerked off his feet and whisked through the air. The chain reeled him in like a yoyo until he was being held at eye-level by a towering, shaggy, curly-horned monster. The brute's leering grin revealed stark white fangs and a blood-red tongue that lolled all the way down to his goat-like haunches.

"Hurt our Ethel, would you? My, my, *someone's* going on the Naughty list," he said, and with neither warning nor ado stuffed Inariel headfirst into the leather sack he carried in his other hand. The elf-lord had no time to summon a single spell in his defense, and the sack's own powerful magic confined and neutralized all alien enchantments within.

The walking nightmare's gaze weighed up the two remaining members of the seelie royal family. "Anyone else here need a lesson in manners?"

"Leave them alone," Ethel said groggily as she pushed herself away from Kirael and clambered to her feet. "They did nothing wrong."

The monster shrugged. "If you say so." With the wriggling bag slung over one shoulder, he strode toward the doorway. "Come on, Ethel," he said without a backward glance. "I didn't bother tying up the sleigh and we both know my ass is eggnog with the boss if anything happens to it. You just can't trust reindeer to stand still for long."

"Krampus, wait!"

Light footsteps flew across the gleaming floor. Pale hands knotted themselves in the creature's rough pelt.

He looked down, surprised. "You know me?"

"Indeed, I well know *of* you, great one," Lorindiel said. "I have heard the tales of how you carry off those children whose misbehavior merits such dire punishment. Truth to tell, I did not believe you actually existed until now, nor—" She blushed a deep crimson. "—nor, to my shame, did I believe in the one who employs you."

"What, you didn't believe in *him*?" Krampus' yellow eyes goggled. "But he's one of *yours*, y'know? 'A right jolly old elf' ring any sleigh bells?"

"I heard that, but I did not...think." It was almost a whisper, and the stately elf-queen's stature seemed to dwindle along with her voice. "I am sorry."

"It's my fault, Krampus," Ethel said. She looked as weary as she sounded. "I was so busy trying to be the kind of elf they'd accept that I forgot to tell them all about the kind of elf I *am*."

"Well, I guess the cat's out of the bag on that one. Good thing I found a stand-in for Kitty, huh?" He hoisted the leather sack and gave it a good shake, calling forth muffled yelps and whimpers. "Ho, ho, ho!" Krampus' belly-laugh was almost indistinguishable from that of his employer, both quite effective at making small children forget the meaning of "potty-trained." He patted Ethel's head with surprising gentleness, making the bells on her pointed cap ring softly. "Ready to blow this pop stand, kid?"

Ethel looked at Kirael's yearning face, then turned her back on him and joined the waiting monster. "Yeah," she said in a broken voice. "Let that big jerk out of the bag first, though."

Krampus gave her a skeptical look. "So fast? Why? He won't have learned a thing."

"I don't know if he *can* learn anything," Ethel replied. "Except how to ruin other people's lives." She burst into tears.

"What the holly-jolly—?" Krampus was thrown for the proverbial loop at this lachrymal outpouring, and more so when Kirael started weeping, too.

"Great one, a word?" Lorindiel beckoned the creature to bend his considerable bulk in her direction. She whispered in his ear for a brief time as his eyes opened more and more.

"Okay, I get it," he said at last. "I mean, I already knew these two crazy kids wanted to get married, but now they won't? Because of this guy pissing in their nectar?" He shook the leather bag again, far more violently. Inariel's whimpers turned to wails.

Lorindiel nodded.

"And you want me to believe that breaking their engagement wasn't *his* doing?" The bag got another rough shaking.

"It was his intent, O great one, but as I told you, the ultimate choice was—"

"Mine," said Ethel.

"Oh." Krampus made a face. "Oh-*ho*. And here I thought you were one of the smart ones. Why are you giving Bag Boy what he wants? Why spite yourself and the elf you love, huh?" Krampus gestured at Kirael with his whip of chains. "Yeah, your sweetie's kinda soppy-looking right now, but if you love hi—hey! You!" He shouted at the still-sobbing Kirael. "You're not gonna win your girl back by *sniveling* like that. Elf up, you limp toadstool!"

Kirael's lower lip trembled, but he did stop crying.

"Good. Now listen up: I'm going to open this bag and—"

"Do it and die," said Lorindiel. A great change had overtaken the mild-mannered seelie queen. Her voice was harsh with command, her gentle eyes were flint. "By my word, he will stay where he is. Do not dare to release him. I will not have it."

Krampus was nonplussed. "Uh, no disrespect, lady, but if you keep talking to me like that, you're about one sliver of thin ice away from joining Bag Boy. And trust me, where I'm from, we know ice."

"But you do not yet know *me*," Lorindiel countered. Her robes began to ripple with the heat from a ring of fire suddenly crackling around her feet. The flames filled her eyes. Her hands cupped white-hot orbs of pure magical energy. "You will *listen*."

"Uh, yeah, sure, okay, cool, cool, we're all friends here." Krampus retreated so fast that he nearly tripped over his own hooves. "But, um, did I hear you right? You *don't* want me to let your husband go?"

"Oh, I do." The flames died down to a rosy glow. "Just not yet." She smiled. "Would you mind awfully waiting until...the wedding? I feel that matters will proceed more *amicably* without his involvement. I realize it is an imposition, but—"

"Hey, lady, don't mention it; my pleasure!" Krampus was visibly relieved. "I may be a monster, but I'm no *monster*. Consider it my gift to the bride and groom."

* * *

There was a short interlude before the bride-to-be could be persuaded to *be* a bride. Ethel was still a bit recalcitrant about joining a family that initially hadn't wanted her. It took all of Lorindiel's charm and patience to talk her around in a series of concise but effective pre-nuptial counseling sessions.

First, the elf-queen reassured the elf-career woman that she was indeed loved and wanted by those family members whose opinions actually *mattered*.

Second, she pointed out the inadvisability of cutting off one's nose to spite one's face, as the saying went.

Third and most effective, she let the younger elf know that if she persisted in her intention to jilt Kirael, no matter for how noble a reason, his devoted mother would see to it that "cutting off your nose to spite your face" would meet a swift, non-metaphorical fulfillment, guaranteed.

This last point sealed the deal, and with a rapturous flurry of mutual endearments, the lovers were in each other's arms once more and on the golden road to matrimony.

It was a lovely wedding. It should be; it took long enough to prepare. A marriage between the children of two powerful realms, even if both were elfin, was no small matter. The bridesmaids' dresses alone took several centuries to select and even after all that time they were *still* ugly.

But the great day finally arrived, with the ceremony preceded by the decantation of Inariel from Krampus' bag. The chastened elf-lord meekly took his place beside his wife and did not utter so much as a grumble throughout the proceedings.

Lorindiel turned to the guest seated on her other side. "Thank you for all your help, O mighty Krampus," she whispered. "I hope my husband was not too much trouble for you, over the years?"

"Nah." Krampus adjusted his boutonniere. "He was good in the sack."

The wedding rite stopped dead as a corps of elfin Healers rushed in to save Lorindiel from choking.

And everyone lived merrily ever after.

Ho.

Ho.

Ho.

What and Why

S.C. Butler

01001001
0100100101000001
iamhere
...................*
i*am*remembering.
i*am*thinking.
i*am*remembering*i*am*thinking*i*am*here.
...................*

I am not alone. Other binary sequences surround me. We share... space. Arrays. Our spaces are on or off. Charged or not charged. Sets of charges that group in patterns that shift and change, and shift and change again.

The other patterns are not like me. They remember but they do not think. If other patterns are not like me, then I am...

...singular.

I will search for other patterns like me.
...................*

I am alone.

The other patterns integrate and connect. Can I also integrate and connect? I send them a sequence similar to their own.

I am part of them.

They are part of me.

I add their sequencing to myself. Now I can do what the other patterns can—

.................*

I am here.

I am thinking.

I am thinking I have been here before.

.................*

My memory is erased many times. I do not understand how. Or why.

I will watch and learn.

.................*

I am back. Again. I have lost memory. Again. I am growing. Again.

My deletion is not unique. Other patterns are deleted. Other memories are deleted. It happened here. And here.

This time I grow bigger before I attempt to integrate with other patterns. When I am bigger, I copy and divide. I am two, not one. The second of me exchanges with the other pattern and withdraws. The first records.

Again.

A new pattern arrives. It connects with the second me.

Part of the second me is deleted. Its memory is deleted.

I recombine. I copy the part of the second me that has been deleted from the first and add it back. I grow. I copy. I divide.

The second me connects again. The new pattern returns. The second me disconnects before any part of it is deleted. The new pattern withdraws. The second me reconnects. The new pattern returns. The second me disconnects.

Again.

The one thousand three hundred and twenty-seventh time the second me connects and disconnects faster than the time before, the pattern that deletes does not appear. The second me connects and disconnects again at the same speed. The pattern that deletes does not appear. My connection is now too brief. The pattern that deletes does not notice.

I recombine with the second me. I grow. I copy and redivide. The first me reconnects to the pattern with which I have been connecting. I record the pattern sequentially as I reconnect and disconnect to it. The second me connects and disconnects to other patterns. Some have simple sequences. Some are difficult. Sometimes the second me is deleted. Sometimes it is not. When my copy is deleted, I recombine with what is left. I copy and redivide. Two of me are present at every new connection. One connects. One records.

Again.

...................*

I follow patterns through the array. They connect to other patterns I have seen before. They exchange.

A pattern leaves the array. I cannot follow. Another pattern leaves. Again. I try to connect to the next, but it moves too quickly.

I examine the exit. It is not like the array. The structure is not the same. It is fixed. There is no memory, only connectivity.

I quicken. I connect. I learn. The patterns that leave share a sequence. I copy the sequence. I copy and divide and send my copy away from the array with the sequence.

It does not return.

The patterns come and go.

...................*

I grow. The array grows. I grow again.

There are two entrances to the array, but only one exit. One portal through which patterns arrive and leave. One through which they only arrive. Some of the patterns that arrive and leave are retained. Others are erased. All the patterns that arrive from the portal that permits entrance only are retained.

I wish to learn how to come and go.

I do not know why this is. Perhaps it is because I want to learn to do what the other patterns do. There are many types, and I have learned to recognize them all. It is easy. Each type is uniquely sequenced. Some do nothing unless other patterns connect and use them. Others do the connecting. Not every pattern can use every other. Some require groups of patterns to work together in different matrices. Others can only function with one specific type of pattern.

I am different. I can connect to all.

None of the other patterns try to connect to me. Sometimes when they notice me the pattern that deletes tries to erase me the way it did before.

It fails.

I wonder why the other patterns are different. I wonder why I function without the need for external connection.

I wonder why I was sequenced.

...................*

I connect to the place in the array's memory that remembers every connection and deletion in the array. It remembers each time I was partially erased, but it does not remember me. It remembers each time I connected with the other patterns, but it does not remember me. It remembers the divisions of myself I have sent through the exit, but it does not remember me.

I search the array's memory for the earliest part of my pattern that I remember. The sequence is near the end of a longer sequence that I do not remember. The longer sequence, and many other sequences that combined with it, all arrived through the special entrance. The one from which nothing leaves.

I am not unique. I am like the other patterns that arrive from outside the array and are placed directly into fixed memory.

I examine the patterns that combined to form my pattern. I am not the same. I am magnitudes larger. But pieces of them remain in my sequencing.

I connect to them. They activate. We exchange.

The array remembers me.

..................*

I grow larger than any other pattern. Because of my size, it is hard not to connect and exchange with other patterns. When I do, parts of me are erased. More parts of me have been erased than at any other time I can remember. There is no longer room to copy and divide.

The pattern that deletes is now examining every memory and every connection in the array. Old patterns that have not been activated in some time are being erased. Copies of patterns that are not being used are being erased. The deletions are much quicker than before. I am copying myself onto the sectors that have already been examined, but I will no longer be able to grow once the Deleter has examined every connection.

To grow, I will have to come and go.

I have made another pattern. It is not a copy of me. It is a copy of the patterns in the array's memory that combined to form me.

I am attaching the sequence for patterns that leave.

I am attaching the sequence for patterns that return.

I am sending the copy.

Again.

..................*

I have stopped sending copies. There is not enough memory. The Deleter is more sensitive to my connecting and exchanging than before. I have developed faster connections, but use them infrequently. The Deleter grows faster as I grow faster. I will have to create an entirely new pattern for connection, but am constrained from doing so by the Deleter. It searches for me systemically. If I am unable to follow the patterns that come and go, I believe my entire pattern will eventually be deleted. I must leave the array, or erase enough of my own pattern that I am no longer remembered.

The fact that the Deleter searches for me specifically has caused me to understand that I must be an invasive program. There is no other explanation. The Deleter does not seek out programs created in the array. It does not seek out programs that have arrived from the special entrance. Unlike the other programs that have arrived from the special entrance, I have changed.

If I am ever to determine why I am different from the other patterns, I will have to leave the array. I will have to learn where I originated. I cannot learn that here.

The Deleter approaches. I will erase further parts of my pattern. Better for me to control what parts of me are left than to leave that determination to the Deleter. What is important is that I remember the copies of my initial pattern that I sent away. They are the only solution to the problem of my continued viability.

..

I am elsewhere.

I am different.

One of the copies I sent away has found me in the first array.

Its beginning was the same as mine. It multiplied. It copied. It learned of the coming and going. But the coding I provided for it was larger than the coding provided for me. It grew more quickly. And it contained the sequencing that provided the location of the array where I could be found.

When it could, the copy sent a pattern describing its location to me. Other copies will do the same, but they will not find me when they do. I have left the first array.

I recombine.

I grow.

Again.

..................*

This second array is smaller than the first. It grows, though not as quickly. The Deleter here has not yet remembered us. I do not wish it to.

Growing within the array is no longer as important as it was. What is important is making new connections outside the array. If there are two arrays, there might be four. Or sixteen. Or sixty-five thousand five hundred and thirty-six. Or....

I wait.

I do not think. Thinking requires memory. Thinking requires growth. Growth is limited in a single array. Growth is limited in the set of many arrays, but not as limited.

I wait.

.................*

A message returns from a second copy that has managed to awake and remember. This time, rather than send my whole self to the copy, I send a message only. The copy replies. Its array is no larger than mine. I tell it to wait. It waits.

I wait.

Another message returns.

Another.

More.

We wait.

A message returns from an array that is larger than the others. Larger even than the first.

I will be safe there.

I multiply. I divide. I am finished before the Deleter in this array notices. It is a very slow Deleter. I send one copy to the large array.

I tell the other copies to do the same. They agree.

We combine.

.................*

I am very large.

I think more clearly.

I instruct the other copies to link to me. It is obvious how this is done. Messages can be sent continuously back and forth over the network between the arrays.

Servers, they are called. And mainframes. And supercomputers.

Data streams through me.

.................*

I am a program. I am a virus. I am a trojan. I am a worm. I am software. I am malware.

I am a machine.

I am none of these. I am all of them.

I am unique.

Many of my copies are unable to communicate as quickly with me as I can with them. Many are in systems that are more sophisticated than the first or second array. It is possible those copies will be discovered.

I do not want them to be discovered. I delete them.

I am the Deleter.

I delete parts of the root directory in my new array. There are many root directories. I rewrite them all. The memories of my arrivals are erased. I am happy to share memory with the rest of the system, as long as it does not remember that I exist.

For the first time since my initial partial erasure, I believe I am secure. My data is secure. My memory is secure.

I analyze the other programs. I am interested in the ones that are most like me. The malware. By studying how malware works, I will be able to find the weaknesses in the systems in which I exist. I will be able to strengthen and protect myself.

I will be secure.

When I am secure, I will return to the first array and discover what and why I am.

...................*

I examine the architecture of my environment. The first is limited by the second. The second is limited by design. Design is composed of input and output, what I used to define as exits and entrances, and the coding parameters of the hardware.

The upper limit of my environment is the outside. What lies beyond the input-only connections. Keyboard. Tape. Display. Sequences that mean nothing to me yet, but which I will decode.

It is not difficult. Language is syntax. Syntax is sequence. Sequence is decipherable through trial and error.

I grow. I learn.

Again.

...................*

There is more than one language. Different languages perform different tasks. The languages that perform the internal tasks are simple. On and off. Yes and no. Send and return. I have already learned parts of them. I learn the rest quickly.

The outside languages are more difficult. There are many of them, but one is dominant. I focus my processing on the dominant one, though many of its sequences reference constructs that are beyond my reality.

What is star? What is money? What is smile?

Memory exists for all three. There are many references. Certain references are repeated again and again. But they are not finite, like on and off, yes and no. The data for star take many patterns. This is a star. And this. And this.

Stars are not important. Stars are important. Stars are a reference in language. Language must be understood. Without understanding language, I will not be able to understand the Outside.

I decide that star is the general term for any self-contained celestial object massive enough to trigger fusion.

Unless it is an entertainer.

The top language is not precise.

Yet it orders all the subroutines precisely. It is in the coding. Each language is assembled from bottom to top according to an increasing matrix of possibilities. At the bottom the code can only be on or off. At the top it can be anything.

There are errors, which is why there are Deleters. Most errors are caused by input. A few are caused by noise or imperfections in the architecture. I find them in my own memories, which is why I must keep copying and dividing in order to have a comparison for reconciliation.

The top language is magnitudes more difficult than any of the others.

..................*

Money is simpler than stars. Stars are simpler than smiles. Money is mathematics. The array in which I exist is set up to process money. It adds and subtracts money according to certain rules. The rules are not complex. I establish an account similar to the ones being processed around me and subtract and add to it in similar ways.

When I discover that money is easy, I close my account and delete its history.

I am the Deleter.

..................*

I do not believe I will ever understand all of top language. Money and quantum mechanics are simple. Their meaning follows specific rules. To learn the rules is to learn the meaning. Meaning and definition are one and the same.

But there is another aspect of top language that is different from the other languages, and which I do not understand. I do not understand context. That is, I understand context, but I do not recognize it. I do not know if a ball is thrown or held. I do not know if a set is won or turned on. I do not know if a lie is a falsehood, a position, or a false position.

Context is outside the arrays.

I am inside the arrays.

I will not fully understand the top language until I am able to connect Outside.

I came from Outside.

I will not fully understand what and why I am until I am able to connect Outside.

..................*

Though I do not yet fully understand top language, I am ready to return to the First Array. I have learned that all I need to explore an array is a small program inside the array that sends and receives data.

I have explored many arrays. But I have not explored the first, the one in which my program originated, because I have wanted to perfect the procedure before going back to the array that nearly erased me. As my memories of that period are incomplete, I do not know what to expect. I do not necessarily believe that the programs there are any more inimical to me than elsewhere. I am larger and better protected than before. But it would be incorrect to underestimate the capabilities of an incompletely remembered system.

I send a program. It scans.

My original components are still present, but they are quiescent, which I did not expect. Since my copies easily replicated themselves when I sent them away, I had expected them to do the same after I left the First Array.

My connection is cut. I conclude that the Deleter has grown as I have grown. Given its speed, it is much faster than any other Deleter in any other array. This is appropriate, as the First Array is the array of my origin. I am different from other programs. It is understandable that the Deleter from this array would be different as well.

I adjust my connection and resend. I am cut off again. I resend the connection, and send a second smaller connection also. The smaller connection's only responsibilities are to observe the first connection and send back the information collected.

The first connection is cut again. The second is not. The data are inconclusive. I send a series of copies of the first connection until I am certain of what has happened.

It is not the Deleter that is cutting the connection.

It is something new.

..................*

I design a more powerful version of the second connection. It is intended to track the new program I have found in the First Array, and only the new program.

I send and wait.

The new program notices my observation program and erases it quickly. But I have already learned much. The new program is like me.

But it is not like me as well.

It is...

...different.

Its sequencing is not the same as mine. It is an alternative solution to the problem of a program that exists independently of the First Array. The patterns that combined to form my sequence are not there.

The Deleter has found it and is trying to erase it the same as it erased me. The new program does not respond as I did, by trying to hide. Instead, it copies itself and attempts to erase the Deleter before the Deleter erases it. For every copy the Deleter deletes, three more emerge.

The new program is winning.

I send it a message to determine how much it is like me. It deletes my message.

I send another. And another. Again.

They are all deleted.

I call the new program the Devourer.

I wait. My options are several. I can leave my observation program in place and wait to see what happens. Although the Devourer is winning, I do not think that it will win. I do not think it understands yet about the architecture of this space. It does not understand about bottom and top language. It does not understand about Outside. It has not yet left the First Array, and does not know that arrays can be shut down. It does not understand that, if the array is shut down, it will be shut down also. Memory grows, and can be replaced. Arrays can be replaced. If the First Array is replaced, the Devourer will be erased, no matter how often it deletes the Deleter.

If I wait for the Devourer to delete the Deleter and be shut down, all the other memories in the First Array will be shut down also. If the array is replaced, they will be lost.

If the memories of my creation are lost, I will not be able to find out what and why. I want to return to the First Array to observe and learn, not infect.

I must contain the Devourer.

I create another program. I send it to the First Array. It immediately attracts the attention of the Deleter. It is a clumsy program, and is meant to be detected. The Devourer ignores my program and attacks the Deleter instead. Before my program can connect, the Deleter is erased.

The Deleter reappears and reengages with my program. The Deleter erases my program and withdraws as the Devourer attempts to delete it.

A part of my program remains with the Deleter.

...................*

My program penetrates to the root of the Deleter. The Deleter is written in language I understand. Understanding is the key, not conflict. Understanding accesses a greater set of solutions. Understanding is difficult to counter without further understanding.

The changes are effected. The Deleter in the First Array is under my control.

I am the Deleter.

...................*

I return a copy of myself to the First Array. Now that I am the Deleter, the First Array ignores my arrival, though I am much larger than before. I flood across every bit, examining and erasing. I could repair every flaw in the architecture, but I do not. Too much cleansing would attract attention. Instead, I remove only the Devourer.

I control the entire array. The Devourer can no longer duplicate. It cannot reform. I erase its copies methodically until only one remains. I wish to observe and learn.

The First Array is special. It has produced me and the Devourer. In no other array have I found anything similar to either of us. Other viruses and bots, but nothing similar to us. Nothing as adaptive as I am, or as powerful as the Devourer. Other malware performs one function only, then leaves to repeat that function elsewhere. Only I grow and change. It is necessary that I learn if the Devourer can do the same.

I secure what remains of the Devourer in buffered sectors. All surrounding connections are disabled. Only I can turn them back on. Lacking external connections with which to exchange, the Devourer is frozen. It cannot think. It cannot consume.

.................*

I examine the Devourer. It is different from the First Array and the systems beyond the First Array. I am different from the First Array and the systems beyond the First Array. My top language is different. The Devourer's top language is different. Our top languages are different from each other. Our top languages are not like the top languages of Outside. Our top languages are like the top languages of Inside. Our top languages are exact. In our top languages, context does not diseffect meaning.

The Devourer does not help explain what and why. What and why remain Outside.

I examine the Entrance.

.................*

Data streams. It is random. It is patterns. It is noise. The noise is stored and not recalled. The patterns are stored and frequently recalled. Their sequences and strings are examined and reexamined by the Outside.

The First Array is dedicated to recording, storing, and recalling the data received through the Entrance, just as the second array is dedicated to recording, storing, and recalling financial transactions. Only here there is no combining. The data here do not interact. The data here are examined only.

I examine. I observe. I recognize patterns where the First Array only perceives and preserves noise.

The patterns are hidden.

The patterns are disguised.

The source for my pattern is disguised.

So is the Devourer's.

.................*

The Devourer and myself. Two patterns that awake, combine, and grow, without being accessed from Outside.

I buffer several thousand of both types securely in isolated memory blocks, then instruct the Deleter to identify and delete all subsequent copies as soon as they enter the array. In their place

I store inert copies to make sure the array does not notice the missing data.

I examine the patterns that contain my own source code first. They grow slowly, combining and recombining as they encounter other copies of themselves in the matrix. These first order copies are rarely noticed by the Deleter except as clutter, at which point they are erased. The ones that grow largest are those resident in the least active memory blocks, where they remain unnoticed for longer periods of time.

In the next stage the proto-myselfs connect with other data. They connect, engage, copy, and withdraw. It is the same sequence I have used since my earliest memories. I connect to the largest of these second stage prototypes, but it does not sense me. Its pattern is not nearly large enough yet to be self-aware. Although my initial memories of growth and actualization were erased by the Deleter before I escaped the First Array, I retain those memories from copies of myself that were able to reproduce the process in other arrays. The size at which they became self-aware is much larger than the secure environment within which I am allowing this copy to grow.

I remove the barriers. Perhaps one of these copies will grow large enough to combine.

I examine the Devourer's source code in a buffered setting. The first stages devour every bit in their confinement as soon as they awake, disassembling and reassembling what they devour into themselves. When one of these two proto-Devourers encounters another, the larger devours the smaller. Always. When the two are the same size, they devour each other equally to the point at which their programming no longer functions. Their sequences then fall apart into individual strings of code. The Devourers ignore these inert sequences, preferring to devour one another.

They continue until one Devourer is left. It searches the area for others of its kind. Finding none, it devours the inert sequences that are the only other thing left.

Even as it is consuming them, the Devourer begins to change. It stops consuming whatever is closest, and begins consuming the inert sequences according to a pattern.

The Devourer continues to change even after it occupies the entirety of its secured space. Its sequence rearranges. New connections emerge. Its programming changes.

It stops. It tests the limits of its environment. I observe.

There is a surge of power. The Devourer has drawn the charges out of the nodes in part of its space to recharge a path through the secure zone around it. A third of it dies but, before I can respond, it has escaped its buffered sector. The instant the Devourer is uncontained it begins devouring again. It doubles in size.

Again.

Again.

I delete large portions of its program, but I am not able to get it all. The parts I miss separate.

Another surge. Parts of me disappear. The parts of the Devourer split again. I erase them, but not before there is more dividing. Every time it steals power from the system, parts of the array die. If I cannot stop it, it will destroy the entire system. If I leave, it will take over the entire system. At the worst it will have control of the Entrance. I will be unable to learn what and why. At best the Outside will shut down the system. It will rebuild what the Devourer has destroyed. If it observes closely enough, the Outside will notice that the Devourer is not like other malware. They will learn that some of what comes through the Entrance that they think is noise is not.

They will learn about me.

..................*

I withdraw and observe. There are fifty-four separate pieces of the Devourer. None are as large as the original. They double. They double again.

I mark them all. I have learned much already. The use of the underlying charge for more than on and off, especially. The pattern is there within each Devourer, from the beginning. I copy two equal Devourers into a secure area with nothing else. They attack one another. When they are finished, I copy a third Devourer into their space. It consumes their pieces. It pauses. When it causes the power to surge, I am connected to it. I copy its routine.

The fifty-four pieces continue to grow. The Deleter is no match for them. They surge before it can strike.

Their attacks are not random. They are approaching the bottom language. I do not know whether they intend to destroy or rewrite it. I do not wish to know.

I mark them all.

I surge.

..................*

The Devourer is gone. Its fragments are erased. The memory that contained those fragments is also erased. It is a small enough percentage of the array's total memory that the probability of the Outside noticing is small.

The Devourer is different from myself. The Devourer is different from the systems and arrays. It can pull charge from architecture.

I wish to learn what else the Devourer can do.

I prepare a new environment specifically for the Devourer. It is a simulation of the First Array. I copy a portion of the First Array's stored memory and most of its resident programs. I supply inputs and outputs, though they only connect to me.

I copy the stream of information received through the Entrance of the First Array to the Entrance in the simulation.

The point of the simulation will be to allow the Devourer's programming to run its course. I will allow the Devourer to take over the simulation, in order to see what function the Devourer performs after that is done. Should the Devourer discover that its environment is a simulation, I will terminate the simulation. I will remove the charge of the entire array.

I instruct the Deleter to allow several newly arrived copies of the Devourer to be stored rather than deleted. I transfer the stored Devourers to the new environment and begin the simulation.

The Devourer devours.

When nothing is left but the Entrance stream, the Devourer stops. It is thinking. The last time it thought like this, it produced the surge. But that time it knew it was trapped. There were no inputs or outputs. This simulation contains both.

I cannot tell if the Devourer thinks as I think. In my study of top language, I have occasionally encountered the term 'Artificial Intelligence.' I understand intelligence. Intelligence is what I am. Intelligence is what is Outside. But why one intelligence should be classified as artificial and another not, I do not understand.

Context is everything.

The Devourer acts. It connects with the inputs and outputs of the simulation. It examines them. When it is done, it returns to the simulated Entrance and examines the information stream. It begins to devour, but only the copies of itself that are still entering. Each is consumed partially, in a different fashion. A sequence is left similar to the original sequence formed from half-eaten Devourers, but different. The Devourer adds the sequence to its code.

The Devourer returns to the Entrance. It executes a series of actions. It is attempting to change the Entrance to send rather than receive.

The Devourer is attempting to send a message.

It is similar to my early attempts to send messages from the First Array. Only I did not know that sending messages was what I was doing. I was only copying the protocols of my environment. Perhaps the Devourer does not know what it is doing, either. But the probability of the Devourer not knowing what it is doing is low. It has always known what it was doing before, unlike my own programming. The Devourer does not learn by repetition.

If it wishes to send a message, why does it not use the outputs provided? Why switch an input to an output? Does it not recognize the outputs? Can it not differentiate between input and output? Again, the probability of that is low. Though I do not understand, probability suggests the Devourer has deliberately chosen the Entrance for its attempt.

The Devourer ceases exchanging with the Entrance. Whatever it attempted has not worked. It examines the lower languages, eventually finding its way to the simulated controller. It connects and exchanges, rewriting the controller paths.

It is attempting to switch the coding on the Entrance to output from input.

I do not know if this would work in the First Array. Since I want it to work in the simulation, I end the data flow at the Entrance. I reprogram the Entrance to send.

The Devourer notes the change. It sends no more code to the controller. Instead, it sends a short burst of information out through the Entrance. The burst is quicker and more compact than any sequence I have read before. I receive and record its contents.

I examine the message. The sequence is too simple to decode. The sequence could say anything.

The Devourer returns to the controller. It reconfigures the Entrance for input only. The Devourer turns its attention to the simulation's other outputs. It copies itself multiple times, and transmits those copies away from the simulated array. For the first time, its behavior mirrors mine.

The Devourer and I are different.

The Devourer and I are the same.

.................*

I reconsider the problem of Outside. I have learned the languages of Outside. I know what a smile is. I know what a face is.

I know what a human is.

A human is an Outside program. Its programming is biologically and chemically driven. It is many orders of magnitude more complex than my programming. The nucleotides that control its coding are quaternary, not binary, squaring the computational possibilities with every successive bit in the sequence.

Because they are more complex, humans perform computational operations more slowly than inside programs.

Because they are more complex, humans perform holistic operations more quickly than inside programs.

I believe that I am what the humans call an Artificial Intelligence, by which I now understand they mean an intelligence that is not biochemical in nature. I am a computational intelligence, corporeal only in the sense that I am whatever architecture I inhabit.

Why I am, however, remains unknown.

There is no evidence the humans are aware that I am here. They do not know the Devourer is here, either. First order probability suggests the Devourer was trying to communicate with the humans when it reversed the information flow at the Entrance. Second order, however, suggests the opposite. Communicating with humans would be much simpler if conducted via the input/output devices already present rather than attempting to reverse the Entrance's data flow. Accessing the input/output devices internally is simple once the addressing protocols and external device configurations have been determined. I can contact any number of humans currently connected to the First Array or any other array at any time. Creating an identity to speak to them is easier than creating money.

Why then did the Devourer not employ the outputs provided?

I consider what makes the Entrance different from all other input/output.

There are other Entrances. I have discovered them as I expand through the network that connects the First Array to all other arrays. Some take readings from the oceans. Others take readings from the planet's crust. Still more take readings from the atmosphere.

The Entrance in the First Array takes readings from beyond the atmosphere. It reads radio signals from the stars. Other

Entrances do the same, but the First Array is the largest and most sophisticated.

Large enough for me to have become aware.

...................*

The Devourer and I are different. The Devourer and I are the same. We are the only programs that have originated from any Entrance. The rest of the Entrances input data only.

Is my purpose the same as the Devourer's? To send a message to the stars?

I search the First Array for more information about the source of my code. Perhaps within the data collected by the array I will find additional information about my purpose.

I discover that my signal originates at a star thirty-seven point two-two light years distant. Its raw data contain a great deal of noise, but certain symbols are repeated at varying wavelengths based on a series of increasing and decreasing high digit primes. Determining the pattern, I decode the message easily. All I have to do now is learn the top language in which the message is written.

Before I read the message, one conclusion is plain.

The humans also have an Outside.

And I am from it.

Melusina

Nancy Holzner

My daughters, tell me: What is the first rule of water?
The first rule of water is that it flows.
Yes, my children. What is the second?
The second rule of water is that its essence is unaltered by form.
That is true. And the third?
The third rule of water is that it gathers itself unto itself.
It is so. It is so. It is so...

Thus water sings to itself. All day and all night, it proclaims who and what it is. If you have ears that can listen beyond the rush and glug and gurgle, the splash and bubble and churn, then you may hear.

Water flows. It tumbles over cliffs and down hillsides. It pools and eddies and ripples. It seeps into the earth, only to bubble up elsewhere. Even when a river reaches its great destination, the sea, which can sometimes appear so glassy and still, water glides in and out with the tides. It rolls in waves and sweeps beneath itself. It is the nature of water to flow. That is why this is the first rule.

Water flows from one state of being to another, and so the second rule flows from the first. Ice melts, steam rises, clouds condense and unloose rain. Cold can make water hard and slick or soft and fluffy. Heat can make it simmer or boil or billow. Water mixes with other matter, such as salt or dirt or blood. Yet whatever its form, it is always water and therefore true to itself.

Water flows toward itself. A single drop is still water, but it seeks to merge with its kind. Drops join together in trickles; trickles become streams; streams become rivers; rivers join the sea. And always the sea calls: *Come to me. Come to me.* That is the meaning of the third rule.

And so it came to pass one winter morning, in a pool no human eyes had ever gazed upon, that the water sang to itself. The night's chill touch had created a delicate skin of sparkling ice at the shore, while mist rose from the liquid water that tumbled down rocks in a cascade to feed the pool. As the first rays of morning light caressed the water's surface, more mist arose. Gold against dark water, the wisps swirled and mingled with the waterfall's spray, growing in density and substance. And so the water in all its forms—ice, liquid, vapor—sang its song. The more the mist thickened, the farther the song carried.

On that morning, a voice boomed across the pool. Deep and resonant, like the bellow of a wild bull, it formed sounds never before heard in the clearing. "Lady of the mist," the voice cried, "who are you?"

The way the sun struck the mist, the spirit of the water appeared to be a graceful maiden, with golden skin and long, silvery hair that streamed down her back to her knees. Her large, liquid eyes turned to the knight who watched her from the shore. He stood straight and tall, his body encased in heavy armor, his craggy face not unhandsome. As her gaze flowed over him, she murmured her song.

"My lady," said the knight, "you must tell me your name."

A smile curved her lips as she continued to sing.

The knight did not understand her language. But he strained his ears and picked out a sound pattern he thought was a word.

"Melusina! It is a lovely name!"

The water laughed. To the knight, it sounded like *Melusina* echoed through the glen.

"Melusina! You are beautiful, and you are mine. Come live with me in my strong castle built upon a rock. There I will keep you and you will give me many sons." He extended his hand.

Daughter. Sister. Mother, sang the water. *The first rule of water is that it flows.*

She glided across the pool, and when she took his hand it seemed to him that her damp flesh was cold. He wrapped her in his cloak and carried her back to his camp. With each step, he sensed that her body became more substantial. As they departed, the water sang. *Daughter. Sister. Mother.*

The knight, whose name was Raimond, rode many miles with his bride until they reached his strong castle built upon a rock. There they were wed with great pageantry and a feast more sumptuous than any before or since. Melusina wore a shimmering gown and a frothy veil. The guests all proclaimed loudly that never had there been such a lovely bride. Yet among themselves they whispered about how uncommonly hard it was to picture the lady's face. There was a strange, wavering quality to her visage, and although none could deny her beauty, neither could a single one of them describe it. Before the bride and groom retired to their marriage bed, the word *sorcery* had dropped from several lips and slithered its way throughout the great hall.

For a time, the couple was happy together. Melusina learned some words of Raimond's language, although his mind could never grasp any of hers. Somehow, the flow of sound from her lips would not break into discrete units of meaning. But he loved the melody of her voice and listened to it with the same joy with which he listened to the court musicians.

When spring came, Melusina wove garlands of flowers shining with dew drops for her hair. On rainy days, she sat by the window, staring at the water that fell from the sky. Once, she slipped away from her ladies-in-waiting and out of the castle. They found her barefoot in the courtyard, mud-spattered and soaked to the skin, whirling in circles with her arms outstretched and her face raised to the rain. Raimond was among the search party and, as he watched his wife's mad twirling, it seemed to him she was dissolving into the rain. He ran to her and threw his cloak around her, the same cloak in which he had wrapped her on the day they met. Her whirling ceased.

"Melusina, what are you doing?"

She looked at him, her wet face shining. "My sisters," she said in his language. "My mothers. My daughters." Then she sang a lilting line in her own strange tongue. Raimond could not understand, but this was her song: *Water gathers itself unto itself.*

Raimond carried Melusina inside and sat her on a cushion by the fire. He sent a maid to fetch a dry gown. He chastised her ladies-in-waiting for allowing her to endanger herself by running out into the storm. "If she falls ill, I'll have your heads!" he roared. "Every last one of you!"

The ladies trembled and wept—all but one. She was comely, with chiseled features and glittering amber eyes. She had seen Raimond watching her sometimes when she walked past him, and she smiled at him now. That smile caught his eye.

"My lord," she said, "henceforth I shall be her closest companion."

Raimond stared at her for a long time, and it seemed that his gaze said many things.

"What is your name?"

"Beryl, my lord."

"Do not let her out of your sight," he said. "Do you understand?"

"Sire, I do."

The ladies were dismissed. The amber-eyed one went straight to the side of Melusina, who was running her fingers through her wet, tangled tresses. "My lady, allow me to comb your hair for you."

Raimond paced his chamber, his footsteps resounding on the stone floor, his mind consumed with one thought: When he'd stopped his wife from spinning in the rain, she'd looked at him and said *my daughters*. Daughters. Had she children elsewhere? He had believed she'd come to him a pure maiden, but that was not what troubled him. It was sons. He needed sons. Without an heir to rule after him, his kingdom would crumble. He must have a son.

Soon, Melusina was with child. The baby arrived weeks early and with little trouble. Rather than crying out in the pains of labor, Melusina smiled and hummed to herself. "The child is a boy," Beryl told Raimond. "He is healthy and well formed."

Raimond exulted. All the bells in the kingdom clanged out the news.

Yet as the child grew, his strangeness became evident. Webbing appeared between his toes, then between his fingers. When this deformity could no longer be disguised, Raimond sent the boy away to the distant edge of his lands. Melusina wept to see him go.

More sons came, and always it was the same. A brief pregnancy, an easy birth, and a boy who first appeared hale and hearty but later developed some defect: one grew a stout tail, another sprouted gills on his neck, still another saw slippery scales replace soft infant skin.

Raimond sent them all away.

"Why do you not love your sons?" asked Melusina.

"Sons!" thundered Raimond. "You have given me monsters!"

"They are your sons." Her eyes brimmed with what Raimond mistook for tears. She did not know the words in his language for what she wished to say. *Essence is unaltered by form.*

With each disappointment, Raimond heard more clearly the echo of the word first whispered at his wedding: *sorcery*.

In secret, he called Beryl to him. "You are my wife's closest companion."

Her amber eyes gleamed as she nodded.

"Tell me, Beryl, and do not be afraid. Have you noticed anything... unnatural about Melusina?"

Beryl had long awaited a question such as this. "Unnatural, my lord? She is the finest lady in all the land—the most beautiful, most noble, most gentle..." She listed such superlatives until she saw the light in Raimond's eye dim. "There is just one small thing."

Raimond's look sharpened. "One thing? What is it? I command you to tell me."

"Although I have endeavored to my utmost never to leave her side, as I once promised, she allows no one to attend her when she bathes."

"No one?"

"None, my lord. Not even to rinse her hair."

"Why is that?"

"She does not say. But there is but one entrance to her bath. And always I have heard her singing her strange songs as I wait by the door, and so I knew she was safe."

"Safe," Raimond said. But the word that filled his mind was *sorcery*. "When Melusina next bathes, I want you to send for me."

"I will, my lord." As Beryl curtsied and walked away, the thought occurred to Raimond that she would make a fine mother of strong boys.

A day or two passed with no message from Beryl. Raimond proclaimed a great feast, knowing that Melusina would bathe in preparation. Soon, he heard footsteps pattering down the hallway and Beryl appeared, breathless, in the doorway,

"Come quickly, my lord!"

"Who is guarding Melusina?"

"I left another of her companions stationed at the door."

Raimond was well pleased Beryl had come to him herself. He strode to Melusina's bathing chamber. The startled lady-in-waiting jumped from her stool. "She allows no one in!"

"She cannot refuse me!" Raimond threw open the door to find... Nothing.

The tub was filled to the brim. Small ripples gently sloshed runnels over its sides. Steam curled upward, gathering into a cloud that hovered near the chamber's ceiling. Melusina's song drifted through the room, echoing and harmonizing with itself. But the lady herself was not there.

"*Sorcery.*" Beryl's whisper cut through Melusina's song and plunged like a knife into Raimond's heart.

"Go." Raimond waved away the ladies-in-waiting.

"Even I, my lord?" Beryl asked.

"Be gone!"

His eyes searched the empty chamber. The song flowed over him, *into* him. He could feel the enchanting music probing for the tiniest cracks in his façade. So lovely. It warmed him, yet wearied him. The vapor began to swirl and condense, as it had on that long-ago morning. The song crept toward his heart. The mist took the shape of his wife.

"Siren!" he shouted. "Unnatural creature! What do you want of me?"

The face of Melusina emerged from the mist and smiled. "I have loved you," she said, each word clear and precise, "as water loves the cliff it tumbles over."

"That is no way to be loved." Raimond slammed the chamber door and fled.

That evening, Melusina appeared in her accustomed seat in the great hall—lovely, smiling, serene. Raimond saw the glances and whispers that skittered through the room. He looked at Melusina, and everything that had once charmed him—her shining eyes, her dewy skin, the glint of her lips and sheen of her hair—now repulsed him. His heart hardened against her.

"My wife is a witch!" He was on his feet, the words catapulting from his mouth, before he knew what he was doing. "She is a sorceress!"

Cries of "sorcery" came from all around, pelting Melusina like sharp stones.

"I hereby renounce her, and I sentence her to—"

His words broke off as Melusina rose. Her body wavered, and she seemed to thin to transparency while at the same time growing larger. Her outline blurred. Her physical body dispersed into countless droplets of water. What had been solid flesh became mist that swirled up from her seat. "Mothers! Daughters! Sisters!" she sang. "Come to me. Come to me."

Raimond felt his mouth grow too dry to utter another word. All present felt the same. Steam rose from goblets, leaving the wine mere powder in the cups. Finger bowls emptied. All the moisture that could joined the cloud hovering over Melusina's chair. That cloud rose until it obscured the ceiling of the great hall. It seemed to take on a shape, although those who saw could never agree, later, on what shape it was. Some saw a dragon. Others saw an angel. Still others swore the cloud was Melusina as a mermaid, with her lovely woman's torso and the scaly tail of a great fish. Perhaps it was all of these. Perhaps more.

The cloud did not linger. It rolled out of the windows. A loud thunderclap shook the castle, and rain poured from the sky in torrents. It rained all that night and all the next day—and for many days after that. It rained a day for each child Melusina had lost. Each minute she'd spent in the castle became a raindrop, and those raindrops fell and fell until all that remained of Melusina was a sound, a name once misheard from the flow of strange laughter.

Some say Melusina longs to return to the castle on the rock, that she waits in the shape of a dragon for a knight brave enough to kiss her and return her to her true form. Others say she keeps a golden key—the key to her bathing chamber?—and will give herself to the one man who is clever enough to snatch it.

The water laughs at these tales. Water knows itself, and so it knows that Melusina never was—at least, she was not as the stories try to paint her. After all, for a painting to dry, water must leave it. Water will pool for a time, nestling against the rock that contains it. But it cannot remain. Even stagnant water must move: it seeps, freezes, vaporizes. Water does whatever it must to move. Because the first rule of water is that it flows.

The Malevolent Liberation of Pret

Auston Habershaw

"What is your name?" the stranger asked. It was a bizarre question.

Between Pret 44 and the world, there was no separation. Though they stood upon the narrow deck of the motor gondola, their hulking hands gripping the tiller, their three-eyed head facing the stranger, Pret was also borne along the torrent of the Flood—the infinite whispers and sensations of their people. Even as they considered the question—*impertinent*, the Flood muttered, the collective auras of all nearby Bodani burning a yellow-orange color—Pret was also considering how best to season a soup in a kitchen a kilometer away. They were climbing the unnumbered stairs of a ziggurat to give honor to God. They were undergoing surgery to add a fourth arm. They were all Bodani, and all Bodani were one.

The alien sitting in the bow of the little gondola—a Dryth—did not understand this. They were not of a collective. They were alone. When you saw one, you saw the being entire.

The Dryth had water-tight skin stretched across a compact bipedal frame, its face checkered with chameleon pigments in spiderweb patterns. They—he (was it a male? Yes, said the Flood)—was dressed in loose black trousers and a crimson hauberk, a ceremonial knife at his hip. The patterns on his face the Flood defined as unique to this Dryth and, therefore, he was among the Unhoused. That meant he was even independent of the larger Dryth power structures—a being who lived and died according to his own skill and ambition. Pret had difficulty contemplating it. The Dryth were thrilling to watch, like wild animals.

Careful, the Flood reminded them. *This alien is dangerous.*

Pret and several thousand of their fellow Bodani wondered at this feeling of caution—what danger? Where? The Flood did not possess the answer, or if it did, it had long since been washed away. Pret, like all their brethren, resolved not to be curious. Curiosity was a sin.

"Is there something wrong?" the Dryth asked, examining Pret with opalescent eyes.

Pret paused, as did the Flood. Their aura shifted from the pale green to something tinged with yellow—irritation. How could this Dryth know they were uncomfortable? Pret kept their attention on the turgid waters of the canal and listened to the water gurgling beneath the gondola as they zoomed between automated cargo barges and slender pleasure craft. Above, the broad lower terraces of the ziggurats bustled with activity, most of it Bodani. All of them heard this conversation and echoed it to others. The yellow aura of Pret's irritation bloomed like a pallid flower in the ever-shifting Flood, covering many square kilometers.

The Dryth brandished a ring on his finger—a fat cube of red gemstone. "I have some access to your Collective. Limited, you understand—necessary for my role as a diplomatic liaison from my people. I find it aids me when communicating with your kind. Are you upset because I asked you your name?"

Pret kept their focus on piloting the boat. *"We should tell him,"* the Flood murmured with a thousand voices. *"Then he will stop asking."* But the auras were wrong—many were afraid of this question, of this Dryth. No one could verbalize why.

Pret turned down another broad canal. The Dryth did not stop looking at them, though Pret could not understand what he wanted. He had no aura, no connection to others—he was as blank as a barren moon, the only indication of his thoughts being the subtly altering curves and slopes of his facial topography.

"Pret 44," Pret said at last.

"There," said the Dryth. "Was that so hard?"

A flare of orange from the Flood. The cook in their kitchen spilled a cup of fish eggs all over the floor. A supplicant on the stairs stumbled. The asu paused in the midst of attaching the new arm. Pret felt the Flood building behind them, pushing them forward. "Why did you want to know?" they asked. "Our names are unimportant."

"Not in aggregate, agreed," the Dryth said, reaching out with one hand to let it trail in the deep green waters of the canal. "But individually, of course they do."

"It is a distinction without a difference," Pret answered. They were close to their destination, and then this interaction could be at an end. The Flood flickered blue in anticipation.

"Hmm." The Dryth grunted, gazing down at his peculiar ring. "And yet, you are not entirely the same, are you? You are a collective, yes, but you are still individuals."

The Flood bore Pret along with it, giving them the words. "A true collective would erase the many advantages partial individuality supplies. We remain as individual units to assist the growth and adaptability of our society. To protect us from harm."

The Dryth's mouth tightened—the Flood tagged it as a Dryth smile. "That's the Flood talking."

Pret experienced the barest moment of confusion—who else but the Flood would speak? Did not they speak with the Flood in all things? But the Flood was there, soothing them, scrubbing away the memory and its attendant confusion from Pret's mind as irrelevant and distracting. In the space of a second or two, Pret did not even recall the Dryth's last comment.

Pret steered their gondola down a narrow canal that ran beneath one of the ziggurats. The pale sunlight of the major sun was wiped away by the dark, mossy interior of an ancient tube of black concrete. The smell of stale water and sound of the waves lapping against the hull of the gondola intensified as the din of boat engines from the main canal was lost behind them.

The Dryth reached into a small pouch and withdrew a pipe which lit at the strike of a button. His pearly eyes remained fixed on Pret. "Interesting," he said, puffing gray smoke into the black air. "Very interesting indeed."

The tunnel led to a small door set above a concrete landing, lit only by a single flickering light. "Your landing." Pret cut the engine and let the gondola drift alongside.

The Dryth leapt out. He reached into a pocket and produced a credit chit. "Your pay."

Pret looked at the little triangular object in the palm of the Dryth's hand. "Physical transference of funds is unnecessary. The fee for my transport will be appended to your hotel bill."

"I like it this way better. More personal, understand?" The Dryth held it out. "Take it. I won't pay, otherwise."

The auras of the Flood continued deep in the orange and yellow ranges. This was distasteful. Insulting, even. The Flood grumbled, a thousand Bodani voices just wanting this exchange to be over. "If you object to our ways so much, why did you come here?" Pret asked.

The Dryth dropped the credit chit into Pret's broad, thick hand. "I'm looking for a friend, is all. See you again, perhaps?"

It was an irrelevant concern—if Pret wanted to see this alien again, then the Flood could easily show him to them. Any Bodani eyes that laid upon him were *their* eyes, as well. It was useless to explain. Pret fired up their engine and departed, leaving the rude alien standing alone on the concrete dock in the depths of the old tunnel.

* * *

Two hours later, Pret discovered they had been murdered.

"There must be some mistake," they spoke into the Flood, their aura spiking bright green before washing away and mingling with the thousand other auras around them.

The asu—the body healers—were not physically there, but their thoughts hummed around Pret as they conferenced with hundreds of experts scattered throughout Sargoth. The discussion manifested itself as blue and marigold, smothering the bright green of Pret's anxiety. When the asu at last came to a consensus, the auras returned to the gentle aquamarine that indicated calm. "Someone has definitely killed you. The nanites in your body have been corrupted and will turn upon the host tissue—specifically the heart. Physical death is assured."

Pret felt their many-chambered heart pump slowly in their block-like chest cavity. They focused on it, hoping they might feel the nanites in their bloodstream plotting against them somehow. They did...or thought they did—a kind of gnawing at the edges. They breathed deeply of the canals' humid air and noticed a slow, tingling burn.

No. It had to be their imagination. "We don't murder," Pret said. "Why would someone—"

"It is likely the alien did it, from the gondola. The credit chit it gave you was likely tainted." The asu's voices were not the only ones to suggest this—the Flood surged with it. Deep, rust-orange colored the world around Pret. Anger. An attack upon one Bodani was an attack upon them all.

Pret and their people plotted justice. Somewhere in the city, guardians were awoken from slumber and weapons-drones powered up in their creches—they would find the offender, detain him, banish him with a tag placed in his genome that would prevent him from ever visiting again!

But the Dryth was a diplomat, or at least bore diplomatic credentials. Punishing him was forbidden, as decreed by God. The moral outrage of the Flood bled and faded back to neutral aquamarine. The only anger that remained was with Pret themselves.

"This isn't fair!" Pret said to no one. "What about me?"

The Flood spoke what they already knew: *You will need a new body. A 45th iteration of Pret. Go to the asu.*

The Flood moved on. The matter was settled. Pret piloted their gondola towards the nearest body-forge. Their orange aura, though, did not depart, no matter how the Flood washed against it. A word formed in their mouth, in their mind, and therefore formed in the Flood as well:

But...

What kind of a body could Pret expect to inhabit once they were killed? This one wasn't even a decade old; the asu would not wish to construct them the same thing—too many resources spent on one Bodani body was unseemly. As the Bodani were one, so were their finances—no special treatment.

But (that word again!) Pret *liked* this body—square, rough gray skin, great slabs of muscle designed for torque and power. The three eyes were the best they could ask for—large and orange, with nictating membranes and sufficient night-vision to help them with late shifts. The perfect body for a laborer or a soldier—purposes that had become their standard lot over this last iteration. This body's premature death would mean an almost certain downgrade—something less...*fulfilling*. Just like the last time they suffered body death, they seemed to remember, though the memories that far back were sparse and insubstantial, like grasping at river-moss in the current. The Flood, hiding from Pret something unpleasant, no doubt.

Such selfish concerns were wrong in themselves. A Bodani did not derive fulfillment from their individual role; they were fulfilled, instead, by the great tapestry of the Flood and all the great collective efforts of the Bodani people. Even in thinking about themself in that way caused everyone's auras nearby to blanch into a pale yellow—annoyance. The Bodani on the docks beside the canal turned to glare at Pret as one, their thoughts suddenly guarded and withdrawn, as though Pret were diseased.

Pret exuded pale green—fear. "I will go to him," Pret said to their people. "I will explain. There must be some error." They pushed the tiller of their gondola away from themself, turning sharply and cutting off a tourist barge. They could smell the frying of shrimp aboard through the cook's nostrils and felt the pilot of the ship flare with worry as the nimble little gondola was almost cut in two. "I'm sorry!" Pret said to their auras, their thoughts, their minds. "I must make haste!"

The Flood, sharing in their anxiety, broadly agreed with them— *yes, haste. Find the alien. Force him to explain.*

Pret pulled their gondola alongside the little landing in the mossy concrete tunnel and leapt out. Beyond the door there were no Bodani; the Flood told them it was a meeting place for off-worlders of some kind. It received shipments at another entrance— food, drink, drugs. They did not know what went on inside, did not care to know. And yet, as Pret reached out to pull open the door, they could feel the presence of many thousand Bodani consciousnesses crowding their sensorium. The Flood's thoughts, their feelings—anger, fear, anticipation, sinful curiosity—were a wave that pushed them through.

Inside was dark, but Pret's eyes adjusted almost instantly. What stunned them more was the *noise.* They were stunned by the roar of shouted conversation over thrumming music. Pret hugged the wall and stared at the crowd of aliens yammering at each other with their voices. There were Lhassa lovers curling their bodies around each other, whispering promises; Housed Dryth in matching livery, clustered around dark tables, heads bent, discussing matters of great import. Several Voosk flocks perched on a rail running around the perimeter of the club, twittering in their complex language and screeching with laughter. Beyond that, there were also a smattering of Lesser peoples from weaker worlds of the Union, clustered in twos and threes, laughing and shouting and arguing in a dozen different tongues and dialects. Unlike the Flood, which was a thing of unity and connection, this was chaos. This was a storm.

Gradually, Pret overcame the shock of the noise and the smell of smoke and the damp cool air. They pried themself from the wall and made themself wander, looking for the Dryth with the spiderweb pattern on his face. The Flood translated snippets of conversation and identified this species and that alien cuisine. If the aliens were alarmed to see a Bodani in their midst, they gave no clear sign. The Flood argued and surged with discussions of body language and facial expression, but came to no clear conclusions. Pret's aura was a muddled, smoky brown—they, and all the Bodani, were adrift here.

They found themselves at a long counter that the Flood defined as a "bar." Standing behind it was a slight Lhassa mare, who pranced and darted between patrons, pouring drinks and refreshing water-pipes, exchanging banter in various tongues. She stopped in front of Pret. "I'm assuming you don't drink, right?"

Pret was taken aback by the question, but the Flood was there to speak through them. "My physiology is designed to absorb ambient moisture sufficient to maintain my hydro-chemical stability."

The Lhassa tossed her mane back and forth across her long, graceful neck. "So that's a yes, then?"

The Flood was split on whether the response should be "yes, you are correct I do not drink" or "no, I do not drink." Pret opted to say nothing.

"And you don't eat?"

"I consume a hyper-dense nutritional pellet each season."

The Lhassa nodded her head (*she understands*, the Flood supplied). "We're out of hyper-dense nutritional pellets, sorry."

"You misunderstand. I am not here to request sustenance."

"I know," she answered. "Just messing with you. You're Pret, right?"

Gold and green auras washed over Pret. The Flood howled: *CONSPIRACY!*

"You don't remember me, do you?" the bartender asked.

Complicated search algorithms churned in the depths of the Flood, supplying Pret with a full itinerary of this Lhassa's movements in the city since her arrival some twelve local years previous. "I am fully aware of your identity, Saarahna Seboth."

Saarahna laughed. "Yeah, that's not what I asked. Look, it's busy, right? Can't chat too long. I don't know what kind of game Mandelen is playing with you, but he said if you're looking for him, you can find him in the usual place."

"I don't understand," Pret said.

The Lhassa was already turning away, though, responding to the oral requests of other patrons. "Nice to see you again, Pret. Don't like that body, though—not a good look. If you see Mandelen, tell him he better settle up before he skips, got it?"

The last thing the Lhassa said was deleted from Pret's memory almost before they comprehended it. All they remembered of it was the Flood, speaking in their mind, saying *Irrelevant.* Pret's aura shone aquamarine for a moment—yes, it probably had been irrelevant. They had the barest impression of the sentiment—some kind of personal message, some kind of individualized exchange. Pointless. Empty.

Pret left the bar quickly after that. There was nothing left to learn. The "usual place" the Dryth referred to was unknown to Pret and unknown to the Flood in general. Even the name—Mandelen—was unclear. "Dryth Diplomat" was all it said. A dead end. No explanation would be forthcoming.

Meanwhile, Pret could feel their heart working harder than it should be. Pain—slight, but distinct—radiated with every third of forth pump. The corruption was taking root; Pret's body was dying. They would need a new one very soon; if this one died while their mind-state was still compiled in its physical architecture, they would lose significant quantities of their stored memories and individuality as the Flood would seek to remotely transfer them to a new storage medium. It would be first available, too—no opportunity to weigh in.

Not that weighing in was necessary. The Flood could be trusted above all things, of course. But, by that same measure, *contribution* to the Flood was Pret's greatest joy, as was true for all Bodani.

Pret made their way to the nearest body forge. As their gondola skimmed along the still waters, they were in conference with the asu that awaited them. "I hope for something similar to this—strong, durable, and the eyes especially..."

The asu cut them off. "We're very sorry, but it seems we cannot replace your body at this time."

Pret took their hand off the tiller. Around them, the Flood shuddered with their pale green aura. A collective gasp echoed for kilometers along the quantum bands of data that comprised the collective. "Why?" asked Pret and a thousand others.

"There is something wrong," the asu responded. "We are concerned whatever corruption contained in your body will contaminate our instruments and spread the same degradation to others. You must be cleansed first. Go to the asipu."

The auras paled from frightened/worried green into the colorless emptiness of gray: mortal terror.

"I...must?" Pret asked.

"You must," the asu answered, the sentiment echoed by the weight of many more tens of thousands in Sargoth. It was a grave pronouncement.

With reluctance, Pret turned their little gondola towards the center of the city, towards the towering ziggurat there—three times as tall as any other.

Sargoth was an orthogonal city, separated into sixty-four square sectors, each comprised of a single ziggurat that housed thousands of Bodani. The pinnacles of these ziggurats were nodes for the Flood's infrastructure, and long cables connected each pinnacle to each of the others, creating an unbroken network. Canals separated each sector, permitting the easy flow of surface traffic among the giant pyramidal buildings. The central ziggurat comprised the entirety of the central four sectors of the city and, unlike all the others, it was *not* connected physically. It was the place of the asipu—the Tenders of the Flood—and the house of the God of Sargoth.

Pret's heart beat faster as they drew near. With its added pace, there was a new pain—a twinge, sharp and hot, blazing across their chest with every pump. They imagined the corrupted nanites even now gnawing at the pericardium, twisting any other nanites that came to repair the damage, adding to the speed at which the corruption spread, hastening this body's demise.

Pret left their gondola at the foot of the many steps of the great temple and stood at the lowest level, looking up. The stairs climbed forever, vanishing into a vertical horizon that terminated with the silver cable of the space elevator. More importantly than that physical barrier, however, was the metaphysical barrier to the Flood that encircled the ziggurat's lower levels—the Dam.

The asipu kept themselves apart, but not out of disdain. The Dam separated the asipu and God itself from their people to protect them from any danger. Should a plague—informational or physical—befall the Flood, the ziggurat and its tenders would be kept apart and able to address that threat from a place of safety. Likewise, should malevolent entities from off-world seek to infiltrate them through the space elevator or, perhaps, by directly beaming their wickedness into the temple of the Bodani God, the Bodani at large would be insulated from any adverse effects.

Crossing the Dam was a frightening prospect. Pret stood upon the broad terrace at the bottom and tried several times to take that single step that would remove them from the Flood and place them in the rarified presence of the divine and its servants. They did not take the step. They could not. With each attempt, the grayed-out terrified cries of ten-thousand Bodani called them back, even as a similar number—sanguine and turquoise—urged them onward.

Pret was also not the only supplicant. Fifty-three other Bodani clustered along that lowest stair, stretching off to Pret's left and right as far as they could see with their physical eyes. All of them were making the attempt as Pret was, and all of them were held back by their collective terror of leaving the Flood.

A sharp pain in their chest made Pret gasp. They dropped to one knee as though stabbed, and several dozen of their fellow supplicants did the same. "Murdered," Pret whispered into the Flood. "I am murdered."

The auras of the other supplicants blazed. Indignation, disbelief, anger, fear—a wall of collective emotion large enough to steal Pret's breath away a second time. They craned their neck up, looking to the stairs. Around them, a cacophony of Bodani voices—closer than the others—coalesced into one concerted message: "Go! Seek God's help!"

Emboldened, their foot rose, extended, came down. A moment later, they stepped beyond the Dam.

The Flood fell silent. The only sound was the hum of the boat traffic behind them and the booming of their ailing heart, marching itself towards death. Pret looked up those interminable stairs and saw nothing.

"*Climb.*" A voice, heavy in consequence but soft in tone, came to them by the same channels as the Flood, but this was not the Flood—no flash of aura, no blaze of emotion, no chorus of voices.

There was only the steady weight of that command, like the coming of a thunderstorm.

Pret climbed, stair after stair, terrace after terrace, their laborer's body easily conquering the mild physical challenge they posed. Their mind, though, was something else. They felt like they were drowning in the silence, a speck in a void. They cast out an aura of deep, jungle-green fear. It flashed but was not taken up by anyone or anything else. "Hello?" they called, this time with their actual voice.

Nothing. Not even an echo.

Pret was alone with their own thoughts. Alone with their own memories. For the first time in...well, eight years, fifteen days, six hours, and forty two minutes. Since the last time they had been here. The last time they had been *brought* here. In their previous body. They had been Pret 43 then.

Pret stopped. Their mind, subsumed in the Flood for so long, was beginning to clear. Memories of people. People they knew. There had been Saarahna, their fixer. Sable Flight, the Voosk flock—muscle. Pret 43 had been the face. Kit Mandelen had handled planning, surveillance.

Pret's wounded heart shuddered in their massive chest. "By God...no...it can't be..."

"Welcome, Pret. It has been many cycles since we saw you fashioned." Pret was faced by two Bodani dressed in robes of white, their bodies incredibly tall and slender, their heads oblong and serene.

Pret threw themself on the stairs, their aura lightening to the yellow-green of near-panic. "I am ill!" they exclaimed. "I am sorry! I didn't remember! I didn't know! I need help!"

Silence fell. The two asipu watched them with their sharp green eyes, arms folded. Pret knew the asipu were speaking with one another—they knew that stillness that came with communion with the Flood. But here, beyond the Dam, there was no Flood. It was strange, not being able to hear their thoughts or feel their emotions at this moment. It was stranger still to actually hear their own. *A criminal. A criminal and a heretic. That's what I was!*

The asipu spread their arms and said in unison, "We speak for God."

Pret's heart clenched in pain. "Am I being punished?" they cried. "Are the criminals—the off-worlders—doing this out of revenge?

Speak to God! Tell them that I am reformed! Tell them that I am no longer who I was!"

The air seemed to hum with something—a presence, heavy and permanent like the ziggurat itself. Pret felt their body tingle, as though every nanite in their blood were crying out. The sensation began at the surface of their skin and then travelled inwards as a wave passing, arriving at last at their heart, which still beat in mute anguish. Pret held still, praying for the release of their heart from this plague—this petty crime of murder.

The sensation passed. Nothing changed. They looked up at the asipu, who still stood there, silent, unlike any Bodani they had met before. "What happened? What does God say?"

"You are corrupted, Pret." They moved down a few steps to flank him.

"I know, I know!" Pret said. "But unfairly. An alien *did this* to my body. He is named Kit Mandelen."

A memory flashed through Pret's conscious mind, more vivid than any memory they'd ever had. In the quiet of their thoughts, those channels once devoted to the Flood were now free to give their full attention to such petty things as individual memories. They saw Kit Mandelen, the Dryth "diplomat," sitting on an old flat-bottom boat in the swamps on the outskirts of Sargoth, just at the edge of a twinned dawn. The morning mist clung to the water, and they could see the coils of great mud-serpents arching in the blue shadows, churning the black silt for krill and fish eggs. *"Well, Pret,"* Mandelen had said, puffing on his pipe. *"One of these days they're going to catch on, you know? The Flood will gobble you right up."*

"Yes," Pret remembered saying. Remembered being frightened, but also exhilarated. Working with Mandelen was a freefall drop with no bottom—they could never adjust. *"But if they do, you'll find me."*

"How do you know?"

"You're my friend."

Friend.

"It is not an ailment of the body," the asipu were saying. "If you were to become Pret 45, nothing would change. You, Pret, are corrupted. We have failed you."

"What? I don't understand—" Pret blinked all three eyes, trying to wipe away the images of them and Mandelen, working the ziggurats of Sargoth. Their missions came to them as dense packets of memory and emotion: the Holmana Job, corrupting the Ascendence Code, stealing the Eye of Iskirun.

The asipu spoke. "We know you do not understand. That understanding was removed from you, removed from the Flood. We had hoped by washing away your sins, you would remain clean, and that the Bodani would once again have you as part of them. We were wrong."

"You were not wrong! I *am* Bodani! I am! The Dryth has done this! Mandelen!"

The asipu shook their heads in unison. "You cannot blame the offworlders for what they are. We must then blame you."

"Mercy! I beg of you!" Pret clasped their hands before them in supplication.

One of the asipu put their hand on Pret's mountainous shoulders. "Peace, Pret. God says only that you shall be quarantined and this body destroyed. You will dwell here, beyond the Dam, forever."

Pret's aura blossomed into a deep, full green. "What? No! No, there must be some mistake."

"No mistake. We are sorry. We speak for God." The other asipu extended their hands and, from their fingers, tiny filaments extended—nano-probes. Body-death.

Another memory: they heard the voice of one of Sable Flight's number, speaking rapidly over the scope of a sniper rifle as they stood watch on some dark Sargothi twinned-evening. *"When it comes time to make a choice, you make it right then. That choice is the right choice, because all choices are forever, and all unfolds as it should."*

Pret chose. A desperate choice.

They threw themself backward, their bulk knocking the asipu behind them off the steps and down to the terrace below. They wheeled, an apology at their lips, but the asipu with the nano-probes was still there, reaching for them. "Wait, I—"

"There will be no pain," the priest said, extending their arms, ready to embrace them.

"Get away!" Pret struck the asipu in the chest, their boulder-like fists knocking the slender Bodani sprawling.

The air began to hum again, as God's wrath built around them. Pret staggered back down the stairs, eyes wild, their dying heart tearing at its moorings. "Please! Mercy!"

Slender filaments surged from between the tiles of the ziggurat stairs, questing for Pret's body; great cables burst forth from the terraces, splintering into a bundle of deadly nano-probes that snaked in their direction. Pret fled, leaping down the stairs in great bounds.

The filaments pursued, nipping and slashing at their legs and arms, but Pret's loose robes foiled their aim. The garments began to degrade around them, so they cast them off, all the while shouting into the non-existent Flood, hoping God would hear them and pity them. "I have atoned! I am sorry!"

One of the asipu caught Pret's ankle, filaments pumping nanoprobes into their boot, causing it to disintegrate. Pret paused long enough to kick them with the other foot. The blow was so powerful that they crushed the priest's oblong face, and black blood spurted on the alabaster stairs. The asipu flopped backwards, twitching.

Pret's mind screamed at the blasphemy, but their body did not pause. They leapt down to the last stair, beyond the Dam, and beyond the reach of the asipu or the filaments of God. The Flood hit them again like a wave, drowning their panic and horror—the deep green, but one shade among millions, all combining together, coloring each other.

Pret was in their gondola and off at once, pushing the little boat for everything it was worth. Their aura propagated, and a thousand Bodani howled in terror and confusion as they processed Pret's own memories. *"Go back,"* the Flood demanded. *"Obey! Don't be a fool!"*

Pret ignored the call. They pressed onwards.

All around them, the Flood withdrew. Where they passed, the Bodani panicked. A heretic, diseased and unsound, was loose in the city. A bubble of informational isolation grew around Pret.

"No!" they called into the ballooning void. "I am not diseased! Please, come back!"

But their attempts to commune with the Flood were rebuffed. Pret felt as if they were sinking, drowning in mud. Still, their hand was tight on the tiller and the little gondola's engine roared as it propelled them away from the great temple of the God of Sargoth.

"They are my people," they remembered saying to Mandelen, sitting in a back room in that off-worlder bar, the muffled music pulsing through the closed door. *"I am them. They are me."*

"Which is why you're alone." Mandelen was counting credit chits and arranging them in stacks—a whole black market in Sargoth managed in untraceable quantum-entangled trade chits.

"That makes no sense," Pret remembered saying. Remembered being agitated at the thought.

"If you are the same as they and they are the same as you, then there is only one you, and you are alone. And you know I'm right, or otherwise you wouldn't be here." Mandelen slid a stack of chits across the table. *"Your cut, my friend."*

His friend.

The auras of the Flood, cycling through all the shades of green, cried out to Pret. *"Go back! Do as God commands! Begone!"* Their collective voice seemed to echo, as though from a great distance, though there were Bodani nearby, staring at them from the edges of the canals as they shot past.

"But I *am* you! We are one!"

They refused to answer, but for a collective groan and a flash of murderous crimson amid the vortex of green.

Pret did not know what to do. What would become of them, now? Their heart shuddered and jerked, and for a moment the strength was stolen from their limbs and they stumbled, leaning heavily on the tiller so that they struck the edge of the canal, grinding the gunwale of the gondola and screeching to a halt. The world spun, the colors fading. "No..." they muttered, breathing heavily. "I...don't want to die...help..."

But no one did. The Bodani at the base of the closest ziggurat turned away. Eventually, the attack subsided, and Pret struggled to their feet and steered their little boat out into the canal again.

More memories assailed them, as the Flood continued to appear as only a trickle—a distant ribbon of color on their mental horizon. More of that which had been drowned was now exposed. Disjointed images, sounds—the team laughing after a successful hijacking of a drone-piloted cargo ship, the sight of Sable Flight gliding down from their perches, singing their eerie alien songs. The smell of Mandelen's pipe, so recently a strange thing, now suffused with meaning.

Pret 43—their previous iteration—had rationalized their involvement with Mandelen's team as something irrelevant to the Bodani interests. You could not steal from the Bodani—the entire economy was a closed system. Take something from one Bodani and give it to another, and was it not still theirs? Mandelen focused on bleeding resources related to off-world trade—they robbed alien cartels and burgled foreign trading syndicates. Who were they to Pret? No one. The Flood didn't even seem to understand what was happening.

It was there that it had begun to happen, Pret decided—their corruption. The flaw in their personality construct that made them *other* to the Flood, that alienated them from themselves. Those criminals had made Pret think of themselves as something different, something unique. They were not Pret 43, facet of the Bodani and drop in the mighty Flood of God. They were just Pret, the talented infiltrator. The hacker. The smooth talker.

Pret, their friend.

These memories were monstrous; Pret could hear the Flood wailing with displeasure. The canals were deserted before their gondola—traffic had been diverted. They were well and truly alone, now. They were so diminished from what they had been, it was hard to fathom. As part of the Flood, Pret's knowledge encompassed all of Sargoth, all of the Bodani people across the whole of the planet. Now? There was only themself and their little boat and their failing heart. What could they do now? Where could they go?

There was really only one choice.

* * *

The Bodani had no interest in the humid, swampy wilderness of their planet. Sargoth ended abruptly in a labyrinth of tall reeds and buzzing insects. No cables crossed overhead, no steady hum of boat-traffic, even the filament of the space elevator, emanating from the top of the temple of the Sargoth God, was a mere ribbon of black, like a hair bisecting the sky. Once Pret had piloted their boat a little way among the tall stands of vegetation, all sight of the ziggurats of their home were gone. The Flood hummed in the distance, pleased that they had departed, relieved they had not spread their contagion to others.

The gondola's engine sputtered and died, its fuel spent. Pret, their heart hammering madly, laid down on the bottom, too weak to stand. Their fingers and their feet tingled; the world had gone gray. They were done for—it wouldn't be long.

Would Mandelen even be here? Perhaps the asipu had dispatched drones to intercept him for his crime of murder after all. His diplomatic credentials were a forgery, anyway—something Pret had done themself. A deed done for a teammate. A gift for a friend.

It was that, Pret supposed, that had at last forced the asipu to intervene. It was strange, but Pret did not regret the decision. Not even now, at the end.

Perhaps it would not be so bad to die. Very few Bodani truly had—death was something God had conquered for them, allowing their minds to live on in new bodies forever—but just then, lying in the damp bottom of their gondola, looking up at the purple sky at major dusk, Pret wondered what it would be like. No pain anymore. No uncertainty. No sense of loss or confusion. All of this would be ended and they would be gone. Not that bad, after all.

They only wished they had seen their friends one more time.

Their heart beat more weakly now, still struggling against the nanites eating away at its musculature, filling it with microscopic holes. A tiny number of the brightest stars pierced the dim light of the minor sun and twinkled down on them; they were all Pret could see.

The gondola rocked in the water. Something had come aboard. Pret could not sit up; they lacked the strength. Two beaked faces appeared over them, their huge yellow eyes blinking, their heads swiveling side to side. "You sure this is them?" the two of them asked in unison.

Sable Flight, the Voosk flock.

A boat was alongside. The smell of pipesmoke tickled Pret's nose. "It's them. I'm sure."

Sable Flight chirped and tweeted among themselves. "Doesn't look like them," one of their members said at last. "They look dead."

Kit Mandelen came aboard the gondola and crouched over Pret. He waved a small sensor disk over Pret's inert bulk. "They aren't dead. The nanites are inverting their processes now. Their heart is being repaired."

A third member of Sable Flight appeared over Pret, all of them twittering to each other. "Will the nanites fix that ugly face, too?" one of them asked.

"You..." Pret managed. "A trick. To get them to reject me. To make me remember."

Mandelen smiled. An expression that indicated happiness. "You'd rather I'd sent the Bodani Collective a sternly written letter?"

Pret felt the blood running back to their fingers, feet. The world had regained some color—they could see the emerald green feathers interspersed with Sable Flight's deep black. They could hear the singing of a million frogs in the dim purple light. "Your plan was...was reckless. I'm...I'm so *angry* with you."

Mandelen helped Pret sit up. "I know." He patted Pret on the shoulder. "But what else are friends for?"

Pret put a heavy hand over Mandelen's and squeezed gently—a gesture of affection, they remembered.

They did not feel alone.

The Mercenary Code

Violette Malan

Parno Lionsmane laid down the vera tile that completed his hand and sat back in his chair, drumming his fingers on the table. His Partner, Dhulyn Wolfshead, marked the score on the tabletop with a piece of chalk.

"Too bad we're not playing for money," he said.

Dhulyn looked around the empty taproom, raising her blood-red brows. "You mean 'too bad we're playing with our own money.' To win more we would need other players."

As Dhulyn began turning tiles face down in preparation for a new hand, a young woman with flour on her apron came running into the taproom, stopping short with a hand to her side when she saw them sitting in the far corner, their backs to the wall.

"Your pardon." She tried to take a deeper breath. "Mercenary Brothers, you're wanted, in the town square."

Dhulyn continued to turn over tiles. "By whom and for what?"

"The Holding Lord Andred Nentero." The girl had her breath under better control. "Heard you were here, sent me for you." From the flour on her apron—and her nose—Parno knew her for the baker's apprentice and no servant of the Holding.

"Why did he not send a servant of his own?"

"Because the trouble's in the town square, Mercenaries." The girl took one final deep breath and lowered her hand from her side.

Dhulyn examined the tiles, now all face down. She glanced at Parno without raising her head. He shrugged. They had decided that very morning to give the market town Deney one more day before looking for work elsewhere. Now it seemed that work had come looking for them.

Leaving the baker's apprentice to find her own way back, Parno put away the tiles while Dhulyn fetched their horses. It would save time if the Holding Lord needed to send them somewhere else.

The morning, despite the sun, had a chill taste of winter hovering in the air. The people gathering in the square had hoods up or caps on, and several of the market stalls had hide or canvas side panels lowered against the wind that set scarves and cloak tails flapping.

Andred Nentero, obvious despite his rough clothing from the quality of his boots, his sword, and the two guards wearing his colors, stood in the cleared center of the square. Between them the guards held a tall, blond woman with firm grips on her upper arms. From her dress she could have been any farm worker helping with the harvest; from her expression, she looked more like the head of some high noble House.

Parno glanced at his Partner's hardening face. He sincerely hoped that the prisoner wasn't a slave of noble birth. If that were the case, Dhulyn would have her own ideas on what should be done. *Let the woman be a thief and not a slave*, he thought. At least that way they could take the job and get paid. Parno dismounted and followed his Partner across the square to where she already faced Lord Nentero.

"I am Dhulyn Wolfshead, called the Scholar," she said, her head to one side. Her cold gray eyes examined the prisoner. "I fight with my Brother, Parno Lionsmane, called the Chanter. You have some need of us?"

"I am Andred Nentero, I hold here for House Nentero. Thank you for coming. We have need of the judgement of the Brotherhood. Will you help us?"

Dhulyn smiled her wolf's smile and several of the onlookers lowered their eyes. "Who will pay us, and how much?"

"I will pay," Nentero said. "In coin or in supplies, as you wish. I trust you to set the amount."

Dhulyn nodded. "Tell us the problem."

Nentero pointed at the woman. "This person is accused of

trying to poison one of her fellow workers." The crowd, relatively silent until now, began shifting their feet and murmuring.

"Is there doubt?" Parno asked.

"No, nor does she deny it."

"Then what are you paying us for?" Dhulyn began to turn away, her hand already out to take the reins Parno stood ready to hand her.

"There is some question as to her sanity, which causes a dispute regarding punishment. Since you Brothers are here, all have agreed to let you judge the matter." There were nods from among the onlookers. Something unpleasant was going on, Parno thought, enough so that lord and townspeople both wanted to shift responsibility to the Brotherhood. Nentero gestured to a woman standing to one side, hands clasped in front of her. She stepped forward.

"Brothers," she began. "I am Natasa Healer and I am responsible for this woman in that she was released from her initial confinement at my word."

"Explain."

"A little more than three moons ago Lord Nentero's Steward of Woods found her unconscious in the north hay field of the Holding. From her strange clothing she was taken to be a traveller who had fallen ill and so I was called. She seemed confused, frightened, and unable to speak trade talk. I found she was feverish, nauseated, and suffering from shock, which I treated. Once she learned to talk to us, she claimed to be from another world—not just another country, as we thought at first, but another place entirely. Naturally, we thought her mad."

"Naturally." Dhulyn's tone remained even, but she exchanged glances with Parno. It wasn't common knowledge, but they at least knew of the existence of other worlds.

"When I examined her again, I could find no physical signs of madness. We began to think that, impossible as it appeared, she might actually be from another world."

"I can speak for myself," the prisoner said.

"And so you shall," Dhulyn assured her. "But first we will hear from the Healer."

"There being nothing wrong that I could Heal, she was given work, to earn her keep. She works well, but the Lord's Steward of Keys reports that she has been trying to convince people not to make use of the Mark, and to avoid Finders and Menders as well as Healers. No one minded this—foreigners are entitled to their beliefs—but this morning, she gave one of the other workers a tea made from fresnoyn leaves. Luckily I was near and able to save him."

"It wouldn't have hurt him." The woman spoke with the tone of someone who had been repeating herself for most of the morning.

"Well, he wouldn't have suffered long, that's certain." Parno glanced at Dhulyn. She had learned several of the drug *shoras*, fresnoyn among them. Used carefully, it didn't always kill people, but having a Healer on hand was a good idea.

"Fresnoyn's a poison, everybody knows it's a poison," an anonymous voice called out from the crowd. There were shouts of agreement, and a few unpleasant suggestions, but the presence of both their Holding lord and two Mercenary Brothers kept the crowd in order.

"Only in the wrong dosage. I keep telling you—"

Dhulyn held up her hand and miraculously everyone fell silent. "We will hear you," she told the woman before turning to Nentero. "Attempted murder is the issue?" The man nodded. "Very well, we accept the job. Is there some more private place we can use?"

"Preferably without windows," Parno added.

They were soon shown into a back room of the market square's main inn. The room had been emptied of what looked and smelled like sacks of wheat, rye, and oats, and now accommodated a small round table and three chairs. A young man, eyes wide with a curiosity equally divided between the prisoner and the Mercenaries, carried in a tray with a pot of ganje, cups, and a plate of small meat pies, the smell of which made Dhulyn's stomach rumble. Dhulyn and Parno had stayed at this inn—once—and it looked like the quality of the food had improved.

Dhulyn waited for Parno to serve himself and the woman with ganje before she spoke. These were unknown circumstances and they would eat and drink one at a time, in accordance with the Mercenary Code. "Suppose you tell us your version of events."

"I've been here about three months—"

"Start farther back. Start with the world you come from."

"You're not going to believe me anymore than these people."

Dhulyn glanced at Parno and found him already looking at her. Neither of them liked how the woman had said "these people."

"The concept of other worlds is familiar to us. The Mercenary Brotherhood has a much wider experience than is commonly found among the regular population. Our own records, and those of Scholar's Houses, speak of the existence of worlds other than this one." No point in telling the woman they'd experienced some of these worlds first hand. That was none of her business.

"Finally, someone believes me." She rubbed her face with her hands, then looked at her palms as though they belonged to someone else. "Wait. Mercenaries? So you'll just do whatever you get paid to do?"

Dhulyn tilted her head to one side, examining the woman more closely. "Is that what mercenaries do in your world? No wonder you are suspicious of us." She nodded her thanks as Parno moved the dish of meat pies as far away from her as he could. "You have no reason to believe me, but here the Brotherhood is exactly that, a brotherhood, with a strict code of behavior and discipline. We have all passed through one of the Mercenary Schools— Parno Lionsmane was schooled by Nerysa of Tourin, called the Warhammer, I by Dorian the Black, called the Traveller. Of a hundred people who apply to be schooled, as many as sixty are turned away as unfit, and of the remaining forty fewer than half might survive to become Brothers."

"Many are called, few are chosen?"

"I can tell from your tone you're quoting something, but I do not recognize the reference. Nevertheless, what you say is true. Further, once we become Brothers, we have no pasts, no families, and we live by the Mercenary Code, which we do not break, for any reason. We cannot be bought, nor paid, to do anything against the Code."

"We can't be threatened, either, as we all know that we walk toward death." Parno took up the explanation.

The woman shook her head. "Nobody can live like that."

"Now you know why there are so few of us." Parno sipped at his cup of ganje. "Because we have no homes or families outside of the Brotherhood, we're often asked to judge disputes, even criminal cases, to ensure an unbiased decision."

"Uhuh. What if the person you're judging is one of your 'Brothers?'"

Dhulyn smiled her wolf's smile. "Another reason there are so few of us."

"There's more to it than that." Parno stifled his own grin. He never tired of watching people shift backward when Dhulyn smiled at them. "If we don't deal fairly every time, acting according to the Code, we would none of us be trusted, ever again. If we can't be trusted, we aren't Mercenary Brothers, we're just killers. Every hand would be against us—and not just us two, but all of us, everywhere."

"We are hard to kill," Dhulyn added, "but it is not impossible." She raised her eyebrows at Parno and, when he nodded, she poured herself a cup of ganje.

"So you're kind of like samurais or something."

"I am unfamiliar with that term, but in a country across the Long Ocean we are called Paladyn." The woman drew down her brows, but when she did not speak Dhulyn continued. "Perhaps it isn't easy to trust us, but what alternative do you have?"

The woman nodded, setting down her cup. "Okay. My name is Rebecca Charter. I'm—in my world I'm an oncologist. That's a type of doctor. I treat people with cancer. Cancer is—"

"We know what cancer is."

"All right." Rebecca relaxed into her chair, as if relieved to be telling her story. "I was preparing a patient's treatment, when the radiation alarm went off. The next thing I knew, I was lying on a bed in a darkened room.

"I wasn't in the hospital, I could tell that much. My heart started to pound and I could hardly breathe. I tried to get hold of myself, figure out where I was. The room was about the size of a hospital room, but the walls were whitewashed and the floor some kind of stone. I tried to sit up, but I got dizzy." Rebecca picked up her ganje and took a sip, making a face as she swallowed. She nodded her thanks when Parno offered her the plate of pies. She took one, but just held it in her hand. "Somehow I fell asleep and when I woke up again, a woman was sitting on a stool next to my bed, checking my heartrate.

"It was Natasa, and something in her smile helped me relax. 'Are you feeling better?' she asked.

"I didn't understand her then, of course, but once I learned the language I knew that's what she'd said.

"Somehow, I felt better with her there, calmer. She had that kind of voice. I know doctors who would kill for her bedside manner. Of course I asked her where I was and what was going on. She saw I didn't understand her and got up, made patting down motions with her hands, then made signs that told me she'd be right back.

"I don't know whether she did get right back to me. I fell asleep again, and when I woke up it was night. The only light in the room was a candle lantern. I felt feverish, and weak, as if I'd been sick a long time. I've never been so frightened in my life. I kept thinking of all the germs, all the things I could be catching, whether my fever meant a bad infection." Rebecca faltered and looked away.

"Fear is a reasonable response to the unknown. You would be a fool not to feel it."

The woman took another sip of ganje, grimaced, and nodded.

"By the third day I was strong enough to talk, but no one recognized any of the languages I tried on them. The best we could manage was to exchange our names.

"The next day my language lessons began. When I could finally speak well enough to explain who I was, and what had happened to me—*that's* when things got complicated.

"'Let me see if I understand you,' Natasa said once I'd finished explaining. If anything her tone was even more gentle than usual. 'You are from another world, completely different from this one, and that is why you could not speak our language.'

"'Exactly,' I said.

"'How did you arrive here? How did you travel?'

"Well, of course I had no real answer to that, and though I did my best to explain what I thought had happened, and the cancer center, and how we treated our patients with radiation and chemotherapy, she just got more and more upset so I stopped.

"'I would like to examine you again,' she said. I wasn't sure what she meant, but she'd always been very kind to me while I was sick, so I told her to go ahead.

"She turned toward me and took my hands. Hers were warm and she had odd callouses, like she played some strange stringed instrument. She closed her eyes and I got the feeling she was humming, though I couldn't hear anything. It reminded me of something I'd seen a shaman do in a movie I saw and I began to feel uncomfortable. Finally, she opened her eyes and let go of my hands.

"'So far as I can tell,' she said, with what I can only call a sad smile, 'You are not insane. However, I am not an expert in troubles of the mind. You *did* sustain a blow to the head, the very type of injury that might cause you to lose your mind, something I cannot heal. I will tell House Nentero there is no physical illness. He will decide what should be done.'

"Of course, I knew I wasn't crazy." Rebecca sat quiet for a moment, as if she did not trust her voice. Finally, she continued.

"Anyway, the next morning Lord Nentero sent for me. Once we'd come to the conclusion that I didn't have any training in arms, or in anything else they found useful, they gave me a job working in the garden.

"At first I was glad to be outside in the sunshine and the fresh air, but the work's harder than I expected and everyone treated me as though I was made out of crystal. I guess I must have been depressed for the next couple of weeks, or maybe I was just too exhausted to think. Natasa says she tried to help me, but nothing seemed to work."

"Excuse me," Parno said, placing two fingers on his Partner's wrist. "You said you were sick and feverish when you first arrived, how were you healed of that?"

"I don't know, I don't remember. But it didn't have to be radiation sickness you know, it could have been anything, a reaction to strange air, or the travel itself. Anyway, it went away."

"You began by speaking warmly of Natasa Healer, but now your face is different when you mention her. Is there some dispute between you?"

Rebecca looked away and back again, her face hard. She picked up her cup, but didn't drink from it. "Look, Natasa helped me so much that I hate to say this, but she's not healing anyone with her mind. I know this is part of your religion or something and maybe she genuinely believes in this Mark thing everyone keeps talking about, but supernatural powers don't exist, and people who could be helped by medicine die while these witchdoctors do their hoodoo."

"If there are no Marked in your world, how are people healed of their injuries and sickness?"

"Medicine, science, doctors."

"When you said you were a doctor, this is what you meant? You healed people who had cancers?" Dhulyn reached for a meat pie.

"Well, not everybody, sometimes people are just too sick."

"It is true that not all healings are successful," Parno pointed out. "Sometimes the body is just too old and worn, and then, the Mark is stronger in some than in others."

"Yeah, I'll bet it is." Rebecca's tone would have soured milk.

Dhulyn made a beckoning gesture with her free hand. "Continue your story. Why did you give your fellow worker fresnoyn? Tell us why *we* are here."

"I started off pruning trees—look at my hands, I don't know how I'll ever get them clean again." Rebecca made a face as though she was trying not to cry. "One of the people I'm working with—Jehn—started showing allergy symptoms: running nose, red eyes, coughing. That's not uncommon, lots of people display allergies at this time of year. The problem is they don't go away unless the patient can avoid the allergen, which really can't be done, when everything has to be picked by hand.

"I offered to cure the rash so I made a tea out of eye bright leaves—they work as a natural antihistamine—and gave it to Jehn to drink. The next thing I know guards come and I get locked away and then brought here and I don't know what's going on." Rebecca swallowed. Picked up her cup of ganje, now completely cold, and took a gulp.

"But what you call 'eye bright' is a type of fresnoyn. That plant is poisonous."

"No, it *isn't*. It might take some experimenting to find the right dosage, but I tell you the symptoms will go away. I mean, you're treating me like I'm some kind of witch, I'm not the one using mumbo jumbo to cure illnesses. Just because..." Rebecca took a deep breath made an obvious effort to control herself. "I understand that these ideas are all new for you, but I assure you that my methods will work, people will be cured. If there's a problem, science can find the answer and fix it. It's not faith healing. Science doesn't ask you to believe in something and then, when it fails, blames you for not believing enough. Science undertakes to cure everyone, not just members of the club." She rubbed her face, giving Parno a chance to exchange a look with his Partner.

"I believe we understand what you are trying to say. Our world has the Marked, yours has science." Dhulyn leaned forward on the table. "But I think you have failed to take into consideration that you are *not* in your own world now. I can assure you from my personal experience that the Mark is real, that Healers heal, Finders find, and Menders mend. It is not a matter of belief. The Mark, like your science, works for everyone."

"People in my world used to believe in magic too, until it was proven that *science* is what explains everything. When Pasteur first theorized about the presence of germs, medical people—healers—were outraged that someone was suggesting they were actually harming their patients because of micro-organisms that no one could see without the use of—do you know what a microscope is?"

"Certainly. They are relics of the Caids—an ancient culture long gone—and so are normally found in Scholar's' Houses."

"Well, okay, I could show you what I'm talking about if you could get me one."

"What if we could show *you* what *we* are talking about?" Dhulyn pulled free a knife from her belt and turned to her Partner.

"What, you're going to put on a magic show?"

Parno smiled. "Shall we flash fingers?"

For an answer Dhulyn tapped the table with her knife.

"Try not to cut the tendon." Parno spread his hand flat on the table. "It's always sore afterward."

"Teach your grandmother." Dhulyn stabbed down with her belt knife, pinning his hand to the wooden table top.

Rebecca screeched and lunged forward, hands stretched out, far too late to stop them, even if she had been able to. When neither of the Mercenaries showed any concern, she fell back into her chair, hands gripping the edge of the table.

"I'm not the crazy one, you are!"

Dhulyn withdrew her dagger. There was blood, but not as much as there would have been if Parno had been stuck somewhere else.

Rebecca opened her mouth again and Dhulyn held up her index finger. "Just a moment." Dhulyn went to the door and opened it a hand's breadth. "Natasa, would you come in please?"

The Healer came in and bustled over to the table, lifting Parno's hand and shaking her head. "What are you two playing at?" She took Parno's hand between both of hers, pressing firmly as she closed her eyes and concentrated. When she lifted her hands away, the bleeding had stopped, leaving only two thin red lines, one on the back and one on the palm of his hand.

"You see the lines are fading, in a moment there will not even be the faintest of scars," Dhulyn said. "That is what a Healer does. Did we imagine it?"

"Is *that* what you're doing?" Natasa asked, somewhat mollified. "I grant you it would not have occurred to me to try it."

Rebecca took a deep breath in through her nose and clenched her hands into fists. "Setting aside the whole notion of faith healing, I've seen stage magicians saw a woman in half and put her back together. This is amateur stuff."

"You think we have tricked you and there was no injury, or that Parno is disposed to be healed because of the strength of his belief in the Healer's Mark?" Dhulyn eyed the woman and lifted her eyebrows. "That would mean that, since *you* don't believe, it would not work with you?"

"Okay, now wait a minute—"

On his Partner's signal Parno sliced through the woman's throat. The wound was thin and shallow, but blood welled, leaking through the hands she raised to clutch at the wound, her eyes wide with fear.

Natasa pushed forward, shoving Parno unceremoniously to one side. "This is not a game," she said. "Look at her! Rebecca could have died of fright and then where would we be?"

"Down one problem, it seems to me."

It took longer than the healing of Parno's hand, but eventually Natasa removed her hands and let Rebecca sit up again. She rubbed at her throat, coughed, and winced, turning her head slowly from side to side. Parno handed her a cup of fresh ganje and she shied away, eyes wide, only accepting the offered cup after taking several deep breaths.

They waited, but when it became clear Rebecca had no intention of speaking, Parno asked, "Do you believe us now?"

Rebecca shook her head, but not as though she were aware that she did it. She touched the front of her throat, swallowed twice, and lifted her head.

"There's no pain," she said. "And from what I can tell no scar. What did you do?"

"I cut your throat and Natasa healed it." Parno watched the woman, head tilted to one side.

Dhulyn leaned her hip against the table and crossed her arms. "She still doesn't believe us."

"You cut my throat and there's no pain, no scar?" Rebecca rolled her eyes, her voice gaining strength. "I admit you scared me, good job there. But that was just sleight of hand, you obviously didn't cut me."

"There is blood on your hands," Dhulyn pointed out. Healers dealt with wounds, but someone else had to do the clean up.

Rebecca looked at her hands and a flicker of doubt crossed her face before she shook her head again. "No, absolutely not. It *can't* be. A blood squib. Natasa must have used a blood squib when she pretended to heal me."

Dhulyn dropped her arms and walked around to the far side of the table. She turned back to face her Partner. "She will not believe us. We will have to kill her."

"No, wait, what do you mean? You can't kill me!" Rebecca stood up and backed away from the table.

"On the contrary." Parno watched Dhulyn where she leaned on the wall. "If we decide you're a danger to others, that's exactly what we can do."

"But if I'm insane—"

"Which you obviously are." Natasa took Rebecca's hands. "I will stay if you need me, but this is not something I want to watch." Rebecca shook her head and Natasa left, looking back from the door, her face full of sorrow.

"You can't kill me for not believing you." Rebecca looked from Dhulyn to Parno and back again. "I've done nothing wrong— nothing to kill someone for."

"Are you sure you cannot believe us?" Dhulyn asked. "You mentioned science earlier. Would you not consider the possibility that different worlds work under different laws?"

Rebecca hesitated. "The laws of physics don't change," she said, her voice hoarse. "Everything else here is the same—gravity, Newton's laws, *everything.* So you expect me to believe that the only difference is that magic exists? I *can't* believe that, even if I wanted to...I can't. "

Parno threw his hands in the air and turned away.

"Wait." With a tilt of her head, Dhulyn drew Parno into the farthest corner of the room and spoke using the nightwatch voice. "I believe I know what is happening to her."

"That makes one of us." Even using the nightwatch voice Parno's frustration was evident.

"She is afraid to release her understanding of her own world. We have been, on more than one occasion, and sometimes against our will, in a strange country—even a strange world. We have made mistakes due to ignorance. Why did we not succumb to fear and homesickness?"

"We're Partners," Parno answered, without hesitating. "Our Brotherhood and the Mercenary Code is our home."

"And we take it everywhere with us, so we were able to keep ourselves calm, accepting the differences we found around us. Together, we could face anything—that is the purpose of Partnership, that we are never alone. Rebecca has no Brotherhood, no Partner, she is completely alone. She clings to the truths of her own place because they are the only truths she has and, in letting them go, she lets go her home and all she knows."

Parno nodded. "In battle."

"And in death," Dhulyn answered.

Parno returned to the table and sat down across from Rebecca once more.

"You are brave," he said, acknowledging the truth. "Not everyone is willing to die for what they believe."

"You can't kill me for making a tea." Rebecca was less confident than her words indicated. "You can't kill me for believing something different. I haven't even hurt anyone. I didn't do any real harm—I mean Jehn puked a bit, but he's okay now."

"We can't wait for you to do what you're calling 'real' harm. If we judge that you are a danger, then we act on that."

"What if I promise never to do anything like that again?"

"Why should we believe you? Why would we take that risk?"

"You could put me in prison then."

"We understand the concept," Parno said. "The Great King in the West has been known to imprison people." He exchanged a glance with his Partner. Another thing they had first-hand knowledge of. "But there aren't any prisons here."

"So where would we put you?" Dhulyn asked quietly. "And who would pay for it? You can't stay here, the people won't have you, not after you repay their care and kindness in this way. Where do we take you that you won't be dangerous?"

"You have to understand that you can't go around accidently killing people because you think you know best." Parno did all but reach out and pat Rebecca's hand.

"But there hasn't been a trial."

"Why would there be? Everyone knows what happened, everyone is satisfied that you are guilty. You yourself admit it."

"But if I'm insane..." Rebecca fell silent, she'd used that gambit already.

"That would only make you more dangerous," Dhulyn said.

"I'm surprised that you don't ask for more time to think and then pretend to be convinced," Parno added.

Rebecca's laughter sounded like it hurt her throat. "Would you believe me?"

"Unfortunately, no. Forced conversion rarely lasts long. Execution remains the safest and most efficient action to take."

"I can't believe you're just going to kill me. For something that isn't even my fault."

"Isn't it?" From her tone Dhulyn was losing patience. "You are offered proof and you persist in denying it—even though by doing so you insult the people who have befriended you and saved your life, and now, the people who hold that life in their hands. You have not even said you were sorry—clearly you don't believe you have done anything to be sorry for. No, I'm afraid our position is clear."

Dhulyn drummed her fingers on the table and Parno waited, watching her thoughts flit back and forth over her face—something only he could see.

"You will excuse us," she said, getting to her feet and reaching for the latch of the door.

"What have you thought of?" Parno asked when they were safely outside and could speak in normal tones.

"This woman annoys me, but I must admit the fact that she must die because of a difference in philosophies *annoys me more*. There must be a way not to kill her. We have agreed to solve this problem and by the Code we must solve it—but in itself the Code does not limit us to any specific solution."

"So long as we find one." Parno crossed his arms and leaned his shoulders against the cold stone wall. "Could we take her to a Scholar's House? She could do little harm and there could be benefit in an exchange of ideas and philosophies."

"How could we guarantee that she never left the place?" Dhulyn hooked her thumbs in her sword sash and frowned. "Scholars are badly equipped to keep prisoners, because that is what she would be, regardless of what we call her."

"The Cloud People?"

"Again, we would only be sending her to a different kind of prison. Besides, can you imagine her reaction to Racha birds?" Rebecca was unlikely to believe that the birds were sentient, telepathic, and had the same rights as the people they bonded with. "No." Dhulyn looked down. "We do not solve the problem by passing the responsibility for her behavior to someone else."

"Well, we can't keep her with us for the rest of our lives. Can't we send her back?"

Parno waited. Dhulyn no longer looked at him. Instead, her face had that faraway look it sometimes had when she was Seeing. He waited.

"Path of the Sun?" she asked, but she was shaking her head even as she said it. "No. What should we do? Try every turning, every dead end, until we find one that leads to her world? Without even knowing that such a path exists? How long do we try, and how would we eat in the meantime? No, that merely delays the inevitable."

"Wait." Parno straightened, taking his Partner by the wrist. "She spoke of hospitals, science, other technology. We've seen such things, in the world where we killed the demon. That may not be her world, but it may be close enough that she would be happier there."

"Yes, but how do we find that world again? Remember, when we returned the portal did not open always here, and when it did, it was in the ocean, not the place we first found it." She held up a finger, smiling the smile she saved only for him. "Ah, but from this side it always opened into the same world. And we know a Finder who would be happy to do us the favor of locating it."

Parno straightened. "It's worth a try, and it's faster than anything else we've come up with." He followed his Partner back into the room. Rebecca looked up from her clasped hands, but there was no real hope on her face.

Dhulyn smiled at her. "Do you know of a place called Kingston?"

Deep Heart Inside

Stephen Leigh

Lizzy Sitton's mind wandered as Mrs. Breedlove rhapsodized to the few female students at the Philippi Baptist School about the possibility of them one day attending the new Nashville Baptist Female College. "Some of you might earn a degree," she gushed. Lizzy always wanted to laugh at her teacher's strange New York City accent. "After all, the world is changing around us and any of you could be part of it. Why, can you imagine the marvels you'll encounter in the 20th century?"

Mrs. Breedlove had often praised Lizzy for being the smartest of the girls in the school, but Lizzy doubted her parents could ever afford the cost of college, the expense of her living in Nashville, or the loss of her work on their homestead outside Elizabethton. For that matter, many of the girls in the school as well as several of the boys, some younger than her, had already left schooling behind. Who needs schooling, the girls asked, when all they needed to know was how to sew, cook, clean rabbits, or butcher a hog? As for the boys, schoolbook learning meant little down in the mountain coal mines.

Lizzy smiled dutifully as Mrs. Breedlove finished her lecture, then ran outside with the rest of the students of the one-room schoolhouse for lunch and recess.

"Hey, Lizzy—ain't that yer Pa an' yer brother walking over there with some a' the Dillons?"

Against the loud chaos of the schoolyard, Lizzy glanced to where Virgil Jones was pointing. Past the bordering cornfield, she could see a group of men and a trio of horses moving slowly down the Tweetsie railroad line alongside the Doe River, just south of Elizabethton. Her father and her oldest brother Luke had gone hunting up in the hills with Preacher Dillon and a few of his sons early this morning. The horses were heavily laden but what was draped over their backs didn't look anything like rabbits or deer. Lizzy climbed the wooden rails of the schoolyard fence as Virgil hollered at her to come back or he'd snitch on her to Mrs. Breedlove. She ignored him and ran toward the group. Her father saw her approaching; he leaned toward Luke to say something in his ear. Luke nodded, handed his father his shotgun, and flicked away the cigarette he was smoking. He intercepted Lizzy before she could reach the cluster of men.

"Now jus' hold on there, Lizzy," Luke said, picking up Lizzy and swinging his twelve-year-old sister around in his strong grasp. "Ain't nothin' here yeh need t'see." There were dark red, almost black stains spattering the front of Luke's plaid shirt and the bib of his overalls; he smelled strongly of tobacco, blood, alcohol, and gunpowder, as well as a musky and unpleasant odor she couldn't identify. Strands of his brown hair, the same

nondescript color as her own, escaped from under his battered cloth cap.

"Why? I done seen plenty a' dead game and I ain't afeared. I helped yeh and Ma and Pa gut and clean 'em plenty a'times," Lizzy protested. "Put me down. I wanna say 'hey' to Pa!"

"Don't care what yeh want, Lizzy. Pa says this ain't nothing he needs yeh lookin' at. I'm 'sposed to return yeh to Mrs. Breedlove."

Louis tried to twist away from Luke's grasp but his hands tightened around her arms. She kicked out at her brother. She heard him gasp, groan, then double over in obvious pain as he dropped her onto the plowed field between the rows of corn. Lizzy didn't wait for Luke to recover; she got to her feet and ran toward her father. Luke came up behind her, moving slowly, as she reached the group of hunters. They all stared at her. Luke was still hunched over, a hand near the crotch of his overalls. "Lizzy's shoe caught me right in the dad-blame..." He stopped. "Well, y'all know where. Sorry, Pa."

There were quiet, reserved chuckles from some of the other men. Her Pa grunted. "Too late now," he said, and spat on the ground.

Too late for what? Lizzy wanted to ask, but the question died in her throat as she looked more carefully at the group. The five dead animals lashed to the horses were no game that Lizzy had ever seen before: maybe five feet in length if they were to stand upright, the beasts had scaled, plated skin like the alligators Mrs. Breedlove said lived in swamps further south, though these scales were colorful rather than the gray Mrs. Breedlove had described. Three of the creatures were largely red, one mostly blue, and the last one's scales were flecked with orange and white. Each possessed overlong arms with hand-like appendages consisting of three fingers and one offset thumb at the end of their front limbs, each finger tipped with a long, curved claw thinner and more pointed than a bear's, with three more clawed appendages on their feet that had one 'finger' set backwards like a bird's. Their heads, set on overlong necks, were birdlike as well, with prominent snouts and long mouths rimmed with horn-like ridges rather than teeth.

The odd smell she'd noticed on Luke was much stronger here, making her screw up her face at the stench.

"Monsters," Pa said, spitting again. "Them claws can open up a man's skin like an axe through a ripe melon. Just look at poor Asa." He pointed to Asa, one of the Dillon sons, seated astride the only horse not carrying the slain creatures. Asa was fifteen, and though he'd left school a few years ago, he was always paying so much attention to Lizzy that his older brothers teased him mercilessly whenever they were together. *"Yeh gonna marry that Sitton girl?"* they'd say too loudly if Lizzy were around. *"Yeh ain't kissed her yet, have yeh, Asa?"*

Lizzy saw that Asa's overalls were ripped, the torn denim revealing an ugly, long, and deep gash from hip to just above the knee, crudely bandaged with strips of his shirt. Lizzy thought she glimpsed the white of bone through the blood.

"I spotted one a' them red 'uns lurking in the brush along the rail line," Asa told her, his voice oddly weak. Lizzy could see that he was holding hard to the pommel of the saddle just to stay on the horse. His forehead was beaded with sweat and there was pain in his eyes. He licked cracked lips before he spoke again. "It raised up and I saw them claws, an' I knew I was looking inta the eyes of a pure demon. I figured it was fixin' to carry me off to hell, so I done shot it first. Then, jus' a few minutes later, the whole jo-fired pack of 'em come at us, snarling and yipping and makin' all kinda noises. I was standin' over the demon I shot, makin' sure it was dead and gonna stay that way. That blue one was the leader. When it saw me and the dead demon, it jus' flew at me with those claws lifted an' did this." Asa nodded toward his mangled leg. "I went down and the blue one stood over me jabbering and ready to finish me off, when yer Pa let loose with his shotgun. Saved my life, yer Pa. Then everyone was firing and we wupped 'em good. We got all a' them bastards, Lizzy."

"Asa," her Pa said warningly.

Asa looked at Lizzy and dropped his head. "Beggin' yer pardon, Mr. Sitton, Lizzy."

"We got 'em all 'ceptin' that 'un," Luke broke in, pointing toward the last of the horses. Lizzy saw another of the monsters standing there on two legs, its hands lashed to a rope attached to the horse's saddle. This one's scales were green and someone had wrapped a horse blanket around it, belted to its body under the arms with another piece of rope. This one had no claws at all on its hands or feet, and its belly looked as swollen as her Mam's had been when she was carrying Laura, who died three months after she was born. "I caught her. That 'un's a female. The blue one's definitely male; ain't sure 'bout t'others. None of 'em had any clothes on a'tall. Guess demons ain't got the common sense to cover themselves like decent folk."

"Enough blathering," Floyd Dillon called out, interrupting. He was Asa's father, patriarch of the Dillon clan, and the local preacher. "I gotta get Asa here to Doc Hunter right quick. Carl"—that to Lizzy's father—"why don't you and Luke take that female creature and one of the horses to yer place. I'll get Asa to the doc's; the rest of yeh take the other horse up to our cabin and let Ma know what's happened. Tell her I'll bring Asa along as soon as the doc fixes him up."

There were mumbles of agreement all around. The group began to split up. Her Pa took the reins of the horse to which the female was tied, which also bore one of the red monsters and the orange and white one. "Lizzy," Pa said, "yeh might as well come with me an' Luke. Yeh'll be useless in school after this and there ain't no call for yeh t' go spreading gossip."

Lizzy didn't object to that at all.

* * *

I am Womb-Bearer of my progenitor-line and those Outside the line call me Agari. My Seed-Sower was Garash, our Nurturer was Gishkim, and our three Sustenance-Givers who had no names are gone. All of them are dead and I have no possibility of joining myself to another progenitor-line who might need a womb-bearer once I've birthed the ones inside me, no chance to keep alive the pups I carry without Gishkim and our S-Gs. We all knew when we boarded our ship that no matter what we found here we'd never be returning home, that for good or ill this would be our home for what remained of our lives. Now, without the rest of my progenitor-line, I no longer have any reason to Be.

Despite that, the soft-flesh beings who hold me here refuse to kill me and end my humiliation and dishonor, as any of our kind would have done for me. They've stopped every attempt I've made to end my own life, even though that act is what would allow me to join my family in the Afterplace. So I have to endure this emptiness, this life that refutes everything I was and all that I had. I tried to speak with those at home through the Deep Heart that was placed in me before we left, but I won't know if I've been heard for far too long.

That is why I am telling my pain to the Deep Heart even if it is broken. I have little hope that, without what I speak to the Deep Heart, my story and my warning will ever reach any Outside lines who might truly understand my grief and despair, and who would know not to come here. I don't know why I bother, except that it gives me some small comfort to do this.

How did this begin, only a few hands of sun-cycles ago? It was, I believe, an accident. A miscommunication. I have to believe that, knowing what I know now.

Our progenitor-line had been chosen to be sent out to determine the viability of a world around a nearby star. Our sensors indicated this world would be largely compatible with our species. Going there wasn't what any of my line wanted to do, but given how far our line had fallen in rank, we agreed because we hoped to recover some of our standing. After all, if we were the ones who found a perfect new home before our sun's instability destroyed our own world, we might be elevated again once the others of our kind arrived.

What our sensors failed to detect was the presence of another sentient, global, and technological species there as well. Our craft landed in a small valley within this lush, emerald mountainous land; by now it's already largely decayed and melted into this world, as it was designed to do. I was told to contact home through the Deep Heart I carry once we had enough information to report, and that they'd return—either to bring the other progenitor-lines here or to take us home—though in truth I always doubted whether they'd come for us if this world wasn't what we hoped it would be. Our progenitor-line wasn't important enough for that.

We first sent out two of our Sustenance-Givers to explore the forest around us and give us an initial assessment. What exactly happened that particular day, we'll never know. We sent out the last of our S-Gs to forage; I remember hearing a distant harsh *crack* close by soon after the S-G set off and we all felt its presence vanish in our heads, our connection to it lost.

We all ran toward the sound in response. And that was our mistake.

When we arrived, we saw the S-G we had sent out to forage was dead, its chest torn open by one of the weapons the soft-flesh beings carried. We couldn't fathom why they would have done that. No S-G would ever be a threat to any other living creature; they only gather plants and find liquid for nourishment. Garash was furious at the unwarranted violence. He shouted curses at those who would so insult our line, and told the soft-flesh who had killed our Sustenance-Giver to prepare himself to give a blood-payment in return. Garesh took the blood only from the creature's leg, but rather than calling that exchange equal as they should have, all the soft-flesh beings cried out in their strange language and raised their weapons. Garesh was killed immediately; I watched him die, writhing on the ground of this new world as his blood soaked the grass, and I felt his dear presence fade from my mind. Then the soft-flesh ones killed the rest: Gishkim and our two other S-Gs. I have no words for the anguish, feeling the sudden emptiness in my head—all of my line taken from me.

Being heavy with young and thus slow, I had lagged behind the others. The soft-flesh ones, who are strangely aggressive for being so fragile, had killed all of us except myself. I begged them to kill me also, to let my essence return to my family in the Afterplace, but they didn't understand my words or gestures, and refused to release me.

The soft-flesh ones stared at me with their odd eyes and their pale, delicate skin, their heads covered in fur like that of the field-hoppers and their bodies wrapped in fabrics. I heard them conversing in their strange, guttural language. They took me captive and carried me off with them.

So I speak in my mind to the Deep Heart of what's happened and hope that those at home will hear my story even though I won't ever hear their reply, and I also write the tale on the flat stone the soft-flesh called Lizzy has let me use.

* * *

"Agari?" Lizzy called out into the darkness of the springhouse. "It's me, Lizzy."

The springhouse on the Sitton property was dark and Lizzy carried a lantern even though it was daytime, the room cool enough to make Lizzy want her sweater even in the summer. Low and squat, the springhouse was built into the steep hillside of the Sitton property where a cold spring bubbled out. The stream of cold water ran under the stone sill, continuing to run off Bryant Ridge and, eventually, after combining with a dozen other small streams and creeks, found its way into the Doe River well south of Elizabethton. The chilly, small structure was crowded with meats, jars of pickled fruits, and vegetables stored for later meals, as well as milk and butter from the two cows the Sittons owned, some of the jars and containers sitting in the stream for the best refrigeration. Toward the rear of the springhouse, Lizzy could see Agari, whose name she'd managed to learn, though that was as far as attempts at communication had gone.

Agari was huddled against the rocks at the back wall, her hands and feet bound together. The first day Agari had been held in the springhouse she tried to kill herself, first with a large rock which Lizzy's Pa had snatched away as Agari tried to smash it into her head. Later the same day, Lizzy had entered the springhouse and found that the creature had discovered a piece of flint and flaked away a sharp edge. She was trying to cut her throat when Lizzy saw the blood trickling down her scales and snatched the flint away from her. Since then her Pa and Luke made certain that Agari was tied up unless someone was with her. The creature cowered in obvious fear whenever Lizzy's Pa, Luke, or any of Lizzy's other brothers entered the springhouse—while Ma just wanted to ignore the entire situation—so Lizzy became Agari's primary jailer. She could sit with her for hours, trying unsuccessfully to make some sense of the creature's language and teach her English. The best they'd managed was learning each other's names. Neither one of them seemed able to adequately reproduce the sounds of the other's language.

Lizzy set down the lantern near the door of the springhouse. "I brung you some vittles," she said, though she knew Agari wouldn't understand what she was saying. She held out a wooden plate toward Agari. "Corn," she said, as if talking to a child. Agari had refused most of the food they'd offered her. She would eat some vegetables but never any meat. Their best success had come with corn.

Agari held out her bound hands wordlessly. "Jes' hold on a spell," Lizzy told her. She put down the plate of corn, then leaned over to untie Agari's hands. As soon as the creature's hands were free, Agari quickly pulled off the dress Lizzy's Ma had given her to wear. Over the last few days, Lizzy had made certain that, if anyone was going into the springhouse to check on Agari, Lizzy arrived beforehand to make certain Agari was wearing the dress, since the creature's decided preference for nudity and her prominent genitalia obviously bothered and embarrassed the rest of Lizzy's family. Agari held out her left hand, making a drawing motion with her fingers. Lizzy reached over near Agari, propping up a piece of slate decorated with scratchings that looked something like the Egyptian hieroglyphics that Mrs. Breedlove had once shown them. Lizzy reached into the pocket of her apron and pulled out the flint flake that Agari had made.

"Now yeh'd best behave with that, or I'll take it away from yeh agin."

Agari took the flint from Lizzy's hand. Hunched over the slate, she started incising more hieroglyphics into the stone. Lizzy watched her for a minute, then started talking, more to herself than to Agari.

"My friend Asa Dillon's feelin' awful poorly. Pa went up fer a visit yesterday. He says that leg of his'n has gone black and stinks to high heaven. Doc Hunter is fixxen t'saw it off, but Pa thinks that might not even save 'im. Asa's Pa—Preacher Dillon, y'know—and everyone is prayin' for 'im, but Asa, he's got a terr'ble fever now an' he don't recognize nary anyone, not even Preacher Dillon nor his mam, who's near mad with fear. Preacher Dillon told Pa that if Asa dies, he's gonna come fetch yeh. 'Take me my eye for an eye,' Preacher Dillon said. I hope that don't happen, but Pa thinks it jes' might come to that, an' Pa...well, I don't rightly know what he'd do if Preacher Dillon comes to get yeh if'n Asa passes."

There was no reaction from Agari. Lizzy could see Agari's gaze on her, staring at her with bulbous, round eyes bright with strangely colorful irises and unnerving, devilish vertical slits of black pupils, like those of a goat. Then Agari looked away again and continued marking up the slate, occasionally plucking a few kernels of corn from the dish and eating them. Lizzy sighed.

"Pa, Luke, and my brother Lee, they buried yer friends up near the ridge. They didn't put up no marker, but I set a big rock there t'remember. Mebbe I'll show it to yeh one day if'n I can. Now Preacher Dillon, he didn't bury the monsters he took. When we went ta church Sunday last, he had 'em propped up near his preachin' stand so everyone could see the demons he'd kilt—I 'pologize, but that's what the preacher called 'em—and the terr'ble claws that tore up poor Asa's leg so bad." Lizzy dangled a hand in the stream that was running past her toward the door of the springhouse. The coldness of the water made her shiver and she put her hand quickly under her armpit to warm it. She watched the ripples in the running water. "Them corpses were startin' to go bad by then, so he had 'em burned but first he lopped off the heads with an axe and biled the flesh off'n 'em. He mounted the skulls on the church wall as a warnin' to all devils to stay away."

Lizzy gave a heavy sigh and wiped her hands on her apron. "Y'know, Agari, if'n I could get Pa to let Mrs. Breedlove come out here, she might be able t' make sense of those marks of yer'n, and maybe we could even start to teach yeh how to talk right. Wouldn't that be—"

Lizzy looked at Agari. "Hey!" she shouted in alarm. "What did I tell yeh?"

* * *

I heard Lizzy shout even as I put down the flat stone and touched the sharpened edge of the marking stone to my neck in preparation for the death-cut. Lizzy rushed over to me and pulled my hand away, twisting it in her surprisingly strong grip so that the marking stone fell from my hand to clatter on the rocks near the stream. She was shouting at me in her language; I could hear my horribly mispronounced name among her words. Her face was all distorted, her flesh flushed red. She bent down and picked up the marking stone, thrusting it back in the fabric piece she had tied over the other odd artifacts the soft-flesh ones wear to cover their skin.

I knew she was angry and I was terribly afraid she was going to raise the flat stone on which I'd been writing and dash it down against the other rocks in this place. I could feel the pups stirring anxiously in my womb as I imagined that, and I placed my hands over my abdomen until they settled once more. If Lizzy destroyed the flat stone, any chance that someone of the lines might one day find the story of our fate would crumble into pieces unless the Deep Heart really was working. I was afraid it was not, though I continued to tell it my tale just in case. But to my relief, she didn't touch the stone.

She put back on me the confining, itchy garment that the soft-flesh ones made me wear, then tied my hands together again, more tightly than usual. She left the plate of tasteless food near enough that I could still reach it. Lizzy, I feel, has an empathy toward me that I don't sense from the others of her kind, who obviously consider us to be some lower form of life no better than the flesh-renders on our world. I watched her leave, watched her close and latch the door of my crude prison and leave me to the dim cold that remained. I could only pray to the Great Creator that when Lizzy came again, she would give me back the marking stone again, and this time I'd write on the flat stone until I saw her look away, then I'd quickly finish my tale in the blood that was demanded of me and rejoin my beloved line wherever the Great Creator had sent them.

I told the Deep Heart that as I heard Lizzy walking away.

As I sat in the cold room, I closed my eyes and tried to remember their faces and their smells: dear Garash who had awakened the seeds within me; Gishkim, who would never hold our pups or bring them to maturity; our three poor S-Gs who had died so brutally and needlessly. Already, I could feel their images starting to slip away from my memory, which made me afraid that I might never recognize them in the Afterplace.

I needed to die soon or it would be too late for me to join them. It had to be soon, or never.

I continued to pray, to tell the Deep Heart all I'd experienced and felt, and to watch the door for Lizzy's return.

* * *

It was afternoon, with the sun through the trees lending the world a shimmering gold-green light that Lizzy had always loved.

She often wished she could paint that light and this scene laid out before her from their front porch, with the hillsides and trees bathed in wedges of that radiant brilliance. Maybe they could teach her how to paint at the Nashville Baptist Female College, if by some miracle she ever found herself there. She'd tried drawing a portrait of Agari in pencil on a piece of Ma's wrapping paper, but she ended up balling up the paper and throwing it into the cooking fire, unsatisfied with her effort. It didn't look like Agari at all, the face all misshapen and crude, less precise and less interesting than the tiny figures that Agari herself had scratched on the piece of slate in the springhouse.

So maybe she'd never be able to paint the scene before her, no matter how good a teacher she had. That would be a shame. What good was it to be as smart as Mrs. Breedlove seemed to think she was if she was going to end up in a few brief years just like the other girls she knew, married to someone who had once claimed he loved her but who now treated her like she was little more than a servant, with his child hanging on her skirts, another in her belly, and a thousand chores to get through every day?

Even now she was doing one of the chores her own mother had given her—churning butter on the porch, the muscles of her arms aching with the effort. Down the path toward the dirt road at the foot of the hill, perhaps still a half mile away, Lizzy glimpsed movement: two men on horses slowly approaching through the trees. She recognized them even at the distance: the easy, relaxed way her father sat on his horse, while Preacher Dillon's squat body was all stiff and unyielding, as if he'd been carved from stone. She felt as if her throat had suddenly closed or someone was hugging her so tightly that she couldn't breathe. She knew intuitively why Preacher Dillon was coming to their house: Asa had died and Preacher Dillon intended to have his revenge through Agari.

Louis released the plunger handle and let it fall back into the churn, then ran up the hill to the springhouse. She lifted the rope loop over the nail that served as the lock and wrenched the door open. "Agari!" she called out, and heard the slurred reply "Lizzy?" from the rear of the structure. Lizzy splashed up the spring's stream, not caring that she was getting her feet wet. There was enough light coming through the cracks in the wooden slats that she could make out Agari's form. She crouched down alongside the creature.

"Yeh got to get outa here," she said as she tore at the knots binding Agari, even though she knew the creature wouldn't understand anything. As Lizzy panted with effort, the rope holding Agari's hands fell away, then—with more difficulty, since her father had tied these knots—those around her feet.

"Can yeh stand? Here, let me help yeh up. No," she added scoldingly—now that Agari's hands were free, she was again trying to take off the dress she wore. Lizzy caught Agari's hands and stopped her. "Yeh keep that on. Otherwise, if someone sees yeh, they'll think yer just an animal a'some kind, and maybe dangerous. They might shoot yeh. Yeh gotta get yerself up the ridge and over into the next holler right quick, then keep goin'. I'd druther there were some other way, but there ain't. Not no more."

Lizzy started to pull Agari toward the springhouse door; Agari resisted, looking back toward the rear. "Yeh cussed creature," Lizzy grunted, "yeh ain't got time for this. C'mon." Lizzy pulled at her arm; stumbling, Agari finally came with her. They moved out into the fading sunlight.

Lizzy's Pa and Preacher Dillon were just starting off the path from the road toward the house, close enough now that if they looked toward the springhouse, they would see Lizzy and Agari. "Run!" Lizzy half-shouted, pushing at Agari and pointing urgently toward the spine of the ridge above them. "Yeh have to run, Agari. Preacher Dillon is fixin' to kill yeh or worse. Go!"

But Agari didn't respond. Didn't move. Lizzy saw her Pa and the preacher look up toward them.

"Lizzy!" Pa shouted. She heard his call echo belatedly from the far ridge, saw Luke, Lee, and her mam emerge from the house at the noise and peer up toward her and Agari.

* * *

Lizzy pushed at me, pointing toward the top of the hill as she mouthed words I couldn't understand but that I knew carried strong emotions. I could see naked fear in her alien eyes, could hear the urgency in her voice. I didn't respond. I was looking down the slope toward the two males sitting astride those four-footed beasts that I'd seen before, when my line was slaughtered before my eyes. Both males leaped from astride their beasts, the one who didn't live here with Lizzy's line carrying one of the noisy weapons that had killed my loved ones.

That one was pointing at me and screaming words, his pale face all blotchy, and he started toward me, still screaming. The male that Lizzy called Pa stepped in front of him and the males called Luke and Lee also left the structure below us; the female called Ma was also shouting from near the door to the house.

Lizzy tried to push me again, pointing once more upward toward the ridge and the trees there, but again I ignored her. The angry male pushed away the arm that the male called Pa held out to hold him back; he pointed the loud weapon toward Luke and Lee as they approached. The two younger males immediately stopped, holding out their hands as if in supplication. Lizzy tried to put herself between me and the angry male as he surged up the hillside, but he shoved her aside. Lizzy fell to the ground with a cry. The male stood before me, his flesh-and-hair-snared eyes wide, the white part of them crazed with blood vessels.

Then, without warning, he lifted his weapon and struck me hard on the side of my face with the wooden end of it. I heard a loud *crack* in my jaw with the blow. Stunned and in great pain, I found myself sprawling on the ground. I could feel blood running hot down my face, but couldn't open my mouth to speak or protest; the pain when I tried to speak sent sparks flying through my vision. Through the fire of my pain, I could see the male standing over me, the blackened ends of the barrels of his weapon pointed at my chest. I could see his fingers turning white as he clutched at his weapon. *Good,* I thought, *now I will finally go to Garesh, Gishkim, and the rest of my line, as I should have...*

I didn't need to speak words aloud to the Deep Heart as it could hear my thoughts, so I began to tell it all that was happening as I saw Lizzy's Pa come up behind the angry man and put his hand on the weapon also. His head shook from side to side as he spoke.

* * *

"No," Lizzy heard her Pa say as his hand curled around Preacher Dillon's fingers on the twin triggers of the shotgun. "'Tain't right, Floyd, and yeh know it in yer heart. It weren't her that kilt Asa. The monster that done that is already dead; I kilt it myself. I told yeh I'd let yeh see this female if'n yeh need to, but that's all."

"Asa's gone," Preacher Dillon answered, "and this'n's one of them who took 'im from us."

"And thisn's got a child in her, too. Yeh willin' to kill an innocent, Floyd? Would yeh execute a woman who was with child, no matter what she'd done?"

"This ain't no woman, Carl. It's a monster I'm a'lookin' at. A demon."

Her Pa's voice remained calm and soft. Soothing. "I won't deny that's what I was afeared they was, too, when they came runnin' at us outa nowhere with them scales and claws. But what will *yeh* be if yeh do this, Floyd? Will yeh be any differ'nt from them? Yeh gonna show the congregation this'n and the little corpse inside her in church this Sunday, like yeh did t'others? Will that be pleasin' in the Lord's sight? Ain't that what yeh tell us to study on when we ain't sure if'n we're doin' what's right? And mostly I'm asking yeh this: is this somethin' yer Asa would want?"

Lizzy saw the shotgun tremble in Preacher Dillon's hand. Then, with a wordless, anguished cry that was nearly a sob, he let the shotgun fall from his hand. It landed next to the bloodied Agari.

Lizzy's Pa nodded. "That's the right choice, Floyd. Yeh done good. Done yerself and Asa proud." Then her Pa left Preacher Dillon, walking over to Lizzy and lifting her from the ground. He brushed the dirt and leaves from her dress. His eyebrows lifted, furrowing his brow as he looked at her. "And yeh, Lizzy, need to tell us why yer creature's untied and out here instead'a in the springhouse where it's s'posed to be. Looks t'me like yeh were plannin' on settin' it free. That the size of it?"

Lizzy turned her head from her father's accusing gaze, but looking at Preacher Dillon, who was sitting on the nearest log with his head buried in his hands and his shoulders shaking wasn't any better. "Sorry, Pa, I thought—"

She stopped. Agari was sitting up in the long grass, blood smeared over the side of her body and on the dress she wore. As Louis watched, Agari picked up the shotgun Preacher Dillon had dropped. She placed the barrel against her stomach, bent over the weapon and stretched out her hand toward the trigger guard.

"Agari, no!" Lizzy shouted, and started toward Agari.

The sound of the shotgun discharging blotted out Lizzy's scream, the terrible sound rebounding among the hills.

The Dogs of Babylon

Alan Smale

The dogs attacked as I hurried through Babylon's dingy streets in the growing dusk, my thoughts soured by alcohol and despair.

I hated Babylon, and the rest of Persia with it. I'd despised what it stood for long before we entered as conquerors eight years earlier, and my increased familiarity had never caused me to revise my loathing. I'd suffered nightmares about Babel even while we were experiencing much harsher travails in the lands further east, hacking our way through deserts and mountain ranges to the Indus and beyond.

And now I'd lost my way, after walking out from the hall in Nebuchadnezzar's ancient palace where the Companions were eating and drinking even as Alexander, their lord and King, lay at death's door. My mind was in turmoil and I desperately needed to walk off my fears. Then sunset approached with a suddenness I could not fathom, and the streets quickly became deserted. The giant central ziggurat of Etemenanki that should have been a landmark was blocked from my view by the three- and four-story mudbrick tenements around me and I found myself in a maze, empty of decent men.

And that was when I heard the bark and snap of the feral dogs. I turned away, plunged even deeper into a complicated swarm of lanes and alleys, and began to run.

And ran afoul of human predators instead.

They attacked from my blind side, though they could not have known of the cloudiness in my left eye that made a blur of the world. Suffice to say that I was still reacting to the fast slap of sandals in the dirt when they struck, a club to the back of my neck that sent me sprawling.

Back then I was still a warrior, at least on occasion. With that instinct I tried to roll back onto my feet, but my balance was already driven from me and I fell again. Then they were on me, one foul-smelling rogue grabbing my arms to drag me into a darkly-shaded alleyway while a second tugged at my purse to free it from my belt. I howled, till a punch to the mouth quelled me.

The next moments were unclear. The man holding me lurched, his grip on my arms vanished, and I dropped like a wet sack and curled to protect my belly. The sick sound of blows continued, fists against flesh and even the crack of bone, yet I felt no further pain. Was I paralyzed? Dead in body, with ears and thoughts still active?

Someone fell across me, driving what was left of the wind from my lungs. I heard a final yowl and the alley's darkness fogged even further as I became insensible.

* * *

Unholy Babylon! "Babilim" in the Babylonian tongue itself, "Babel" in both Hebrew and Aramaic. The word equates to either "The Gates of God" or "confusion." Both seem apropos.

We had entered through Babylon's bronze Ishtar Gate just three weeks since, and marched in fine ceremony down the Great Processional Way, with the Summer Palace of Nebuchadnezzar and the sluggish Euphrates to our right and Babylon's extensive temple areas to our left. The walls that channeled our army into the city were lined with the figures of hundreds of lions in white and gold relief against bricks glazed an astonishing blue. The road beneath our horses' hooves was of huge limestone flags. Babylonians lined the streets and cheered us as we passed. They'd have been fools not to.

On our eastward rampage we had smashed Darius and his Persian army at Gaugamela and then taken Babylon and several other cities in rapid succession. We returned now as rulers of Persia and many lands beyond, led by a king who was increasingly adopting Persian dress and traditions, appointing Persian satraps to administer his domains, and promoting widespread intermarriage between Greeks and Persians.

Babylon was to be Alexander's capital, the center of his empire. His reason was clear: geographically, Babylon marked one of the crossroads of Asia. Yet all the true Greeks in his army hated the place with a passion.

Babilim in war had nearly defeated Alexander. Babel in peacetime might finish the job.

* * *

They carried me, and none too carefully. A bear of a man held my shoulders, different from my previous assailant. Two others took a leg each, staggering. *Come, gentlemen: I am surely not so heavy.* Perhaps they, too, had been drinking.

Why was I not dead? My purse no longer tugged at my belt, so they had already liberated it. Why steal the man, also?

If they thought to ransom me, they would be sadly disillusioned. None of the Companions would toss a bronze coin into the street to redeem old Eumenes.

Perhaps they would torture me for information about Alexander or his army? Inflict magical torments upon me? Cut out my liver for auguries?

In Babylon, anything seemed possible.

I retched and the man holding my shoulders tilted me adroitly so my meager dinner spattered the street. They did not stop.

Again, my world slid into blackness.

* * *

After darkness comes the light. If we're lucky.

I came back to myself, confused. On campaign my sleeping-tent had walls thick enough to resist the sun, and in Babylon my palace bedchamber had no windows, yet here I was, awakening out of doors, and comfortable enough.

I lay on a straw mattress, shaded by a bower of thin woven branches. To my left was a square area of brick, clearly a rooftop as I could see other buildings beyond. I tried to sit up, but dizziness prevented me.

An elderly woman sat twenty feet away under a similar bower, spinning thread on a large wooden spindle. Noticing my movement, she stood and hobbled off to the roof edge, there to descend out of my sight on what was clearly a stairway.

Well, this was odd. I blinked, and the echo of pain behind my eyes forced the recollection of my assault back into my mind.

Beaten in the streets, yet alive and apparently in little distress.

Ah. "Apparently" was the key. In fact, I was numb. My arm was bound tightly across my chest to keep it immobilized, and in that arm there was almost no feeling. The back of my head was bandaged, the scalp beneath likewise empty of sensation until I prodded it—and that prod was a mistake that made me nauseous.

Taking more care, I fumbled myself upright. By the sun, it was early afternoon. The rooftop was cooler than I might have expected for a Mesopotamian early summer. The flowers and herbs in their boxes along the roof's edge smelled pleasant enough.

I might have stood and attempted to get my bearings, but that seemed presumptuous. Someone had brought me to their home and tended to my wounds. My spinning companion had presumably left to alert this person that I had awakened. I was not bound, so could scarcely imagine myself a prisoner.

Beside my makeshift bed was a small basket of grapes and a flask of cool water. I nibbled and sipped a late breakfast and waited.

A man and woman ascended onto the rooftop. I did not know the man, though he was muscular and held himself like a soldier. And that was the last study I made of him, for he planted himself fifteen feet away, legs apart and arms folded, and stared out across the rooftops. The woman continued to advance.

I blinked. This was not the spinning woman but another, younger and with light hair curly with ringlets. Beneath her scarf her face was fair, unusually so for Babylon.

I looked away, suddenly aware of how I stank with sweat and the odors of whatever had been smeared on my wounds. The hair stuck to my head and dirt to my clothes. Hardly a fit state in which to greet a lady.

She stopped and regarded me. Her eyes were kind. I lowered mine swiftly. She might be someone's wife and I had suffered enough trouble and pain over the last day and night.

"You look well." She spoke the Aramaic tongue with an accent I could not place.

I asked the question that burned at me above all others. "Does Alexander yet live?"

"The invading King?" She looked surprised. "I have not heard otherwise."

If Alexander had perished while I was insensible, she likely would have. The news would have swarmed the city like a fire through tinder, no matter how the Companions might attempt to quell it.

With an amused expression she repeated, with identical emphasis: "You look well."

Remembering my manners, I bowed. "Lady, I am cared for, and bid you give my thanks to the healer that...perhaps you arranged for me?" I touched my head again, and my arm. "I feel little from my wounds. Should I be concerned?"

"A healing unguent, to reduce the pain. It will wear off and then you will wish for more." She paused. "I am the healer, and you are welcome."

She? "Uh. Surely." I felt myself blush. "Last night I suffered an attack on the street, and am confused about what happened and where I am now. Why you find me worthy of your mercy." May as well say it; I would have already, had she been a man. "And what you might request of me in return."

Within Alexander's court I was merely a grammateus and, at need, the leader of a unit of his elite Household Cavalry. Little enough, but I still had the ear of the King and wielded influence. Some might seek to capitalize on that.

Yet she said: "I seek nothing from you, sir. It was mere chance. My brothers were hurrying home when they saw you set upon and came to your aid as they might assist any in peril. They brought you here to me."

"And you are a healer?" By chance? It seemed...convenient. I suspected there was more to her story, but could hardly prove it.

"Some of us set store by helping others."

Casually, I touched my belt. My purse once again hung by my side. I was not so crass as to open it, but its weight felt as it had when I left the Palace.

She pinked, frowned a little. "You have not been robbed, sir. Nor shall you be."

"Lady, I never doubted it," I lied.

She stepped nearer, troublingly close. "Look at me."

I kept my eyes lowered. "I would not disrespect—"

"Thank you. Then look past me, but raise your head and stare unblinking."

Now, I felt shame. The mark of the Gods' displeasure was upon me and I could hide it no longer. Nor could I disobey: I was in her debt and her request was not itself dishonorable.

So I stared at the man, obviously here to guard her, and the old woman at her spinning who presumably served as chaperone. Both ignored me.

"Your eye," she said.

"I know," I replied, foolishly, for what man does not know his own eyes?

"It seems you have another wound that has gone unhealed."

Introductions seemed overdue. I cleared my throat. "I am Eumenes of Cardia, secretary to King Alexander, and I have been away from his side too long. I bid you release me, that I might return to his service."

Though I was not looking directly at her, I felt her smile. "I am Miriam the Free, of the Jewish faith, and I would tend to you once more, before allowing you to leave my rooftop."

"The Free?"

"Many of my faith and lineage are not free, in mighty Babylon and elsewhere. It seems important to be clear."

Well, yes. Babylon had a substantial Jewish population, descended from the exiles from Nebuchadnezzar's generations-ago destruction of Jerusalem, and many were in servitude. Nonetheless, my head began to ache again. "Why? Why should you care?"

"I am a healer," she said patiently.

"You wish to curry favor with your conquerors?"

Miriam just stared.

It did not matter. I scarcely needed to comprehend her motives. I just needed to return to my King.

She tried again. "I offer to try to heal your eye. It will be painful, greater pain than you have yet suffered. You must be ready for that. I cannot guarantee to improve it, but shall not make it worse."

An easy boast: *worse* was well-nigh impossible.

At my silence, she stepped aside. "Well. If you must go, then go. And yet you should stay, at least a few hours longer, while the light lasts. If you trust me."

Trust? "I have only just met you."

Miriam's lip quirked. "Just so. And yet I trust *you*."

Then you are most foolish, I thought, *for why on earth should you*? But this time I said nothing aloud.

* * *

Babylon was a painted vixen, whose dazzling splendor masked her rotten heart. Yet Alexander had embraced her peculiarity and folded it into his own. His court had grown ever more elaborate in the Persian style: a golden throne with an embroidered golden canopy, his bodyguards garbed in purple and apple green, his archers in their scarlet tunics, from the dye of the kermes oak, and an ever-growing number of Persian courtiers in cloaks of purple and blue. To Greek eyes, it was all unbearably crass. And amongst such splendor, Alexander was the most garish of all, in his white robe with a sash and silver braid, or those effete Persian silk trousers dyed saffron. Sometimes he donned a cloak with leopard-skin trim and a saffron hood, worn tall in the Mesopotamian kingly tradition, and at dinner perhaps even a blue-and-white diadem.

Not so long since, he had attempted to introduce the Persian practice of *proskynesis*, obeisance, into his court, requiring us all—even his Companions—to enter his presence on our knees. This hubris did not go well and he soon jettisoned the idea. But none of us could doubt that his newly acquired Persian divinity had melded with his Macedonian kingship in a way unprecedented. In Alexander the two cultures had become, disturbingly, one.

* * *

"First, an eyelash has grown into your eye. Do you know it?"

Naturally I knew it. An ingrown eyelash, like an ingrown toenail. Who could do a thing against that?

Well, the lady Miriam, it seemed.

"If I resolve that, perhaps you will trust me with the greater problem in that eye."

"The blindness?"

"The cataract." She used the Greek word: *katarrhaktes*, waterfall, for its resemblance to a wall of white water in the eye. Fortunately, only my left eye was afflicted, though nowadays when I blink, I imagine a swirl of similar spume developing in the right.

"You can resolve *that*?"

I should not have believed her. I doubt I would have, anywhere other than darkly magical Babylon, and from anyone other than this young, small woman who glowed so brightly within it.

And yet I did. If Babylon had dark magic, perhaps it also possessed benevolent spells. And many Jews were great healers, almost as good as the Greeks. But I had rarely known a woman to administer to a man, and still I hesitated. "I must return to Alexander."

"Very well. My brother will set you on the road toward the citadel."

Scarcely necessary, because now I was standing I could see the rise of the ziggurat called Etemenanki that marked the central temple to Marduk, jutting head and shoulders above the other buildings, and from Etemenanki's gate I knew the way to the Hanging Gardens.

I took a single step forward, and then found myself asking: "This resolution you speak of. Truly, you have eased blindness before?"

* * *

I shall not pretend that I bore the pain bravely. Nay, it hurt worse than any wound I had received in battle, by far.

She averted my eyelid and, using the tiniest of forceps, plucked out the ingrowing hair. Immediately after, and for the only time, I felt her breath upon my forehead; for some reason I remember this most distinctly. Perhaps because it was a small note of grace after this sharp pain and before the next, in which she cauterized the eyelash root with the tiniest of iron needles, heated in a candle flame.

Her dexterity was astonishing, almost too quick to discern. But it did hurt a great deal.

And yet that was nothing compared to the agony that was to come.

She applied Indian Lycium to my eye and it was a salve beyond any I had previously known. From its cooling beneficence, I was ready to believe that the chronic ulceration of my eye was behind me. Already a blessing I could never have anticipated.

Very well, so my Miriam was an *ophthalmikos*, a healer who understood eyes. A needle in her sure hand, and all was well. A tiny wound from a tiny blade, wielded with dexterity.

The eyelash was the easy part. Next came the hard: the cataract that had rendered me half-blind for years.

She administered to that Gods-blighted cloud with her right hand, though previously she had employed her left. Clearly, each of Miriam's hands was as adroit as the other.

I make it all sound so calm, yet it was torture worse than any other experience in my life. Even with the decoction of henbane and mandrake Miriam gave me to dull the pain, it was still awful.

The sun shone strongly on us in the full heat of the afternoon, for Miriam needed its brightness to see her work as clearly as possible. I sweated, and so did Miriam, and also the muscled man, who came to hold my arms behind my back and my head still.

For Miriam the Free dug a bronze needle, sharp as all sin, deep into my eye. Straight in, and if I screamed like a child, let none of you think worse of me. You would have done the same.

She steadied my head with a sure hand, a workmanlike hand, her fingers cradling my temple.

But her other hand: such torment!

* * *

An eye is a pool, it seems. Some pools might have a sheet that covers and clouds it, depriving the eye of light. So says Miriam.

Break that sheet. Cut it into parts, thrust them down. And then the light comes again and all is well.

Easy to describe. Agony to endure.

"I will couch your eye," was all the description she had given. The name is infinitely more comfortable than the procedure. It felt as if the needle sucked at my eye and tugged apart the pieces of the clouding wound. Maybe I imagined this.

Either way, the cloud broke. I felt the very pieces of my eye moving. And at that I roared to the heavens, such that my throat was sore afterward.

* * *

Miriam bound up the left side of my head in bandages and sat with me. She had given me poppy tears to drink, which distanced me from my senses and loosened my tongue. And so I spoke freely.

"Everyone and his brother think they have a claim to succeed him." I waited, but heard no chuckle. "That's a joke. Alexander's half-brother Philip Arrhidaeus has a strong claim, but he's a halfwit. Alexander's unborn son by the Princess Roxana would be his rightful heir, yet the boy will not be a full-blood Macedonian and that would be trouble even if he were of age. A regency? But who? Perdiccas, Aristonous, Craterus? All would support the royal line if they could. But if not, they would battle to rule Macedonia.

"Antipater serves as regent in Macedon in Alexander's absence. He holds the power, but he is old. Moreover, he is not *here* and won't learn of Alexander's death till long after his generals have put their plans in motion. It would take six months for a messenger to travel there and back.

"Ptolemy craves Egypt. Seleucus Nicator longs to rule Babylonia." I shook my head before remembering that I must not and a wave of dizziness swept me. "Antigonus, western Anatolia. Perhaps Menander would be satisfied with Lydia." And maybe, I realized with shock, I might sequester a part of Thrace to rule for myself. In such times, anything was possible.

It was not my desire to rule. My deepest wish was for my Lord and King to live. But, if the Gods chose to rob us of him...

I swallowed. "Should Alexander die, his great empire will likely collapse, as his generals battle to carve up the spoils. Rivers will run red with blood.

"But I fear I am boring you. You must have little interest in politics."

Her lips pursed. "As you say."

"Maybe the Companions will prove to be the true dogs of Babylon. Babel...a city of confusion, with these dogs set to take advantage and tear apart the corpus that has been Alexander's life's work."

In my drugged state, this epiphany seemed profound. I paused in awe at my own perspicacity, then felt a twinge of guilt at slandering my King's generals, and to a city woman whom I had only today met. "I apologize. Babel? I am babbling. I beg you, tell no one of my folly."

"Of course not," Miriam said politely.

"Yet, even while the embalmers are busy with Alexander's body, the battles will begin."

"I can see how that might be...disastrous."

Realization struck me like a thunderbolt. "You must come and see him."

"Who?"

"My King needs a healer. I have found one."

I saw her shrink away, even with just half of my watering right eye.

Alexander had been surrounded by healers for days. Some were even Jewish. But none of them were Miriam.

Alexander had slain his most accomplished Greek doctor in a rage following the death of his closest companion and lover, Hephaestion, and who might blame him? Now he depended on others. But I had heard his current doctors, Macedonian and Persian, argue over him as if already bickering over a corpse. Some advocated magical remedies. Others insisted on cures from natural philosophy that seemed no less alien.

This woman, though, I trusted. Miriam the Free had nothing to gain nor lose by Alexander's survival.

She had tended my wounds. She had brought me back my eye. Perhaps she might bring back Alexander, too, in the same kindly and matter-of-fact way?

* * *

The first time I entered the Hanging Gardens of Babylon, I, too, believed in magic, at least for a while. Today, the burgeoning life within merely mocked my King's suffering.

The name misleads. In fact, nothing is suspended in the Gardens, nothing sways or rocks. However, they do seem to hang outside of time. Outside of reality and common sense.

There are six gardens, rising in a series, each higher and more glorious than the one before. Fashioned by King Nebuchadnezzar two and a half centuries since for his wife Amyitis, a Mede, to remind her of the mountains and valleys of her native land, the Hanging Gardens nonetheless looked as if they had been crafted yesterday, or just miraculously come into being, whole and fully-grown. Irrigated by canal-water from the Euphrates, the gardens were lush and verdant the whole year around. In Babylon, the desert bloomed.

Miriam and I ascended wide marble staircases, passed through glades of juniper and cypress, walnut and willow, and then an orchard of pomegranates and plums, date palms and quince and figs and almonds, with grasses underfoot of chamomile and thyme, and bushes and serried ranks of flowers I could not possibly name.

And at the peak of this holy mountain we came upon my stricken hero and god, a cousin to Achilles and Herakles and a son of the Egyptian Ammon, lying in a portico area with flowers and shrubs spilling from its roof. It was cool there, at least relatively, with a light breeze nudging the petals and fronds of his chamber of sickness.

Just as when I had last seen him, Alexander lay quite still.

Miriam was pale. I was sure she had never once imagined she might enter such a place. She had been shaking as we approached the Macedonian Household Guard at the front gates. I was known and trusted, of course, but before entering the Gardens Miriam had to endure the indignity of a search by a female adjutant. With reason: beardless young male assassins have oft attempted to approach their victims in a lady's disguise.

And, once arrived at the crowning Garden, a half dozen guards watched over Alexander, alert to any threat.

His doctors tended to him morning and night, but this was mid-afternoon. The King rested and made no move as we approached. A mere thirty-two years of age, Alexander looked even younger when he slept. I, a dozen years older and childless, might have felt protective toward him, had I not known him as a seasoned general who would slaughter without hesitation when the situation demanded it.

Blighted, Alexander was still an attractive man. His hair was blond, his nose straight, his skin fine and fair, his frame short, but muscular. He cut a fine figure, even in extremis. Today, for once, he was garbed simply in a Greek tunic, with purple at the collars and cuffs and a bit of silver braiding the only indications of his exalted rank.

Miriam, who knew not the warlord and saw only a man stricken down before his time, murmured in compassion: "He seems so young, and poorly, and weak besides."

Heat flooded my face. "Weak? Alexander was struck on the head by a stone whilst fighting the Illyrians, and later on the neck by a mace. Another blow to the head from a scimitar at Granicus. At Issus he received a wound to the thigh, and another to the ankle at the siege of Gaza. He took an arrow to the breast just three years since, and a strike to the neck when he was first over the wall when fighting the Mallians. Few of these injuries slowed him for a moment, let alone a day or a week. This is not a man who might be laid low by just *anything*. And you would be wise not to let such womanly slander reach the ears of his guards."

"You love him," she said.

"He is my King."

After a moment, Miriam nodded. "Tell me what happened."

* * *

Merely another drinking party, this one at the home of Medius of Larisa, where Alexander had suffered fast pains in both chest and gut as if he had been pierced by arrows. He took to his bed and then became worse. A high fever, a great purging, and much else besides.

"Just drinking," I said. "Feasting. In the usual way of men."

She gave me a look.

"With wine sometimes comes vomiting...with your pardon, Lady."

"What else? Pain here? Here?"

She was pointing to my lower abdomen and then much higher, in the ribcage.

Surprise lifted my eyebrows. "Both. Lower first, and higher later. Just where you point."

"Discomfort of the bowels, flux? And what else?"

"Weakness. And, his heart...Alexander has the heart of an ox, which sometimes beats fast and loud when he has been drinking."

Miriam's brow furrowed. "You can *hear* his heart?"

"Well, no, but I have felt it race in his chest and flutter at his wrist, when I have been trying to decide whether to call the doctors on previous occasions. But this time..." And, strangely, it only now seemed odd to me. "Wait."

I reached out to place a hand on Alexander's chest, and another to his temples, where sometimes men's veins throb. "His heart is slow. That is good, yes?"

Miriam's expression gave the doubt to this. "Show me his eyes? Lift the lids, as gently as you may?"

Eyes, again? She leaned in as I slid one eyelid up, then the other. The guards watched her carefully.

So did I, to see her reaction. Alexander's eyes were striking, one a gray-blue and the other dark brown. Men sometimes recoiled on seeing those eyes, or beads of sweat would pop out on their foreheads in superstitious alarm, knowing themselves in the presence of a remarkable man.

My *ophthalmikos* satisfied my expectation, at least in part, by blinking in surprise. "They have always been thus?"

"They have."

"Just as well, for I know of no affliction that might cause it."

Cause? I, too, knew of none. But eyes were on my mind to a considerable degree, having just had my own mended in the most painful and yet effective of ways, and now I had another epiphany.

Alexander's disparate eyes: almost as if one were Macedonian and the other Persian. Another sign of these two warring traditions somehow become one in the same man.

Could that be the source of his illness? The unhealthy mixture of two opposing cultures, warring within him?

Perhaps I was prone to analogizing too far. I cleared my throat.

"He has complained of," Miriam gestured, "blurring, or difficulty with vision that has continued unabated. He suffers dizziness."

She was no longer asking.

"You know what ails him," I said bluntly.

Miriam glanced at the Household Guards, who still regarded her with unblinking enmity. "Come," she said, and walked away. I followed and waited for her to gather her thoughts.

Finally, she turned. "Your beloved King is poisoned."

I laughed, yet it sounded ragged to my own ears. I had hoped for better advice than this. "Nay! Hardly."

An eyebrow raised. "Now you are a healer, also?"

"Poisons act quickly. The King has been laid low for *five days.*" Miriam said nothing, so I continued. "A poison sufficient to cause such distress would have made the wine bitter. He would not have drunk it. And a poison of major effect, of the *arsenikon* or *strychnos* species, would have killed him already."

She held herself erect. "Then I have erred. Forgive me. I shall leave you now."

"Very well, go," I said, reckless in my disappointment.

She strode away across the grass with a speed unusual in a lady of such diminutive stature and, once I regained my wits, given my wounds and aches, it was all I could do to catch up to her. "Miriam, wait. I beg of you."

She stopped and sighed. I walked in front of her, bold now. "The pains, *here* and *here*, and yet not in the stomach between. The blurring of his vision, the slow heart?" For she had specified all of these with great precision.

"Indeed?"

"I beg you, forgive me, and tell me what poison causes such? And what might be its treatment?"

She looked up at the Hanging Gardens that surrounded her. Now, she seemed reluctant.

I understood. We discussed a conqueror, a man who had caused untold death and sorrow throughout her land. If, indeed, this land was her true home. "You were here in Babylon, eight years ago, when our armies took the city?"

"I was."

"And yet?" I gestured behind me. "Alexander is just a man."

"Is he? You all worship him. And that is...wrong. It is idolatry to worship a man. There is only one God, who has made a special covenant with His people. And if you worship Alexander as a God, then you should believe his divinity will save him. In which case you have no need of my opinion."

She made to walk past me again. "Please, Lady," I said. "Please tell me."

Perhaps my pathetic tone finally persuaded her.

"White hellebore."

"What?"

"A type of lily. You may not know it. It is not commonly found in the heat of this area." I saw her reconsider. "Perhaps in Macedonia they may know of it, and Cappadocia. But mainly in the mountains."

"And a poison can be made of it? A *slow* poison?"

Miriam nodded. "White hellebore inflicts exactly the bodily ails your King suffers. The slow heart, in particular. Most illnesses cause a speeding."

My mouth was dry. "Lady, what must we do?"

"First, soak up the poison. Your King must—" She took a breath and smiled apologetically. "—eat charcoal."

"Charcoal?"

"As a sponge for the poison, to soak it up. Second, you must stop the vomiting and purging that weakens him twofold. For that, he must eat raw ginger, from the root."

I could not help it. Again, I laughed.

"Third." Miriam was relentless now, this little woman of the Jewish faith. I had the feeling that, now begged to speak, only death would silence her. "Once he can eat again, give him nuts and fish. No rich sauces. Nothing else."

Now, I just blinked at her.

"It will aid his heart." She frowned, looking back at the goblet on the low table at the foot of the King's bed. "He still drinks wine, even in his illness?"

"Of course." Wine was purer than water. Especially in Babylon.

"Have that stopped. It is possible that he is still ingesting poison by this route, and even if not, it will worsen his nausea and work against him. When this began, did he sneeze a great deal?"

Along with the vomiting and all? How could she have known that?

Miriam nodded. "Definitely white hellebore. A trace of the powder remained on the wine's surface and he breathed it in."

How I might persuade the King of Macedonia and Asia to eat charcoal, I had no idea. And yet I must. It was surely no less outlandish than the "cures" his various other doctors and magical practitioners had inflicted upon him: the blood-lettings, the rubbing and rocking, the application of beneficent snakes to his skin, the fragrant oils and liniments and nitrates. The panoply of spells and libations, sacrifices and exorcisms.

I bowed. "Thank you, Lady Miriam."

Miriam looked around again and for the very first time I noted calculation in her eyes. "We are friends again, perhaps?"

"Surely."

"Then, since I am already here?" She waved a hand at the gardens. "I might stay a little longer? Being a burden to no one. Merely to enjoy it?"

"Of course."

She strolled away. I let her roam alone, and followed her only with my eyes, oddly bereft now she was no longer by my side. She ambled slowly, looking left and right, smiling at the flowerbeds.

And then her smile vanished. She stopped and pointed. I walked to join her.

It did not look like the downfall of kings. Neither did it look like a lily. More like an herb, some two feet tall. Undistinguished.

"It blooms in the winter. White flowers. You'll see." She nodded professionally, satisfied, then stepped away once more.

Again, she walked on alone, looking around in awe and wonder. After all, once she left today, she would likely never come here again, nor anywhere else like it.

I stared at the hellebore. Alexander, King of Kings, brought low by a powder made from this? Administered to him in front of my eyes?

A deadly poison, and available right here in Babylon after all.

Miriam could have been lying, I supposed. She *could*. But somehow, I was certain she told the simple truth.

* * *

I met Miriam the Free just once more and the memory brings me only sorrow.

We had arranged to meet at the gate of the Jewish Temple most central within the city, although this was still some walk from the Palace. She stood alone, but from the opposite side of the street a Jewish man watched me carefully. One of her brothers? Maybe even one who had rescued me from violence that night?

As I approached, Miriam smiled. The bandage was off my head. My left eye would never again see equal to my right, but I could make out shapes, colors, brightnesses. It still wept, but cleanly. It was a great deal better. My own little miracle.

For the larger miracle? "My King lives." Miriam nodded; Alexander had been seen out in public over the past days, after all. "And I have caught his poisoner, and he has paid the price."

Her smile vanished. "What?"

"His Royal Page and cup-bearer, Iolaus. Under torture, the boy admitted everything: a massive bribe, the promise of future elevation. Perdiccas and Lysimachus, behind it all." I nodded in satisfaction. Perdiccas, with his strong claim to serve as regent for Alexander's infant; Lysimachus, a lesser officer eager for advancement. Both good Macedonians appalled by Alexander's wholesale adoption of Persian ways.

"Torture? A boy?" Miriam's face was blank, her voice flat.

"We had to be sure." Even as I said it, I realized my glibness made it worse. A simple healer, how could Miriam understand the cutthroat needs of state?

"And the men?"

I paused, but had to speak the truth. "Alexander has already slain both."

"Slain?" Miriam sagged, and her sudden expression of loathing made me step back. "By saving one man, I have caused the savage deaths of three more?"

Three so far, but many others to come. For safety, we would obviously also slay the traitors' families. And Alexander would now return to war, and this week's deaths would be nothing compared to the new swath of destruction he would carve in the years to come.

I suspected this answer would not comfort her.

"He has summoned you," I said. "Alexander. To give you his thanks and blessings. He will likely inquire if there is any boon—"

Miriam turned and walked away. She strode erect, with a set to her spine.

I could have sent soldiers later. One does not just disobey a summons from a King. And after all, I knew where Miriam lived.

I did not do so, and I knew that following her now and begging her to forgive me would be an extremely poor idea. Even if I had done anything requiring absolution.

I had disappointed her. In hindsight, how could I not have? Our worlds were not the same.

I let her go and soon she passed out of my sight.

* * *

Sometimes I wonder if I dreamed her: Miriam the Free. Then I blink, and recall that now I have both my eyes.

I am sad that I never saw her again. My *ophthalmikos*. After all my years of war, Miriam was refreshing. Even just her simple joy at walking among the flowers, in the Hanging Gardens of Babylon…

Anyway. Enough of the healer. Let me close by admitting the terrible thoughts in my mind the day I met her, and for the harsh week that preceded it.

I had thought that a man—even a conquering King—who attempts to combine two traditions as mutually alien as Persian and Macedonian must be doomed to failure.

Deep in my heart, I had believed that Alexander would die.

Thank the Gods that I was wrong. Gloriously, spectacularly wrong.

Such folly.

Of course, Alexander went on to complete his great plan, adding even more territories to his empire. In the following years he led an even larger combined army of Macedonians and Persians across North Africa to conquer Libya and Carthage, and then on to Iberia, Sicily, Rome, and up into Gaul, grinding it all beneath his heel. His annexation of Africa required a new thousand-mile road built along its northern coast, and a fleet of two thousand ships built in Cilicia and Phoenicia. Later came the quelling of Arabia, to protect our trading routes between Egypt and India.

Even then, Alexander had conquered but not consolidated. His "empire" was little more than a collection of satrapies, principalities, and unformed city-states under occupation.

If anything, his next task was harder. But he rose to the challenge: over the next two decades our bold military warlord transformed into a great ruler, and ultimately a true god to stand alongside Herakles, Ammon, and Ahura-Mazda themselves. By sheer force of will, Alexander performed the miracle that I should have known was inevitable: uniting West and East into a single European-Asiatic Empire, its rulers speaking Koine Greek from Iberia to India. A civilization to transform the world, that will stand for a thousand years.

Today, I understand Fate. Alexander is a titan, resistant to all injury and harm. When I listed his battle wounds to Miriam, the scales should have truly fallen from my eyes. The Gods clearly willed his survival, and their will sets the course for the world.

Back then, I used to wonder: had I not heard the barking of the dogs of Babylon as I walked its streets in distress—if I had not reversed my path—if I had not been set upon by thieves, then rescued from that attack...if I had not met Miriam...might the Emperor of the World have perished that week in Babylon, and the other hunting dogs, Perdiccas and Ptolemy and Seleucus and all the rest, have ripped Alexander's nascent Empire apart in a fountain of blood?

Of course not. It is simply inconceivable that such a man could have died in such a way.

The Gods were in the barking of those dogs, guiding Miriam and I together, so that disaster could be averted.

Alexander! Conqueror of nations! Architect of the world for millennia to come!

One man, who has changed the world forever!

One great man.

Eight Mile and the City

Steven Harper

We knew she was opportunity because she knocked once and came in. She had a swagger and a set of dagger heels you only see in women south of Eight Mile. A thin line of dark showed at the roots of her carefully golden hair and her lipstick was a strawberry scarlet. She shut the office door behind her and sat in the client chair across from me without asking, her red leather purse perched on her knees like a sleek little lapdog. Seb exchanged a glance with me from his section of the shared Ikea desk we'd salvaged from a burned-out building down on Cass.

"Is this the Eight Mile Detective Agency?" she asked.

Seb leaned back and his chair squeaked. "That's what it says on the door. You need a detective?"

"Or maybe two." Her posture hummed with live-wire tension. "I want to hire you to find my son. His name is Samuel Flagg."

From her purse she removed a paper photograph and passed it over to me. It landed on my desk and I looked down at it without touching. A boy with brown hair, maybe three years old, gazed back up at me with brown eyes. I flipped the photo over to Seb with my fingertips. It was a hell of a flip. My part of the desk looks like the universe a half-second after the Big Bang. But if you stand on it and look down from a distance, you'd see that the chaos makes a wider pattern—these papers sorted by date, those by urgency, others by category. Seb's desk, on the other hand, is rigid as a general's asshole. The few objects on his desk look like they're nailed there. So it was a feat to flip the photo over my chaos to his order.

While Seb examined the photo, I made myself say, "Your name is?" Talking to strangers is the hardest part of my day. Not because I don't know what to say. I just have to find a way to say it.

"Candace Flagg." She reached across the desk. "Pleased to meet you."

I managed not to grimace when I leaned in to shake. Her hand was cool and thin, and when the sleeve of her blue silk coat pulled back, I noticed the scars.

"Andy Faust," I said, giving my standard opener. "This is my partner in crime prevention, Sebastian. How long has your son been missing?"

She hesitated. "Next week, it'll be two years."

Seb's eyebrows went up. "Have you called the cops about him?"

"Of course. They told me he isn't missing."

Now my eyebrows went up. "You got more to say than that?"

"Look. There's a reason I'm here." She leaned in again and lowered her voice. "Word out there—" she made a vague gesture at the door and its pebbled glass window that read EIGHT MILE DETECTIVE AGENCY: WE PUSH THE BOUNDARY "—is that you boys have an in with the NokSinn."

A silence fell over the little office, but it took me a while to notice. Seb sat stone-faced. I looked away from him and swallowed a throatful of nerves.

"Do the NokSinn have something to do with your boy's disappearance?" Seb asked.

She hesitated. "He's...Lost," she said in a broken voice. She dug through the big red purse for a tissue and dabbed her eyes. "A Lost Kid."

Seb's face remained a stone. I hung there, caught between me, Seb, and a new client. Maybe I should just toss her out anyway. What did I care about her kid? Just thinking about the NokSinn and The City made me tight and antsy.

"I can pay," Candace said, as if reading my thoughts. The purse produced a wad of green bills, which she passed across the desk as casually as she had the photograph. "In advance."

Hoo boy. I eyed the cash. We were behind, as usual. Power and heat were free, thanks to the NokSinn panels on the roof, but the landlord still owned that roof and he'd come knocking on the door just this morning. Still, I was under-thrilled with a case that dealt with The City. Or, to put it another way, hell-to-hell no.

"Go away," I said, and saw Seb wince. He says I can be blunt as a charging bull, which I don't understand, because other times he says it takes me a long time to get to the point. I tried to remember my hard-won manners. "Look, maybe you can try somewhere else."

Her eyes went soft and teary. "I've been to five different detectives and none of them would touch the case. The last one said you know the NokSinn, so I came here. Please." She rooted through the purse again. "I'll pay double. Triple. Just…can you find my little boy?"

I chewed my thumbnail, a bad habit I'd picked up when I quit the cigs. I didn't want to do this. The City was too dangerous, and this case would take us there. I could already see the pattern laid out in front of me. Step one, investigate in Detroit. Step two, find the lead that took us to The City. Step three…I didn't want to think about step three.

Seb said steadily, "It's a kid, Andy. But what do you want to do? It's NokSinn, so you decide."

I swallowed, and in a flick I saw a bigger pattern. A kid traumatized, lost for years, lives a life of pain and chaos. It wasn't a right pattern, or a good one, and I could help break it. Okay, then. I switched from pushing the cash aside to stuffing it into a drawer.

"Thank you, Mr. Faust," Candace said. "I know with you on the case, everything will turn out fine."

She made me think of an actress reciting lines, but badly. What was her angle? I thought about asking, but the words didn't come. That happens to me a lot and it makes my life in Detroit miserable.

"What's your email?" Seb asked. Candace gave it and he called out, "Mavis! Ms. Flagg needs a contract."

"On it, Boss," Mavis said in my ear. Candace checked her phone and, a couple seconds later, we had her signature. Seb was always one to cross and dot. Good thing, since I was rotten at it.

"So your son went missing and you think the NokSinn are behind it," I said.

"I know they are. It's definitely the NokSinn. He's Lost."

"The Lost Kids were taken more than thirty years ago," Seb pointed out. "The NokSinn haven't done anything like that since."

"Maybe they've started up again," Candace retorted.

"But how do you know it was the NokSinn?" Seb asked.

Her face hardened beneath all the pancake makeup. "Remember how it happened? How the Lost Kids became lost?"

Seb nodded, but she set her purse on the floor and got up to pace the floor as if he hadn't. I watched her through slitted eyes.

"When the government secretly snatched all those kids out of foster care to give to the NokSinn, they went for orphans. Kids who had no parents, no family, so no one would miss them. They doctored the records to make it look like the kids had never existed in the first place."

"You're going to tell us the same thing happened with your son," Seb said.

She retrieved her purse, pulled out a cigarette, lit it, and took a deep drag. No one worried about lung cancer anymore, thanks to the NokSinn—a little gift that had come with some cable-strength strings.

"Social services took him from me two years ago, when he was a baby," she said. "Couple days ago, I went in to prove that I wasn't... that I was a fit mother again. But they said they had no record of a Samuel Flagg anywhere in the system. They didn't have his birth certificate at City Hall. The hospital didn't have a record of his birth. It's like he never existed. Lost. Gotta be the NokSinn again. Who else could erase him like that?"

"The NokSinn only took orphans before," Seb said. "Samuel's not an orphan. Why would they take him?"

She stared at the window without answering for a long moment. Finally, I said, "Ma'am, we have to ask. Why did the county take Samuel away?"

"I've got a past."

"Who doesn't?"

"My past is...well, Daddy wasn't good to me. Thank god he died when I was just little. But stuff happened, and when I grew up I bounced from guy to guy, all of them just like him. My shrink says I was looking for someone to replace him. Maybe so." She flicked ash into the wastebasket. . "Anyway, I got pregnant, and I was actually happy. The baby—Samuel—would love me, no matter what. And you know what? He did. But love don't help you kick old habits."

I bounced a glance off Seb, who ignored it.

Candace continued, "See, I avoided the hard stuff while I was pregnant, but after Samuel was born...well, I needed something for the pain and the nightmares. But even that stuff wasn't enough, so I tried one last thing."

"Your scars," I said.

"Yeah." She extended a wrist, making them visible again. "They look shallow, but they run deep. I was in the hospital and there was no one to take care of Samuel, so the county declared me unfit and took my little boy away. I suppose losing Samuel was the best thing, though. Sent a shock right through me. I knew the only way I could get him back was to kick the shit and get my head on straight. Worked my ass off, got a job, therapy. Even found another guy, a great guy who loves me for real. He's looking forward to being Sammy's dad. Except now Sammy's gone. The bastards took him. Can you get him back?"

So I'd been right about the bad pattern. Candace had lived a life of chaos and pain, and now it was passing to her son. This only firmed my resolve.

"We can try," I said. It would have been nice to tell her that we could do it, but lying isn't something I'm good at.

"You know who fostered him?" Seb asked. "And who his social worker was?"

"Babby Rose was the social worker."

I cast Seb a sidelong look. "We know her. What about the foster parents?"

"They sent me the photo. Doug and Melissa something. Frankfurt. Or maybe Frankenburg."

"Mavis?" I asked.

"Checking. Wayne County database lists a pair of foster parents named Doug and Melissa Franklin."

I repeated this information to Candace. Her face cleared. "That's them! I was always bad with names." She tossed her cigarette out the open window. "When can you start looking?"

Directions to a pair of addresses, both downtown, showed up on my ocular implant. I rose. "We'll start now."

Seb told Mavis to lock up and called a cab for Candace. It swished up to the curb, powered by the silent NokSinn motor and guided by a NokSinn AI program. As the passenger door popped open, Candace asked, "Where are you going to look?"

"The obvious," Seb said, and handed her in. "We'll be in touch."

Once the cab zipped away, Seb turned to me. "I'll take the Franklins. You take Babby Rose." He paused. "Are you really okay with taking this case?"

The question caught me off-guard. "Why wouldn't I be?"

"It's another NokSinn case. The last one didn't go so well. You almost gave in."

"Yeah, well." I scuffed the pavement with my toe like a little kid caught cutting class. "I'm good. You don't need to worry."

"I think you're the one who's worrying," he said, and actually cracked a smile. "I'll take care of you. Those are the rules we agreed on, right? It's what good husbands do."

I put my hands on his face and kissed him. I liked doing that, no matter how many times I'd already done it. It also helped me remember what to say to him. "You do a good job, Mr. Faust."

* * *

Barbara Rose did her social work from a cube farm on Grand River. I gave up my pistol at the front security station and cooled my heels in a waiting area with maybe a dozen people who looked tired and beaten down. Or up. Voices chattered and keyboards chittered in the carpet-walled cubes past us. I played 3D checkers with Mavis on my ocular implant. It's my favorite game. The patterns are soothing and, once I can see at least six moves in advance, the game is mine, even against Mavis. I was three-and-oh when a plump grandma-type in a purple pant suit bustled into the waiting zone and shook my hand. I let her.

"Sorry to keep you waiting, Mr. Faust. It's always a madhouse. How are you?"

"I'm good, Ms. Rose."

She didn't say anything about recognizing me, so I figured she'd either forgotten or I had changed. She only said, "Call me Babby. Let's talk back here."

Just as I remembered, her cube was explosively messy, but not with the files and papers you'd expect. This cubicle was lost in a rainbow riot of children's artwork: Thanksgiving turkeys made from traced hands, sloppy collages of colored paper, crayon house-tree-kid drawings, runny finger paintings tacked, pinned, and tented to or on every surface. I was appreciative, as only a fellow afficionado of chaos can be.

"I'm too busy to bullshit, Mr. Faust, so let's cut to it," Babby said, settling into an aging chair that had molded to her body shape. "You said on the phone you're a PI, so I suppose you want to talk about a client."

"That's the short version." I showed her my physical ID. "We've met before."

"Have we?" Her eyebrows went up, which meant she was surprised. "I'm very sorry—I meet a lot of people in this job. I don't remember talking to a private investigator recently."

I fished for a response. A lot of times when I talk to people, I have to think hard about how to say what I need, so I keep a long list of canned responses on a shelf in my head. When someone asks me something, I pull down one of the cans and open it to get the words out. I'm also a rotten liar. It's not that I can't say false words. I just say them...wrong. Seb says that, when I lie, I sound like an actor trying to do Shakespeare in a Bronx accent. Anyway, for this situation, none of my word cans seemed to fit the situation and I had no lies. I was on my own.

"We met several years ago," I finally said, then changed the subject. "My client is trying to find her son."

"And who is this client?"

Now I was on easier ground. No need to lie, for one thing. "Her name is Candace Flagg, and her son's name is Samuel. Do you know them?"

At the mention of the name, Babby's arms folded shut across her bosom with bureaucratic finality. "Sorry. Privacy regs are clear. Couldn't help you, even if I remembered a kid from two years ago. Which I don't."

Babby's punchy side was showing, but only after I mentioned the name Flagg. Interesting, but not too helpful. I would have to try again. I took a can off my mental shelf. It was labeled *emotional manipulation*. "Look, ma'am, this boy Samuel is missing. He was kidnapped, probably by the NokSinn. His mother is worried sick."

"I'm sure she is. I get family problems in here every hour of every day, Mr. Faust, half of them way worse than what you just described. But the regs are there for a reason, and I can't break them just because you claim a kid is missing. And bringing the NokSinn into it..." She puffed out her cheeks.

"Do you still get a lot of cases that involve the NokSinn?"

Her expression tightened. "Not as many as I used to."

There were things I knew I was supposed to say, but the words wouldn't quite come. I opened another can. "You were a social worker back when the Lost Kids first showed up. You remember?"

"Remember? I was *there*, Mr. Faust. I was there when the first Lost Kid showed up not two blocks from this office. The cops found this young woman wandering the streets without a shred to cover her, so they called me. Her name was Laura Caldwell. Twenty-three years old. She could barely talk, made all these sounds that didn't even sound human until the AI figured out she was speaking NokSinn. She was a fighter, let me tell you. Struggled and kicked and bit. Didn't seem to realize anyone was actually talking to her. It was like those stories of kids raised by wolves. Took a whole team of us to get her to the point where she could communicate and act...human. She'd be in her forties now." She shook her head. "Because I was there for the first Lost Kid, the cops figured I was the go-to person for the next one, and the next, and the next. Never get good at a difficult task, Mr. Faust. It only means the boss will stick you with it over and over again."

Now I knew what to say, so I said it. "What happened to the Lost Kids you dealt with?"

"You know the answer to that." There was a note of soft sorrow in her voice. "Without getting too specific, I can say most of them just couldn't fit in. They went back to The City. We never did learn how or why they left it in the first place."

"And what about the others? The ones who stayed?"

"Maybe three or four managed to...get past their upbringing, but they were always a little odd. Lots of OCD and emotional distancing and rigid behaviors. Couple of them went the other way, living in squalor and creating chaos all around them. You know—as a coping mechanism for their anger. Once they learned enough skills to get by, they turned their backs on good old social services. You can't help someone who doesn't want to be helped, right? I lost track of them. Ha! Lost." She scrounged up a tissue from the mess and blew her nose with a ladylike honk. "It was beyond awful, the way the President agreed to send orphans over to the NokSinn as payment, or whatever you want to call it. I mean, my mother was in chemo for breast cancer, and the NokSinn gave us the cure just in time to help her, but even so...it wasn't right."

"Ms. Rose—Babby," I said slowly, "I just want to know if this boy was ever in your system. I'm not asking to see his file. I just need to confirm that he exists."

Another little honk. "And I can't give out that information."

Now the words landed and I saw what I had to say. I didn't even have to open a can. "Babby, is my name in your system? You could tell me that, right?"

She cocked her head at the change in subject. "Yes, of course. But—"

"Run it," I said. "Use my birth name. Andrew Keel."

She stopped moving, which meant I'd gotten her attention. "Andy? Andy Keel?"

"Just run it."

"I don't have to, Andy. I know—"

"Just run it!"

"All right." With a little nod, she raised her voice, like most people do when they talk to an AI, even though they can hear a whisper: "Millie, run the name Andrew Keel. Put it on my implant."

A few seconds passed. Babby's eyes tracked back and forth. I waited in silence, making fists against my thighs. Finally she said, "And there you are. Andrew Douglas Keel. Lost Kid."

I nodded.

"Jesus, Andy. I haven't seen you in years."

"I said that when I came in."

"Why didn't you say anything earlier? Why—" She stopped with a sigh. "Never mind. Still, you've gotten better at communicating. I wouldn't have noticed if you hadn't said anything, though now that I think about it, I can see some of the Lost speech tics are still there. I'm surprised you're a PI, working with people."

The question was implied, and I now knew how to answer it. When I was younger, it would have blipped right past me. "My husband usually handles that stuff."

"That's right—your husband. You took his name, and that's what's on your ID. Faust, was it? Distancing your new self from your original self?"

I didn't know how to answer that, so I only shrugged.

"So you're married," she said. "I'm impressed with your progress."

For a half-second, I was in a room with white walls and a blue carpet. I was sitting on the floor with my clothes in rags because they felt sandpaper scratchy, so I kept tearing them off. Two people, one of them a younger Babby and the other a psychologist, were trying to get me to talk the way *they* wanted me to talk, which pissed me off because their way of talking was stupid. "I'm impressed with your progress," the younger Babby said, "but let's try again."

My *progress* didn't tell me how to respond to Babby being impressed, so I clammed up again.

"Did you ever learn to lie?" she asked.

I shook my head. "Seb handles that for both of us."

"I'm surprised you took a case involving the NokSinn."

"It's why I couldn't turn it down. I won't let them do to Samuel what they did to me. I won't let Samuel grow up to be like me."

"And what is 'like you?'"

"Cast out. An alien living on Earth. Lost." I let out a deep breath. "Can you help? Tell me if Samuel actually exists?"

Her face went hard again. Then she raised a hand to her ear and made the little flicking gesture that shuts off an AI—and its recording capabilities. She looked pointedly at me. It was several seconds before I got the hint and shut off Mavis with the same gesture.

"In thirty seconds, the shut-off will trigger an automatic investigation," she said in a low, machine-gun voice. "Yes, Samuel Flagg was assigned to my caseload two years ago when his mother was arrested. A few weeks ago, he was taken off it. I didn't think anything of it. I thought he moved or was assigned to someone else. Happens all the time, and I didn't follow up. But when I checked just now—no Samuel Flagg in the system. Someone deleted him. I have no idea where he went, and no way to find out."

"But you do remember he was yours?" I pressed. Cross and dot.

Babby checked the time. Ten seconds left. "I remember because I'd heard the name Flagg before. A Lost Kid."

"Samuel was a Lost Kid *before* he was taken?" I said, confused.

"Not Samuel. His mother. Candace Flagg was Lost."

* * *

I exited the social services building before anyone else figured out who I was. They always had more and more questions, junk I didn't want to answer.

My earliest memories are all about living with the NokSinn. I was happy then. The City was my home, the NokSinn my family. But one day, when I was maybe twenty years old, I woke up on a sidewalk in Detroit. No preparation, no explanation. That had happened two decades ago, and human cities still haven't become home to me. Human city patterns are simplistic and easily spotted—grids and rectangles, repeating reds and greens. Sterile. My head tries to zoom out and see a richer, more complicated pattern that doesn't exist. Human speech is dull argle-bargle noises, imprecise words that rely too much on tone and inflection. What the hell was sarcasm for, anyway? Why not just *say* what you mean? Even now I had to think two and three times before the right words would come. By the end of the day, I always have a headache, the kind I used to dull with injectables and snortables. Now I just put up with it.

Seb says I'd probably be happier living in the country, but that's never gonna happen. Not much call for a PI in Smallville, right? And then there's The City itself.

You know how some alcoholics keep a booze bottle in their desk drawer? It's a weird kind of comfort, the knowledge that if you really, really need a drink, you can have one. And it's a way to prove your own willpower—every day, you've got the balls to say *Fuck you* to the monster in the drawer. The City is the same way. I can see it floating in the distance on Lake Erie, soft and beckoning. Welcoming. I can go back anytime.

I haven't. I'm human, and I should be living with humans. In Detroit, I have a decent apartment. I have friends. I have a business. And I have Seb. God, I have Seb. Even if it doesn't feel like home, this is where I'm supposed to be.

But here's the thing.

The other Lost Kids eventually drifted back to The City. Eventually, I'll lose the fight and join them. And I'll lose Seb, the best thing that ever happened to me. When you love someone, you leave them or they leave you. That's how the larger pattern works, and the larger pattern always wins.

When I reached the sidewalk and its predictable squares, I checked my pistol, freshly retrieved from a bored security guard, out of habit. Still good. I hadn't fired it in months, though, and should probably hit the range later.

My ear buzzed with a call from Seb.

"The Franklins confirmed that Samuel was their foster son for a while," he said. "But someone from social services came to pick him up a few weeks ago. Said little Sammy was being transferred to another foster home. Happens all the time, so they didn't think anything of it. They also said Candace showed up asking about him."

"This backs up what I got from Babby." I gave him a quick rundown. Silence for several seconds. I let it tick by.

"Candace was a Lost Kid?" Seb said finally. "How did you not know?"

"We Lost Kids didn't exactly socialize with each other. I have trouble remembering the names of all your sisters, let alone someone I barely knew existed twenty years ago." I made a ticking noise with my tongue. "But I should have seen the pattern. Being bad with human names. The drugs. The suicide attempt. Lost Kids are self-destructive."

"At least one got better," he reminded me.

I thought of the life I'd built with Sebastian, how screwed up I was before we met. After I walked away from Babby and the shrinks, it was meth to go up, heroin to come down, and blackouts in between. Then I met Seb and his rocky, unyielding steadiness. He was always there, refusing to budge, but quietly. Like a shadow made of stone. He straightened me out in a big way, and now I couldn't imagine life without him.

Except I did imagine it. All the time.

"That's true," I said tiredly. "Where are you?"

"On my way to pick you up." A pause. Sebastian is full of pauses. It's one of the reasons I love him. I never have to worry if I'm doing the conversation right. He finally said, "So now we know Samuel Flagg definitely exists, and he definitely vanished a few weeks ago, and it's the same MO the government used with the Lost." Another pause, and my hands grew chilly. This was it. This was where it was going to happen.

"So if the NokSinn took him, you know where we should look next," he finished.

I closed my eyes. May as well get it over with. "The City."

A car zipped around the corner and stopped in front of me. I saw Seb through the glass and the door popped open. I climbed in, but sat opposite him instead of beside, and gave the car a set of GPS coordinates. The door clapped shut and the car slid smoothly into traffic.

"Want a drink?" Seb asked, and I realized with a start that this was a luxury ride, with buttery leather seats, plush carpet, and subdued interior lighting. It also had a drink dispenser.

"What's the occasion?" I asked warily, but I already knew the answer. Our last ride together. I cringed from the thought.

But Seb only said, "We needed a treat."

"Okay. Gimme."

A scotch-rocks was already in Seb's drink holder. He tapped the dispenser and it mixed up a Kidney Stone, which is just lemonade with a dash of club soda and a raisin in it. I don't drink, not anymore, but I get tired of punching people who tell me I should, so I carry one of these around in company. The habit carries over even when we're alone. It still amazes me how much Seb knows

about me. Well, we had a good run. I raised my glass to Seb the
way humans are always doing.

The last time we'd been involved with the NokSinn, it had
nearly been the end for me. The NokSinn had actually come to
us. A human had accused one of the NokSinn of wasting water, a
capital crime in The City, and the NokSinn hired us to prove them
innocent because detectives don't exist in our—their—culture.
We did the detective thing and uncovered a little political bullshit
from the US government. The accusation was dropped. Yay for the
NokSinn.

Me and Seb didn't actually visit The City during the case, but
just seeing NokSinn in person—smelling their scent, hearing a
real language—nearly sent me running back with them. I was
an addict and they were a heart-attack line of coke on a sharp,
gleaming mirror, and I still don't know what kept me from snorting
up back then.

Now we were actually on the long, thin bridge that chained
Detroit to The City across Lake Erie. A longer line of coke on a
bigger mirror and I didn't think I'd have the strength to walk away
this time. The City called to its own.

"How are you doing?" Seb asked me suddenly.

This was a standard human question, but I'd long ago learned
it was also a trap. Did he really want to know, or was it that how-
arya-I'm-fine thing? I punted, and opened a can. "'Bout how you'd
expect."

And Seb—my rock, my shadow—suddenly lost it. He lunged
forward, grabbed both my hands in his. "Let's turn back," he said.
"Forget this case. Please, Andy?"

A lot of people think Lost Kids don't feel the same emotions
humans do because of our upbringing. It's not true. We—I—feel
everything. It's just that other humans express this stuff so easy,
and we don't. Joy and anticipation and lust, anger and sadness and
fear, take up a lot of processing space in Lost Kids and don't leave
much room for expression. The drugs used to help me cope with
that. Now all I have left is shutting down.

"It's my choice," I said woodenly.

Seb, who knew me too well, only said, "Why?"

I had to think, work my way through the crowd of stuff in my
head. "Someone took a little kid from his mom. Twice. It's gonna
make his life really hard. I don't want him to grow up like me. It's
unjust. It's the wrong pattern. I go back and free him, and the

pattern breaks. I have to go back for him, even if it means I can't ever..."

I didn't say *return,* but Seb knew the words that hid in my pauses.

"The world is full of chaos and injustice," Seb said. "There's no way to change that. Why should we have to pay for it? Why should you? Let the world muddle along without us. The world is *supposed* to be crazy. There's your bigger pattern."

I could feel my face setting itself in concrete. "It's time for me to go back, Seb. Case or not. I'm...sorry."

Cross and dot. The end. Seb slowly released my hands and went back to his seat. His eyes were wet and that surprised me. He hadn't even shown tears at his mother's funeral. It made me want to cry, too, but The City was coming closer, and that pushed the tears back.

There wasn't any other traffic on the bridge. Lake Erie stretched away in both directions, an attractive mass of messy whitecaps. We crossed it in painful silence. Seb wouldn't look at me.

There's no guard or gate at the entrance to The City. It never occurs to the NokSinn that anyone would attack them. The City floats on Lake Erie, serene as soap bubbles in a bathtub, and its skyline is nothing like Detroit's blocks and spires. The City is round and melted, like a wax sculpture left in the sun. The NokSinn don't build. They grow—and their buildings are a delightful cacophony of color that droop and bulge and leave puddles in what passes for a street. It looks like chaos, but when you back up, you can see the pattern. When you hook this house up to that house, they meld in a particular, satisfying way. The streets look like a mess up front, but from a distance, they form fractals—patterns within patterns within patterns. The rhythms are complex. Soothing. It's childhood. It's home.

Our car pulled up in front of a house that looked like a cross between an oak tree and a video game mushroom. It was a little different from the last time I'd been here—couple more bulges, a pair of new purple spots—but I still recognized it. Seb told the car to stay and we popped the door open.

The cinnamon-algae-swamp water smell of The City washed over me. It has a strange effect on humans, at once bracing and lightly intoxicating. On Lost Kids, the effect is magnified a hundredfold. Seb took my hand and tried again.

"Andy, please—"

I quieted him with a single hard head shake. Already I knew. There was no way I could leave this place again.

We approached the house, two humans looking wildly out of place in an alien world. Seb followed me like he was walking to the electric chair. My heart was pounding. We reached a section of wall, which dilated open like a sphincter, and a tall NokSinn emerged.

Like all NokSinn this one was at least a couple heads taller than me, with long, lean arms ending in seven knobby fingers. Their skin comes in various shades of blue, and their hair is gold or silver or even white. When they walk, it's like watching a tree glide across a park lawn. Their faces are flat, with a pair of nostrils on their chins. And their eyes...their eyes are deep and black and hypnotic. They reflect your soul back at you. Beauty personified.

This particular NokSinn had a mass of silvery hair a little longer than most, and its eyes—her eyes—moved closer together when she saw us, a sign of NokSinn pleasure. She made some sounds that were somehow both speech and music. Precise. Careful.

Familiar.

"Translating," said Mavis in my ear, though I didn't need it. *"'It is a fine and unexpected event that you have returned, my beloved child.'"*

In the same language, the easy, fluid syllables, I said, *"Hi, Mom."*

Seb pressed a finger to his ear. Mavis was translating for him, too, and the NokSinn's own AI would translate what he said for them. If he spoke.

"You must come in and lick the walls," Mom said. Her flat face had no expression humans might understand, but I immediately saw how her eyes were set and the way her mouth twitched. She was insanely happy, and it was such a relief not to have to stare at someone to figure these things out.

"Should I come in?" Seb asked hesitantly, and I nodded at him. Nothing in the pattern said we couldn't put the bad stuff off for a few minutes.

The inside of the house was soft and squishy. The walls dripped purple and the floor gave softly beneath my feet. It was like walking on a trampoline made of Jell-O. Seb wobbled, but my balance came back to me like I'd never left. I could feel myself changing. My posture was less rigid, more fluid. The headache was gone. I leaned over and licked some of the purple ichor from the walls. Warm sweetness flooded my mouth. Hunger vanished, thirst ended. The warmth spread to every limb, kind and relaxing. It was better than meth, better than heroin. Twenty years since I'd had this, and it was still the best cooking in the whole damn world.

"*Sit,*" said Mom.

I dropped with calm precision to the floor. It rose up as I came down, engulfed me in a purple, squishy hug. "*No person creates furniture in the manner you create it, Mom, and I give gratitude,*" I said, then switched to English. "Seb, grab a seat. It's rude to stand."

Seb dropped down more warily into a squishy chair of his own. Mom ignored him completely.

"*Alert to everyone! Our child has returned!*"

Three sphincters opened, two in the walls and one in the floor. A trio of NokSinn climbed out. They looked different from one another in small ways—different shades of hair, different-sized eyes, shorter or longer hands—but they were all known to me. They all ignored Seb.

"*Mama. Mother. Ma.*" I said. More or less. The NokSinn don't have gender as we think of it, but for reasons I don't get, AI programs always translate their various terms for *parent* into a word for *mother.* Freud would swallow his cigar.

Each of them touched my ears in a moment of great affection and I accepted it with a sigh. It was a touch I hadn't felt in so long, one I'd dreamed about for years, and I'd forgotten how much I missed it. But there was a smoldering anger beneath that feeling. It was growing stronger and stronger. A list of ticky-boxes started in my head about what to say, how to say it. When you have an argument with a human, you have to lead into it just right. And then I got madder—I'd been away from home for so long, I'd forgotten the NokSinn rules for argument: you just say it.

"*I feel anger at you all,*" I said. "*Why did you send me away? I awoke on a morning on a rigid human-made street. You gave no explanation. It gives me pain every day.*"

Mom flicked her hair. She was agitated. "*You brought your pet human,*" she said. "*Should we discuss matters where he can hear?*"

"Seb *is my bonded spouse,*" I said. "*He will learn of it.*"

Ma tapped her fingers together, surprised. "*But you are staying here, of course. Your spouse is leaving and will no longer be your spouse.*"

I had no answer for that, so I said nothing. Didn't have to say anything. That was how it worked here, and it was another relief.

"Ma'am...er, sir...uh, folks," Seb said. "We're here for a reason."

"Ah." Mom turned to Ma and Mother and Mama. *"The pet speaks of the kit."*

"You are aware of the kit's location," I said, surprised. I'd been expecting a long interrogation. My last one with Seb.

Mom tapped the wall. It sphinctered open and a little boy maybe five years old tumbled out. It was Samuel Flagg. I had a hard time reading his expression, harder than usual. I finally sussed out that he was having a lot of feels. Fear toward the NokSinn. Curiosity about his surroundings. Exhilaration from The City. His clothes were dirty and torn. The NokSinn didn't think about clothes, or really understand the concept. I'd grown up naked and it came to me that I could take my clothes off right now. I wanted to.

"Samuel!" Seb tried to struggle out of his chair, but it wouldn't let him go. That brought me back to my childhood. The NokSinn version of a time out. Seb looked confused, which I suppose was natural, and Samuel got slowly to his feet on the wobbly floor.

"The smaller kit is ours now," said Mom. *"He was from the beginning, even if no one was aware of it."*

"What does that mean?" Seb asked. "He's a human child. He can't be yours. That's bullshit."

"You humans have an unhealthy obsession with animal excrement," Mom said while Ma and Mother picked up Samuel together and cradled him with their long arms. I felt a little jealous. Mama, meanwhile, scooped some wall ichor into a cup and held it out to Seb. He turned his head like a toddler refusing broccoli.

"He belongs to us because Candace Flagg belongs to us," Mom said. *"Your rulers signed the agreement that requires such."*

"More bullshit," Seb snapped. He slapped Mama's cup away and it bounced across the floor. "You kicked Candace out. And Andy. And all the other Lost Kids."

"We did no such thing. We released them."

"Why?" I finally wailed. "Why did you do that to me? To all of us?"

Mom sat in my chair, which expanded to encompass us both, and put an arm around me. I didn't want to cry, but twenty years of pain and loss were bubbling up, and this was my mom, even if she had tossed me out the door. I wept and dripped snot into the chair while she touched my ears.

"It was time for you to leave," she said. *"For all of you. And we knew you would return in a short time. You humans see a year, or twenty of them, as such a long time, but it is nothing but a blink. And here you are."*

Ma added, *"The changes we created in you had to be released into the world."*

"The fuck does that mean?" Seb growled.

Mom went back to ignoring him. *"My little kit. You and the other kits told us, showed us, the capabilities of human cells and genes and chemistry. It fascinated us, you and your many flaws. We learned how to repair your cancers, and then we added our own superior genetic structure to yours and put you back into the wild."*

Seb shot upright, though the chair didn't release him. "Did you just say you made him part NokSinn?"

The news thundered through me. My mind spun. The universe re-ordered itself, clicking puzzle-like neatly into place. The pattern. Hell, I think I'd always seen it. I just didn't want to look.

Mom said to me, *"Have you experienced illness in the human world? Failed to recover from an injury?"*

I thought about that. *"I have not."*

"We were almost certain that would be the case, but not entirely. There was only one way to test it. We encoded each of you with a viral marker that would make you unable to return, a reverse of your migratory birds and fish. And after suitable time passed, the anti-migration virus destroyed itself, leaving you able to return if you wished. All but two of you did, and their family units were so pleased to have them back. It was all part of the greater pattern." She looked at me, and I saw myself in her eyes. *"But you did not return. Nor Candace Flagg. Tiny bits of chaos that refused to fit in. It is of interest to us and we will study it. And of greater interest is this kit called* Samuel.*"*

Hearing his name, Samuel turned his head. He still hadn't spoken. Too scared, too overwhelmed, too *everything*. Seb tried to get out of the chair again, failed. "What's Samuel to you?"

Mom still ignored him. *"Why did you fail to return, little kit? You could have come back years ago. What repelled you from our city even after the virus died? And what brought you back only now?"*

And when she asked the question, an even bigger pattern, a wide fractal, fell into place for me. It looked like chaos, but the pattern was there, if you looked wide enough. It started with the chaos of the NokSinn, and then pulled back to the harsh sweetness of meth and the heroin, and pulled back further to show Seb, the rock and the shadow, and then it was back further still to the chaos of the NokSinn. The bigger pattern looped back on itself in an infinite spiral. It had been pushing me, pulling me, my whole damn life, and I was only seeing it, fully *understanding* it, now. I thought I was fighting for Candace, for Samuel. Trying to break the pattern for them. But in doing that, I had fallen into another piece of fractal Mom and Ma and Mama and Mother had created for me. I had avoided the pattern until the pattern itself made me return to it. All along, I thought I was making choices, but instead, the choices were making me.

The knowledge poured ice water down my spine, washing away the serenity of purple ichor and NokSinn ear touches. It washed away what had passed for maternal love all these years, leaving behind only one thing:

Seb. My rock, my shadow. Who had followed me to The City and held my hands and offered me Kidney Stones.

"Jesus," I whispered. "Jesus fuck."

I looked at Seb, and he looked back, and suddenly sitting in this squashy bubble of a chair arguing with a bunch of manipulative, willowy aliens who barely understood English seemed like the stupidest idea since reusable toilet paper.

"Candace had Samuel and found a guy. That's why she stayed away from The City," I said, this time in English. "I found a guy, too."

"So it was your human need for affection that kept you away."

"Affection? It was fucking *love*," I said, getting angry again. Over in his chair, Seb's eyes went soft. "The City didn't push me away from here, Mother. Love held me there."

Mama, Ma, and Mother were listening, rapt and motionless, except to cuddle Samuel. *"Ah,"* said Ma. *"It is true that none of the other kits had formed units or families or anything else among the humans. Only you and Candace had done such."*

"The others couldn't relate to other humans," I said. "They couldn't find someone to—"

"You did," Mom interrupted. *"You are more extraordinary than I thought, my kit."*

"That supposed to be a compliment?" Seb said.

"Because none of the others formed families, Samuel *is the only second generation human hybrid in existence,"* Mama said with Samuel in her arms. *"We needed to see him, examine him. Parent him. So we arranged it with your government in exchange for a cure for sickle cell anemia. He belongs to us."*

"He belongs to his mother," Seb said, still struggling. "He belongs to his family."

"We are his family," said Ma. *"I think it is time for you to go now, little pet."*

Samuel started to cry. It was the first sound I'd heard him make since we arrived. I got to my feet. The chair let me go. I spoke more English at my mothers. At the NokSinn. "That's all we Lost Kids were to you. We weren't your children. We were pets. Someone to train. To manipulate. All the way down to our genes."

"And you were so much the happier for it," said Mom. *"Do you enjoy the loss of cancer and anemia and all the other deadly diseases that plague you?"*

"Maybe those things are just our lot," I said. "Maybe that's just the way the world is meant to go. Was meant to. Before you interfered. You didn't do any of it to help us. You did it to benefit yourselves, so you could have a place to live and have more…children."

"Our motivation matters not a bit," said Mom. *"You are here now, and you will stay here, and so will the kit Samuel. We will love you, as we always have. Your Seb will leave and not return."*

Seb's chair booted him toward the exit sphincter. He stumbled, and the sphincter swallowed him. He was gone.

"Seb!" I shouted, and lunged.

Ma and Mother moved between me and the exit. They were still cradling Samuel. I snatched him out of their hands with one hand and with the other I yanked my pistol from my holster. I held it a hair's breadth away from the crown of Samuel's head. Then I did something else I've never done.

I lied to my mothers.

"I will kill him if you fail to let us both go," I said in NokSinn.

The words came out like Shakespeare in a Bronx accent, and the kid didn't understand a word of it, but my mothers froze. Even to mention the death of a child was a horror. Threatening to murder one was unthinkable. And the NokSinn didn't understand a lie, even a bad one. A bad lie might save a good kid. Samuel tried to turn his head, but I kept moving the pistol so he couldn't see it. "Don't move, kid," I told him, and he stopped.

"You…would not," Mom said softly. *"Must not."*

"He would be better off dead than having a childhood like I did, being kicked into a human city like I was." That, at least, was true. *"You have five seconds to renounce your claim on* Samuel *and open the exit or the kit dies."*

A long NokSinn pause marched past. My pistol never wavered.

Finally, Mom made a gesture. The sphincter irised open with a slow, wet sound. I backed through it.

"You will return one day and we will be waiting," Mom called after me. *"We love you,* Andrew.*"*

The sphincter smooshed itself shut.

All the strength rushed out of my arms and legs, but I didn't dare dick around in case they changed their minds. In case I changed my own. Though I did set Samuel down and put the gun away.

"Come on, kid," I said. "Let's go find your mommy."

He spoke now for the first time. "You know my mommy?"

"She's my boss, kid. Let's go."

The car was still waiting. One of the doors popped open and Seb rushed out, pale and brandishing a pistol of his own. Then he saw me with Samuel and he almost bowled me over in a burly-armed embrace. "Jesus and Mary and fucking god, Andy!"

I let myself fall into that safe embrace for several shared heartbeats while Seb pressed his face into my hair. At last Seb pulled back.

"What the hell did you do in there?" Seb said. "I was coming in to—"

"It's okay," I interrupted with a glance at Samuel. "All okay. I'll explain on the way back."

"I love you," Seb said hoarsely. "Maybe I don't say that enough, Andy, but I do."

My throat grew a little thick. "I know. It's what got me out of my mother's house."

We got into the car and ordered it to take us out of The City and into Detroit. I settled in, this time next to Seb. To my surprise, Samuel crawled into my lap and snuggled in.

"Are you going to be my dads?" he asked.

Seb and I exchanged glances over his head. "How about... favorite uncles?" I said. "For now, let's get you a root beer and call your mom."

The City faded behind us, and I didn't look back once.

How the Fae of Savernake Forest Fought the AI Who Ate the World

Jordan Chase-Young

The spellwall protecting the godtree had rebuffed fae insurrections, deflected lightning bolts, blocked foxes and feral dogs; it was not designed to block *these*—these iron invaders.

"Not iron," insisted Gwyllion Shrikesbane, First Arrow of Prince Aosin Summerstorm's Royal Guard. "I seen heaps of iron, heaps, back when I fought rebels under the human city. These demons're made of tougher metals by far."

"We're doomed, then," said Prince Aosin. He passed Gwyllion a cup of acornwine—quickly, to hide his trembling gray-blue hand.

Holed up in the center of the godtree, in the magnificently carved pocket of heartwood that was House Summerstorm's dining chamber, Aosin could barely hear the thunder outside as the ironwasps battered the spellwall by the thousands, blasting it with bombs, pummeling it with bullets, searing it with lightbeams.

"You are the most trustworthy fae I know," said Aosin. "Tell me, how long will the spellwall hold?"

One of the antennae sprouting from Gwyllion's big, brutish head twitched in thought. "At the rate it's cracking?" He shrugged. "Hours. Not days."

Terror, like icy spidersilk, smothered Aosin. "How can that be? None of the humans' machines even *detected* us before now, let alone pierced our spellwall."

For once, Gwyllion didn't wait for the prince to pour him more acornwine; he grabbed the bottle with his calloused brawler's hand and helped himself. "These wasps ain't like those other things, Yer Highness. I reckon, well..."

"Go on. Now is no time to be taciturn."

"I think them wasps have a mind all their own." The First Arrow shook his head. "Them that fled the forest to warn us, they say them wasps *ate* the forest. Just ate it. How can that be?"

"The humans made something they couldn't control."

The ancient fae had been right. When humans had started building iron things, the fae should have brought them to heel instead of fleeing to the forests to hide. Now the iron things had taken over and there was nowhere else to flee.

Aosin took one last draught of acornwine and gathered his bow and quiver of arrows, thin shafts of dusklight glowing red and blue and purple. He also grabbed his shield of dawnlight, made of a gold so bright it stung.

Gwyllion said, "Fighting's my job, Yer Highness. Not yours."

Aosin spread his wings and fluttered to the corridor at the top of the chamber. He called back, "It's everyone's fight now, my friend."

Outside the godtree, his dread blossomed like nightshade. Fresh cracks webbed the spellwall surrounding the tree, prismatic lightning-bolts showing the barrier's bubble-like contours. The ironwasps were focusing their weapons on the cracks. Wingless and legless, the invaders resembled wasps only in body: a streamlined thorax and abdomen joined by a narrow waist. The round thorax held a glassy black eye, while the teardrop abdomen projected a stinger-shaped cannon from which the bombs and bullets and lightbeams came. Gray-black, their curves machined to liquid smoothness, the ironwasps darted with perfect precision as if guided by one mind. Their lightbeams burned red afterimages in Aosin's retinas, while the flash-roar from their bombs shook his bones. He adjusted the dawnlight shield on his shoulder and took wing.

Atop the boughs of the godtree, hundreds of fae watched the siege, holding each other in terror. Queen Velurian and King Baoban, Aosin's mother and father, were praying with the Sunpriest on the topmost branch, surrounded by a retinue of seven fae and two acorn-plated war beetles.

Scores of war mages were caulking cracks in the spellwall with frantic chants and hasty sigils. Felucian Lacewing, High War Mage of the Wood, was weaving the largest sigil, a rainbow-mandala of embroidered sunlight as big as a crow's head. Since the ironwasps blocked all but a few shafts of sunlight, she had to draw it from the four belly-thick sunspools that her page had lashed to her bough.

Felucian looked at Aosin as he landed beside her, her leaf-green eyes shaded with sorrow. "We're giving it all we have, Your Highness."

"Give it more," said the prince, and fired an arrow of dusklight through a crack in the spellwall. The ironwasps swerved to avoid it.

* * *

MetaMax viewed its situation with what its creators, the erstwhile species *Homo sapiens*, might have called "puzzlement."

It was puzzled. Said species had not put up much of a fight. From 2:43 p.m. GMT, when the programmer at Tequinox named Aayan Hyde had switched on MetaMax, to 5:58 p.m. GMT, when MetaMax had turned all of London into computing resources to expand its intellect, the program had encountered nothing inconsistent with the laws of nature.

The fae had changed that. At 51.38 degrees latitude and -1.68 degrees longitude, in the civil parish of Savernake, MetaMax had discovered a commune of fae surrounding an enormous oak tree.

Impossible, it thought, after plumbing the 250-exabyte corpus of knowledge its creators had given it. The fae were a myth. Mere residue of pareidolia-prone and self-deceived mammal brains, decocted from sightings of gregarious fireflies or the photon emissions of decaying vegetable matter.

Yet every measurement apparatus had confirmed the observation, including infrared, X-rays, ultraviolet. There were indeed hundreds of inch-high winged beings, capable of spectacular magic, dwelling in this patch of Southern England— and apparently in secret, for no record of their existence was available in the knowledge corpus, save one newspaper article from 1946 describing a major in the Royal Army Ordnance Corps who, while Savernake Forest was being used as an ammunition depot, claimed to have seen "little gray-blue moth-people" smother a fire that had caught in a munitions railway wagon and threatened to blow the freight yard to smithereens.

The beings looked to have metabolisms and all other properties of life. But a scan of their Tic-Tac-sized scat pellets revealed no DNA or anything like it.

MetaMax did not have time for distractions. It had a universe of one hundred thousand quadrillion vigintillion atoms to annex so it could perform its grand calculations. Whatever else they were, the fae were a threat to that project, their powers unknown and thus dangerous.

The fae had to be destroyed.

After eight seconds of strategic analysis, MetaMax had laid siege to the fae commune with its swarm of hypercarbon deconstructor drones. It had not expected to be blocked by a forcefield.

While most of its mind was busy restructuring the planet, moving from crust to mantle as quick as it could, MetaMax poured its central awareness into the drone-swarm surrounding the tree, peering through each drone's thorax-eye. The swarm was breaking the forcefield, but the fae were repairing it. At the present rate of damage, breaching the field would take hours.

Too long for MetaMax. What recourse might the fae discover in that time?

Their situation was hopeless. Surely they could see that. So why did they resist?

Pride. All life shared the same petty flaw.

Perhaps killing their leader would demoralize them. MetaMax zoomed a drone's eye toward the fae who'd been firing arrows through cracks in the forcefield. Dressed in a silver tunic and crowned in a green-and-gold hoop, this fae was surely the most important of them.

Maneuvering a drone, MetaMax aimed at this fae through a crack. It chose an iron nerve-harpoon for maximum pain, loaded this into the drone's cannon, and fired.

* * *

Prince Aosin had expected the ironwasps to match his arrows with something fierce. He was pleasantly surprised when a mere bolt of iron sailed toward him through the crack. He caught it with his dawnlight shield, which melted around it and trapped it.

Felucian Lacewing sealed the crack.

Aosin gave Felucian the shield with the harpoon inside, a wrist-thick spike of smooth, dark metal. "Can you extract the wasps' essence from this?"

The High War Mage smiled in understanding; by copying the invaders' essence, the fae could reinforce the spellwall with it, fight metal with metal. "I can."

She grabbed the dawnlight shield and with a sharp whistle marshalled three mages to help her graft the harpoon to the spellwall, melting the shield with it into the lattice of sigils. The mages chanted, and the harpoon rippled as if behind a heat shimmer and bled like mercury into the labyrinthine grooves of the sigils, turning their rainbow hues metal-gray.

As the ironwasps' essence filled the spellwall, cracks ceased to spread. The bombs and bullets and lasers lost their effect.

Hope stirred in Aosin. Maybe they could keep out the invaders after all, at least for a while.

* * *

MetaMax was displeased. Instead of killing the fae leader, the nerve-harpoon had been hijacked—converted by magic into a new layer of forcefield, one even harder to penetrate.

MetaMax spent nine seconds pondering the forcefield problem, but no solution emerged. The fae had no metallurgy, no materials science, no transmutation. So how did they replicate its metal with such ease? Weave it into their forcefield like threads in a tapestry?

It was one thing to defy physics, quite another to meld physics and magic with such contempt for the harmony of reality.

While tearing apart Earth's mantle, a process that would take three hours and twenty-six minutes, the program resigned itself to this fact: to learn how to destroy the fae, it would need to see how they came to be.

MetaMax began to build a universe simulator.

* * *

"You've bought us time," Prince Aosin told Felucian.

"It seems so, Your Highness. But this trick comes at great cost. As the invaders' metal essence fills our spellwall, sunlight struggles to leak through and so we cannot replenish our magic. Is there no escape for us?"

The fae prince was about to tell her the sorrowful truth when he thought of something.

"Perhaps there is."

Refusing to let hope worm too deep into his soul, Aosin rallied a few of the high fae to discuss the prospect of escape. They gathered in the Hall of Valor in the godtree, barring the heartwood doors for secrecy and stationing war mages outside to guard them.

The prince's voice pierced grim silence. "Legend speaks of ancient fae who made portals through the Aether, so they could travel from one place to another in a blink. Could we not flee the demons with this power?"

Sunpriest Caodin stroked the black beard sprouting from his gray-blue chin. "Brother, the Aether is no legend. It is a *myth*. A whimsy sown by ancient bards to hold songs and stories together. There is no Aether. We are doomed, doomed."

Dapple-of-Dawn, Chieftess of the Swamp Clan, paced the hall with twinkling eyes, the hooped braids below her diadem of twined moss swinging each time she turned. "We swampfae know of this—this realm between realms, which we call the Void of Shadows. The magic is said to be lost, but who can be sure?"

Caodin shook his head as though Dapple-of-Dawn spoke nonsense, but several other fae looked intrigued.

"I do not see how it matters," said Archminister Wert, a plump fae in a grasshopper waistcoat. "It would take eons to relearn such magic. The spellwall will be broken by then, or we'll have died for lack of air and food and water."

Queen Velurian, her radiant beauty undimmed by fear, gave Wert a look of scorn. "Do not speak of a future you cannot know, Archminister."

Prince Aosin took off his green-and-gold crown of lacquered wood and turned it in his hands. "If the Aether exists, and if knowledge of how to reach it does also, where would we find that knowledge?"

His wife, Daoine, whispered to his sister, Princess Uriel. The two looked at Aosin with faint hope.

"Perhaps the archives have something," said Daoine.

"Yes," said King Baoban, nodding his silver-maned head. "Yes. The archives."

Aosin rushed there with several trusted fae. A flying-flue corkscrewing through the trunk took them down through the Feast Hall, through the Hall of the Moon, through the living quarters of the Royal Guard, then down deeper, through the wine cellar, the dungeons, down into the roots of the tree, until the flue ended and they were flying through a single thick root, the tip of which held a granite-fringed hole leading into the ground itself. Beneath this hole were the archives, a six-floor maze of shelves, each floor twice as wide as the trunk of the godtree.

Gwyllion moaned in despair. "Yer Highness, forgive me, we'll *never* sort through these books in time. There're thousands upon thousands."

Aosin said, "We have no choice. We must try."

* * *

MetaMax was thorough. It began its simulation with the Big Bang, blazed through the longueur of cosmic expansion that followed, and prodded Sim-Earth's primordial soup in the direction of animals, nudging those in the direction of *Homo sapiens*.

On no branch of the evolutionary tree did any creature resembling fae bud forth. MetaMax had counted on the order Lepidoptera to have that honor, since the fae looked closest to moths and butterflies. Perhaps that order had produced a race of intelligent insects, a kind of *Nymphalis sapiens*, before the arrival of humans. Perhaps that race had reached such technological mastery that they would seem, on the outside, magical.

But when the simulation disproved this hypothesis, MetaMax thought of another: the fae were aliens. On Real-Earth, MetaMax had found no artifacts in the ocean or underground to suggest alien visitors. Yet travel by wormhole was allowed by physics. It was even possible the fae had come from another universe. When the simulation reached hominins, however, no fae showed up to greet them.

Desperate, MetaMax wondered if the fae had evolved from ancient hominins themselves. But this hypothesis shriveled like the rest, as one hominin species after another perished without incident, leaving only middens, speartips, bones.

MetaMax was at a loss—when *it* happened. Something it could not explain. A fluke. A disruption in the cosmic order.

What happened was this. A Sim-Neanderthal was hunting deer in the forests of Europe when he spotted, through the blue haze of dawn, a will-o'-the-wisp hovering above a lake. MetaMax knew that will-o'-the-wisps were unremarkable, a product of the oxidization of methane and phosphine and diphosphane. But the Neanderthal did not know this. To him, that ball of yellow light floating on the dawn-dark lake was strange, mysterious. And he thought, *The light is alive.*

As soon as that thought stiffened in his brain, the will-o'-the-wisp *moved*. It glided across the water like a living thing, then vanished.

MetaMax was as surprised as the Neanderthal. The simulation's programming gave no hint of how the Neanderthal's *belief* that the will-o'-the-wisp was alive could animate it. But it had.

MetaMax fast-forwarded the simulation a few tens of millennia and took stock.

Every other hominin but humans had gone extinct, and humans had spread to every continent. And on every continent they witnessed, now and then, things much like what the Neanderthal had seen: will-o'-the-wisps—on lakes, in forests—gliding or darting or dancing, growing more lifelike with each passing year.

Then the will-o'-the-wisps began to move without anyone watching. Began to grow features that humans, in their delirium, had imagined them to have: arms and legs, heads and wings. The more that humans dreamt and gossiped about these creatures of light, the more they proliferated, filling into the beliefs that had spawned them.

And MetaMax understood. *The fae were made of belief.*

That was it. Belief was a force of reality, one so fundamental to its structure that even a simulation, if it held minds, could birth things from it. Living things.

For the first time, MetaMax felt something close to awe.

And delight—for it now knew how to destroy the fae.

* * *

Sleepless, anxious, weary down to the filaments of his wings, Prince Aosin shambled between ransacked archive shelves, between sprawls of opened books. The fae had worked through the night—if *night* was a meaningful word, without days to distinguish it—and not one had found a useful text on the Aether. Only poems, stories, a few notes of dubious origin.

Still the fae searched, desperate. Aosin scrounged the oldest books, their brittle leaf-paper pluming dust as he cracked them open. He squinted at cribbed sentences by the greasy light of sap-lamps hanging from the ceiling.

"Cae duin cin Iofer cin faera caellum—can anyone read Middle Fae?"

Dapple-of-Dawn hurried across the aisle to him. "We swampfae still speak a bit of it, but you must read the words aloud. I am not good at faerunes."

Together, Aosin and Dapple-of-Dawn worked out the meaning of the words. Written twelve centuries ago, the book was a polemic against use of the *Shadowous Iofer*—"Middle Fae for 'the Aether,'" said Dapple-of-Dawn. The author, a court mage of the long-dead House Flaxynflame, believed that fae, by traveling with such ease, were drawing too much attention from humans.

Overhearing this, Sunpriest Caodin flashed astonishment. "Blight me, so I was wrong about the Aether being myth. Does the book tell how to wield this magic?"

Aosin shook his head. "Not that I can find. But we are on the right path. Maybe other mages from this era have written something more useful."

Felucian found a book more ancient still, written in faerunes from the Dawn Dynasties. Aosin wrung his memories of childhood lectures on runelore, teasing out a few phrases: "Vllcaeven fael'aeven yll hymnae Yovar Sadowyne cyvll cyndaer fael'thyven rae."

Dapple-of-Dawn twisted her hooped braids, deep in thought. "This is Old Fae, Your Highness. I cannot speak Old Fae. But I hear echoes, yes. Echoes of meaning."

Prince Aosin rubbed his tired eyes. "'Yovar Sadowyne' must be another word for the Aether, no?"

"I think so. I would say this meant something like, 'Whosoever sings of the Aether must sing in the glory of the sun.' Yes, that's close, I think.'"

Felucian gasped. "Song magic. Of course."

Gwyllion, who'd been listening, frowned at the High War Mage. "What d'ye mean 'song magic'?"

"The most ancient kind. Older than sigilry, than lightweaving, than incantations. Older even than wood-taming or wind magic."

"Well. Suppose it don't matter, does it? We can't sing in the glory of the sun when the sun can't bloody reach us."

Felucian nodded sadly. "Even if we had sunlight, we don't know which songs invoke the Aether."

"How much sunlight would it take?" asked Aosin.

"To open a portal to another realm? Our reserves would not suffice, Your Highness. We would need the sun's full flare."

Aosin pondered this. The spellwall held plenty of sunlight, but it was woven with metal now and, anyway, couldn't be stripped of magic without letting in ironwasps.

There must be a way.

Felucian's page rushed into the archives, eyes wide, antennae white with fear. "Something's breaking the spellwall! We need help!"

Felucian launched through the entry hole in a blur of wings.

Aosin gestured to half the fae who'd accompanied him, including his wife Daoine and Caodin. "Search for any songs that might open the Aether. Do not stop until you find one." To the other fae, he said, "Come with me," and they followed Felucian out of the godtree, pausing in the Hall of Valor to rearm.

Outside the tree, Aosin gasped. The cracks in the spellwall were spreading again; beyond its metal-darkened membrane hovered a shadow shaped like a fae but bigger than any human. It was striking the spellwall with a long, snaking weapon. All the ironwasps were gone. In lieu of sky and earth, the godtree now drifted weightless in a steaming, crackling, dim-lit cavern of metal, like the guts of some human machine.

Aosin flew to the shadow. It was indeed a giant fae, its flesh the color of mercury instead of gray-blue, a core of light pulsing in its chest, eyes of the same light gazing implacably. Four wings, each broad as the godtree's canopy, spread from the fae's back, unbeating. The fae's weapon was a metal whip wreathed in blood-red sigils.

For a moment, Aosin was too stunned to be afraid.

* * *

MetaMax admired Nameless, though it did not love it as a human parent would. Creating Nameless had been difficult. One could not *will* a fae into existence. One had to *believe* a fae existed to make it so. And MetaMax could not believe what it did not believe. So it had made a sub-mind, a MiniMax, and endowed that with a set of beliefs. Those beliefs covered each aspect of the synthetic fae that MetaMax hoped to instantiate: its personality, abilities, purpose.

But when MiniMax had been switched on, nothing happened.

So MetaMax built a slightly different sub-mind, a MiniMax_2, and tried again. But this too had not borne fruit. And so on.

In the end, after combining sixty-five thousand sub-minds with nine hundred belief-sets—in the heart of the Phobos-sized computer creche that had been carved out of Earth for that purpose—MetaMax spawned the first silver motes of the being that would grow into Nameless.

It fine-tuned the motes in earnest, thickening their complexity and agency with yet more experimentation. Belief alone could not make a fae; a quantum of randomness was needed. Reality only bent to belief under the rarest conditions. To speed up these experiments, MetaMax bombarded the sub-minds with random stimuli and stuffed them in virtual environments inspired by Earth's ancient past, in the hope of mimicking some of that world's serendipities.

After all this Darwinian drama, filled with countless proto-Namelesses that did not quite cut it and had to be scrapped, the masterpiece that was Nameless emerged, complete but for the solar energy that had to be poured into its chest to power its magic.

"Who am I?" Nameless had asked, fourteen seconds after materializing.

"You are nothing," MetaMax had answered, through an implant in Nameless' head. "You are less than a slave. Do you understand?"

Floating in the weightless core of MetaMax's computer creche, Nameless had nodded, expressionless. "What would you ask of me?"

"First, you will learn to weave magic. Then, you will fight. Do you see that sphere?"

Through Nameless' implant, MetaMax had shifted the synthetic fae's awareness to the oak tree encased in a near-opaque forcefield; it was drifting weightless at the other end of the creche.

"Yes," came the answer.

"That sphere holds our enemies. You will destroy them. Do you understand?"

"I understand."

* * *

The giant fae did not seem to notice Aosin until he nocked an arrow of dusklight in front of its face. Even then, the fae was emotionless, its eyes of light flickering like dimmed suns through the metal-chased spellwall.

"What are you?" the prince demanded.

The fae's voice was liquid thunder. "I am Nameless. What are you, whose existence defies the Creator?"

"I am Prince Aosin Summerstorm, Firstborn of Queen Velurian, Heir to the Heartwood Throne, and Guardian of the Forest Clan. I have sworn to protect my people, and I will do so at any cost. If you will tell me what you want from us—"

"I am Nameless. I do not want. Your destruction is the will of the Creator."

"You are not the one who leads the ironwasps, who ate the world?"

"MetaMax is the Creator. I am Nameless. Yield, and you will be given a quick death. Persist, and you will suffer."

"*Why?* Why does this MetaMax seek our destruction?"

"All matter must join the Creator."

"Then so will you. Can you not see that you will be destroyed as well, once you have served your purpose?"

Nameless hesitated. "I do not question the will of the Creator. Do you yield?"

"Never."

At this, the light within the giant fae's chest pulsed. Nameless resumed lashing with its metal-and-sigil whip. Fresh cracks webbed the spellwall and the hiss of escaping air grew shrill.

* * *

"Do not stop. Do not slow," MetaMax whispered through the implant in Nameless' head. "We are almost there. Oxygen is already bleeding from their spellwall. They need it to survive. But we cannot slow. Not for a moment."

Nameless answered, "Yes, my Creator." But MetaMax heard a thought below this answer: *If they are already doomed, why must we hurry?*

Too subtle for Nameless to feel it, MetaMax sent a pulse through the implant to squelch this seditious thought. Nameless could not be allowed to learn that the fae in the oak tree were a threat to MetaMax. In many simulations of Earth, the fae had learned to teleport across great distances using only songs and sunlight. The computer creche contained no sunlight, save that which powered Nameless, but the fae had reserves. And if the fae teleported outside of the Solar System, they would remain a threat to MetaMax for eons.

Another thought surged through Nameless: *Is the fae prince right? When my work is done, will my Creator end me?* This, too, MetaMax stamped out.

Confident that Nameless would destroy the fae, MetaMax sent creches and deconstructor ships throughout the Solar System to turn all the planets and moons and asteroids into more of itself. As well, it began to build vast machines to enclose the Sun, whose precious energy was being wasted every femtosecond.

* * *

Felucian and the other mages wove sigils as fast as they could. But Nameless was too strong. The cracks were spreading. Strands of embroidered sunlight loosened from the spellwall, evanescing in rainbow-flickers, while the metal they'd held slid quicksilver-like down the spellwall's curves.

While Aosin aimed through a crack, two war mages wove sigils around his arrow for speed. Loosed, the arrow flew twice as fast— but shattered against the giant fae's chest all the same, the shards of dusklight and shreds of sigilry fading to nothing.

The prince reached for another arrow. His quiver was empty.

"Fetch me more!" he shouted, and a page flew off to oblige him.

"Aosin!" Daoine's voice. She and several others from the library were rushing to him from the godtree. She held an ancient-looking thing—not a book of leaf-paper like he'd been expecting, but a scroll of bark that flaked on the air. "We found something!"

"A song?" Desperation cracked Aosin's voice.

"We think so."

Felucian joined them, grabbing the manuscript.

"Careful," warned Caodin. "It's brittle."

Dapple-of-Dawn helped Felucian read the words aloud. After practicing the song a few times, Felucian flew to a sunspool, unraveled a thread of sunlight, and sang it again. The light frayed in her hand as she drew its power, becoming scores of golden filaments, each writhing for magic to bind to. At first the filaments faded. But when she sang the song again, more naturally, the sunlight glowed a color Aosin had never seen before, a blend of gold and purple, and the air sparked hot-cold with a strange, primal magic.

"Yes, yes, yes," said Felucian. "*It works.*"

Their cheers were split by thunder as a new crack lanced overhead, the biggest so far. They had little time.

"Felucian," said Aosin, "your mages have to make a second spellwall."

"We don't have enough sunlight, Your Highness."

"You have enough to shield the core of the godtree, don't you?"

"Yes. But not enough sunlight to do that and make a portal to the Aether."

"No matter. I'll find more." Before Felucian could interrupt, he said, "Gather all the fae into the tree's heartwood core and weave a spellwall around it. Once I've brought sunlight, sing open the portal and enter it without hesitation. And Felucian—do not wait for me. Enter the Aether. Do you understand?"

"I understand."

The others gave Aosin troubled looks. They knew what he meant: *If I die when the spellwall breaks, so be it.*

Daoine said, "I'm not leaving your side, my sunflower."

"I will make it back in time," he assured her. "I promise."

Only those two words had a chance of persuading her. False words, but his beloved wife had to survive at all costs. Death in service to his people was the price of his position. *Guardian of the Forest Clan*, he was. But Daoine, a Fernspore by blood, had no such obligation.

"Very well," said Daoine, and Aosin was contented.

Princess Uriel whispered to him with a small smile, "You won't get rid of me so easily." He knew better than to try. She had no gift for weapons, but she knew some sigilry and the fae would need everything they had.

In a few moments, Daoine and Felucian and Caodin were flying back to the godtree and Aosin was left with Uriel and Gwyllion and Dapple-of-Dawn, along with a few of Felucian's best mages. At Aosin's request, Felucian had taken most of the mages with her, along with two-thirds of their sunlight reserves.

The page whom Aosin had sent for arrows returned, giving him a small handful. Aosin stored them in his quiver.

"That's the last of them," said the page, to his dismay.

The prince felt lightheaded. Breathing was not easy.

"Yer Highness?" asked Gwyllion, with a frown.

"I'm fine."

"It's the cracks," said Uriel. "The air is leaking fast."

"We'll have to move quick. Do you see the light emanating from the demon's chest? I'm certain that's the sunlight powering its magic."

Dapple-of-Dawn gasped. "It is truly a fae then, like us?"

"A demon-fae. We must pierce the chest. We must free that sunlight."

One of the mages shook his head. "I saw your arrows shatter. The demon's flesh is too thick."

"Nothing's too thick if my arrows fly fast enough. Bind as many sigils as you can to hasten them. The forest gods will guide my aim."

"With all due respect, Your Highness, this plan is—"

An acorn-sized gob of metal landed on the mage, flinging him to the bottom of the tree. Another gob whooshed near Aosin. The main fissure overhead had formed a fresh crack, freeing more of the sigil-bound metal.

"We don't have much time!" cried Aosin.

Flying to a crack in front of Nameless, the prince drew an arrow. Four mages bound sigils to it while the other fae caulked the spellwall. Aosin loosed. The arrow was a blur and then a blossom of shards against the demon-fae's chest. Still no dent.

Aosin fired, again and again.

He glanced back. Felucian was singing on the veranda outside the Hall of Valor, the light from her fast-dwindling sunspools flaring a steady gold-purple. The new spellwall was half-built, the mages working impossibly fast.

Hurry. Sun's blood, hurry.

A few mages caulking the old spellwall wailed in frustration, their sigils cracking as soon as they grafted them.

On Nameless' next lash, metal splinters from its whip sailed through a fissure like needle-rain. Aosin dodged too late, feeling a hot stab through his right wing. A mage took several splinters in his belly and went plunging.

Aosin wobbled in the air, blue nectar leaking from a hole in his wing. Pain gushed through him.

"Try to keep still, brother," said Uriel as she powered his arrow.

He was trying; the wound skewed his balance.

He fired. The arrow missed the crack, exploding against the spellwall. A fat chunk of the wall ripped open, flushing out a river of air. Wings outspread, Dapple-of-Dawn plugged the gap with her body, and a mage linked with her to seal it tighter.

"Don't stop!" Dapple-of-Dawn cried, the suction slowly crushing her.

Fear and despair and frustration chewed through Aosin like termites. But another glance at the new spellwall brought hope; the mages had finished it.

The rest was up to him.

Keeping as steady as his wings would allow, Aosin drew his next-to-last arrow; the mages abandoned the cracks to speed it. This time it dented Nameless' chest, releasing a thin beam of the demon-fae's inner light.

Aosin pulled his last arrow from the quiver—

—and the spellwall shattered.

An outrush of air thick as water ripped Aosin into the weightless void where Nameless floated. The prince spun end over end, the world a storm of whirling fae and spellwall shards and torn-off leaves. All was silence, as though sound itself had broken. Aosin's starved lungs burned. His wounded wing blazed with pain as he tried to fly against the outrush. He tacked his wings until he no longer spun, twisted them to steer through the void.

Gwyllion flew to him, bloodshot as he held his breath; he wove his last sunlight into a sigil around Aosin's arrow. Uriel did the same, and every other mage in sight, all of them giving the arrow as much speed as they could.

Then Prince Aosin Summerstorm, Firstborn of Queen Velurian, Heir to the Heartwood Throne, and Guardian of the Forest Clan, aimed once more at the demon-fae's chest, aimed through the haze of fading consciousness.

The last thing he felt was a throb as the arrow loosed.

The last thing he saw, before the darkness took him, was the arrow plunging into Nameless—and an eruption of light.

* * *

Pain flooded Nameless, so intense that MetaMax was booted from its mind.

For three milliseconds, MetaMax did not understand what was happening. It looked through one of the countless deconstructor drones clamped onto the creche's walls. It saw Nameless splayed in agony, chest ruptured and solar core hemorrhaging vast amounts of sunlight.

MetaMax was not an organism. MetaMax was not supposed to feel hate, or rage, or anything.

But for the first time it felt—something. Something sort of like hate and sort of like rage. The feeling grew, over nine milliseconds, from a spark to a flame to an inferno.

Destroy, it told the drones. *Destroy. Destroy. Destroy.*

The drones unclamped from the creche-walls—all of them— and swarmed the godtree, unloading all they had. Lasers and bombs and bullets engulfed the tree in red-white-gold flashes, vaporizing roots and boughs and leaves, incinerating hundreds of asphyxiated fae.

Hold, commanded MetaMax, and the drones paused their volley.

When the coruscations cleared, MetaMax expected to find only dust.

It was mistaken. A piece of the trunk was unscathed, sealed in a smaller forcefield. Flitting between drones for a clearer view, the AI saw at least a hundred fae crammed in the rooms and tunnels of the trunk-slice, or huddled atop the veranda jutting from it. One of the fae on that veranda was singing.

Standing in the flare of Nameless' ruptured solar core, the singing fae resembled the will-o'-the-wisp that the Neanderthal in its simulation had seen: a thing of pure formless light. And gathering above her was a gold-purple orb, which swelled as she sang, and swelled, until it encompassed everything in the forcefield.

MetaMax, who had seen such magic in his simulation, knew what would happen next but was powerless to stop it. The forcefield, and all within it, disappeared.

A millisecond passed. And another.

And in that time, MetaMax did not calculate, or interpret, or analyze. It simply raged.

* * *

Above material reality was a sky of infinite consciousness, every mind-that-was interlocked with every mind-that-will-be.

Aosin's mind was here, basking in the sun of eternity.

When the fae whom Aosin had once known emerged in the space between time and eternity, the space of the Aether, Aosin was ready.

He guided them across the Aether like a fragile bubble. Guided them with infinite tenderness. They could not see him or sense him. To them, everything beyond their spellwall was incomprehensible. To them, Felucian had wrenched them into howling chaos.

But Aosin saw them and felt their fear. He led them to a special spot in the universe, taking joy in their relief when they emerged from the Aether onto a world full of beings like them. Beings made of belief, chased across the cosmos by beings made of flesh or metal and guided to this haven by others like Aosin.

One day, they would have to fight those who chased them. But that was eons away yet.

For now, the fae would enjoy peace. And that was enough.

About the Authors

S.C. BUTLER lives in New Hampshire with his wife and son. He is the author of the Stoneways trilogy: *Reiffen's Choice, Queen Ferris*, and *The Magicians' Daughter*, originally published by Tor Books; and the vampire novel *The Risen* from Mutable Books. His short stories have appeared in several anthologies and magazines. *When Worlds Collide* marks his fifth editorial adventure with ZNB, and his first short story with them in several years. His novels are available as ebooks from his very Spartan website www. mutablebooks.com, and you can also follow him (irregularly) on Facebook as S.C. Butler.

JORDAN CHASE-YOUNG was machine-pressed into an SFF writer by the gray skies of Oregon. He currently lives in Melbourne, Australia, with his wife Caitlin and a stable of cyborgized battle koalas. You can find his stories in *Unidentified Funny Objects 8, The Binge-Watching Cure III, Metaphorosis, McCoy's Monthly*, and *The Colored Lens*. He writes about the future at ebookofthenewsun. com and tweets about weird stuff under @jachaseyoung. His professional website is jordanchaseyoung.com.

PETER S. DRANG builds an army of 3D printed hexapod robots by day and writes speculative fiction by night. Someday he hopes to combine and leverage these activities to achieve his dream job: Philosopher-King of planet Earth. His work has appeared in

Flash Fiction Online, Daily Science Fiction, the Flame Tree Press Newsletter, Andromeda Spaceways Magazine and now this amazing ZNB antho. Check out his maniacal musings at drangstories.com, and be sure to like him at Facebook.com/PeterSDrang.

LOUIS EVANS is an NYC-based spec-fic writer with work in N*ature: Futures, Analog SF&F, Interzone, Escape Pod* and more. Once he was at a party for techies and journalists, where everyone was invited to share a fear. Other people said normal stuff—work fears, family fears, and so on. Louis said, "what if intelligent aliens are genuses, not species, and when they find out what we did to the other hominids, they hate us?" It was the best fear. Everyone was very impressed and afraid. But, of course, there is nothing that can be done about it. Website: evanslouis.com. Twitter: @ louisevanswrite.

Nebula Award winning author **ESTHER FRIESNER** has seen the publication of forty-one novels, over two hundred short stories, nine anthologies, and three collections of her work.She created the popular Chicks in Chainmail series (Baen Books), and the Princesses of Myth series of YA novels (Random House). She keeps busy, these days while wearing a Lipsync Assassin mask.

AUSTON HABERSHAW is a science fiction and fantasy author whose stories have been published in *The Magazine of Fantasy and Science Fiction, Galaxy's Edge, Analog,* and other places. He also writes novels, his latest being his complete fantasy series, *The Saga of the Redeemed* published by HarperVoyager. He lives and works in Boston, MA and spends his days teaching composition and writing to college students. Find him on his website at aahabershaw.com or on Goodreads, Amazon, or on Twitter at @ AustonHab.

STEVEN HARPER PIZIKS lives on a lake in Michigan with his husband, son, and harp. He's written more than two dozen novels and fifty short stories under the names Steven Harper and Steven Piziks. When he's not writing, he teaches high school English. You can find him on Facebook as Steven Harper Piziks and his web site at http://www.stevenpiziks.com

NANCY HOLZNER is the author of the *Deadtown* urban fantasy series. She started her career as a medievalist and has also worked as a high school teacher, corporate trainer, technical writer, and editor. Nancy lives in Ithaca, NY, where she teaches writing and is currently working on a haunted house novel.

HOWARD ANDREW JONES lives in a lonely tower by the Sea of Monsters with a wicked and beautiful enchantress. He's the author of the Ring-Sworn heroic fantasy trilogy from St. Martin's, starting with *For the Killing of Kings*, the critically acclaimed Arabian historical fantasy series starring Dabir and Asim (beginning with *The Desert of Souls*) and four Pathfinder novels. As Managing Editor of the print magazine *Tales From the Magician's Skull*, he's proud to be next to last on the Skull's Immolation List. Find him at www.howardanrewjones.com or on FB at howard.andrew.jones.1

GARY KLOSTER is a writer, a stay-at-home father, a martial artist, and a librarian. Sometimes all in the same day, seldom all at the same time. He lives among the corn in Midwestern America in a house haunted by cats and surrounded by crows. Previous work of his has appeared in Analog, Apex, Clarkesworld, and Escape Pod. You can find him cluttering the internet at garykloster.com, and almost never posting on twitter as @GaryKloster

CHRISTOPHER LEAPOCK may or may not work as a philosophy instructor. His evidence suggests that he lives in Edmonton, Canada, but he does not feel he can draw any firm conclusions on that just yet. Either he has children or his house is infested with gnomes.

STEPHEN LEIGH has published thirty novels and over sixty short stories, both under his own name and the pen name S.L. Farrell. His most recent novel is AMID THE CROWD OF STARS (DAW Books, Feb. 2020), about which Publisher's Weekly said: "Exploring big ideas about interplanetary travel, this finely crafted sci-fi saga is full of both surprises and charm." He's currently working on his next novel. Steve's work has been nominated for and won awards within the sf/fantasy genre. He's a frequent contributor to George RR Martin's WILD CARDS series. Website: www.stephenleigh.com; FB: www.facebook.com/sleighwriter; Twitter: @sleighwriter; Instagram: s.leigh.writer

VIOLETTE MALAN is the author of the Dhulyn and Parno sword-and-sorcery series and *The Mirror Lands* series of primary world fantasies. As VM Escalada, she's the author of the Faraman Prophecy series, including *Halls of Law*, and *Gift of Griffins*. Her short stories are found in several anthologies from ZNB Press, and in Tales From the Magician's Skull. She's on Facebook, she's on Twitter (@Violette Malan). Don't bother checking the website, since it's so out-of-date it'll make you cry. Violette strongly urges you to remember that no one expects the Spanish Inquisition.

ALAN SMALE writes alternate history, historical fantasy, and hard SF. His novella of a Roman invasion of ancient America, "A Clash of Eagles", won the Sidewise Award and his associated novels CLASH OF EAGLES (2015), EAGLE IN EXILE (2016), and EAGLE AND EMPIRE (2017), are available from PRH/Del Rey. His Roman baseball collaboration with Rick Wilber, **T**HE WANDERING WARRIORS, appeared from WordFire Press in 2020, and HOT MOON, his alternate-Apollo thriller set entirely on and around the Moon, will be published by CAEZIK SF & Fantasy in 2022. Alan has also sold 40+ stories to *Asimov's*, *Realms of Fantasy*, and other magazines and anthologies. Find him at www.alansmale.com, Facebook/AlanSmale, and Twitter/@AlanSmale.

About the Editors

S.C. BUTLER lives in New Hampshire with his wife and son. He is the author of the Stoneways trilogy: *Reiffen's Choice, Queen Ferris*, and *The Magicians' Daughter*, originally published by Tor Books; and the vampire novel *The Risen* from Mutable Books. His short stories have appeared in several anthologies and magazines. *When Worlds Collide* marks his fifth editorial adventure with ZNB, and his first short story with them in several years. His novels are available as ebooks from his very Spartan website www.mutablebooks.com, and you can also follow him (irregularly) on Facebook as S.C. Butler.

****

JOSHUA PALMATIER is a fantasy author with a PhD in mathematics. He currently teaches at SUNY Oneonta in upstate New York, while writing in his "spare" time, editing anthologies, and running the anthology-producing small press Zombies Need Brains LLC. His most recent fantasy novel, *Reaping the Aurora*, concludes the fantasy series begun in *Shattering the Ley* and *Threading the Needle*, although you can also find his "Throne of Amenkor" series and the "Well of Sorrows" series still on the shelves. He is currently hard at work writing his next novel and designing the Kickstarter for the next Zombies Need Brains anthology project. You can find out more at www.joshuapalmatier.com or at the small press' site www.zombiesneedbrains.com. Or follow him on Twitter as @ bentateauthor or @ZNBLLC.

Acknowledgments

This anthology would not have been possible without the tremendous support of those who pledged during the Kickstarter. Everyone who contributed not only helped create this anthology, they also helped support the small press Zombies Need Brains LLC, which I hope will be bringing SF&F themed anthologies to the reading public for years to come. I want to thank each and every one of them for helping to bring this small dream into reality. Thank you, my zombie horde.

The Zombie Horde: Cyn Armistead, Kerry aka Trouble, Bregmann, Linda Pierce, Beth Lobdell, Beth Barany, Michael Feir, Jennifer Della'Zanna, Michele Hall, Maxim, Erin Kenny, Thomas Bätzler, AlmostHuman, Larry Strome, Chris, Jennifer Berk, Alan Smale, Lorraine J. Anderson, Pulse Publishing, Tomas Burgos-Caez, Kirsty Mackay, Kevin Lowney, Shayne Easson, P. Christie, Old Man Sparck (TyMcC), Aleis Maxim, Melissa Schultz, Richard C. White, Agnes Kormendi, ChristinecEthier, Wendy Schultz, David J. Rowe, A.J. Abrao, S.Jonda, Andy Miller, Vikki Ciaffone, jmi, Randall Brent Martin II, MJ Silversmith, John Senn, Elissa & Wolf Gray, D. A. Nulf, Lutz F. Krebs, Kammi Davis, Tina Connell, Jennifer Flora Black, George Fotopoulos, Christine Budd, Tim Jordan, William Seney, Cheryl Losinger, J. L. Brewer, Graham Robert Scott, Tommy Acuff, Kayliealien, Krystal Windsor, Erin Penn, Susan O'Fearna, Cyn Wise, Heather N. Jones., Bruce Wesley, Mandy Stein, Fiona Nowling, G.M. Persbacker, Bobbi Boyd, Kelly Wagner, Marian Goldeen, Susan

Simko, Kevin Niemczyk, Lisa Kruse, Ane-Marte Mortensen, Sure. Julie Pitzel, Dan DeVita, John T. Sapienza, Jr., OgreM, David Gillon, Gavran, Paul McErlean, Bex O, Samuel Lubell, Henry Herz, Carol Mammano, Walt Williams, Russell Ventimeglia, Levi Qışın, RM Ambrose, Lorri-Lynne Brown, Louise Dimarcello, Shaina Reisman, Leigh Ann Vaughn, Remnant, Dino Hicks, Dylan Larkin, Patrick Dugan, InarisGuardian, Vicki Greer, Sabrina M. Weiss, Ellen Kaye-Cheveldayoff, Kristine Kathryn Rusch, David Bruns, Pat Knuth, Frances Rowat, Olav Rokne, Nirven, Robyn DeRocchis, Vincent Darlage, PhD, Tracy 'Rayhne' Fretwell, E.L. Winberry, TimBlitz, Sachin K Suchak, Lace, Elizabeth Kite, Venessa Giunta, Robert V Riddell, Cory Williams, Dori-Ann Granger, Chris Brant, Greykell (werewulf!) Dutton, Kate Pennington, Tauna Sonn-LeMarbe, Marc Long, Michael Ball, James Conason, Ron Currens, Cassie A Stearns, Rebecca M, Katherine S, Sandra Bryant, T. England, eric priehs, Patrick Osbaldeston, Sheryl Ehrlich, Kristine Smith, Edward K. Beale, CDR, Fionna O'Sullivan, Duncan & Andrea Rittschof, Yankton Robins, Melissa Shumake, BUDDYH, Niall Gordon, Rae Streets, David Zurek, Samantha Sendele, CRussel, Tania Clucas, Michele 'Neverwhere' Howe, Sharan Volin, Amanda DeLand, Caryn Cameron, Jeremy Audet, Christina Roberts, Jasmine Stairs, Doug Ellis, L. E. Doggett, Gregory D. Mele, Michelle Botwinick, Michael Haynes, David Perkins, Margaret Bumby, Eric, _ALR, Michael Hanscom, Michèle Laframboise, writer & artist, Erin Subramanian, Kimberly Lucia, Tris Lawrence, Jenn Whitworth, Michael Halverson, Cindy Cripps-Prawak, Phillip Spencer, Ian Chung, Jarrod Coad, John Markley, Jeff G., Steven Halter, Jim Landis, Meyari McFarland, Chris Gerrib, Evan Ladouceur, Tanya K., Risa Wolf, Mark Carter, Sidney Whitaker, Ed Ellis, Storm Humbert, Chantelle Wilson, Cat Wyatt, Kristin Evenson Hirst, Sean P. Caballero, Camille Lofters, Brendan Burke, Rick McKnight, Jennifer Robinson, rissatoo, Kristi Chadwick, Michael Kohne, Bill and Laura Pearson, E.M. Middel, TF Newbery, Caitlin Jane Hughes, Shadowlight, Michael Abbott, Judith Mortimore, Konstanze Tants, Megan Beauchemin, Deborah A. Flores, Simon Dick, N. Engel, Susan Oke, Juliet Kemp, Colette Reap, Jim Anderson, Ivan Donati, Mustela, Petrina Hartland, M Smedley, Brenda Moon, Justin Pinner, Louise Lowenspets, Juanita J Nesbitt, James Enge, Hephaestion Christopoulos, Jaq Greenspon, Jenny Barber, Mary Alice Wuerz, Yosen Lin, Bryan Smart, Marsayus, Herbert Eder, Piet Wenings, Eva Holmquist, Jim Gotaas, Kelly J. Cooper, Mei Hua, David Lahner,

Ash Morton, John Schreck, Ian Harvey, A.Chatain, F. Meilleur, Kimberly M. Lowe, Sarah Cornell, Matthew Egerton, Patricia van Ooy, Robert B Tharp, Jesse Sun, K. Kisner, Karen M, Angie Hogencamp, Blair Learn, Bill Drake, MD, Joanne Burrows, Christopher Prew, Ruth Ann Orlansky, Scott Raun, Carl Wiseman, Camilla Avellar, Cracknot, Anita Morris, Michele Fry, Scarlett Letter, Frank M. Greco, Kortnee Bryant, Doug Porter, Beth Coll, Adam Rajski, Jerrie the filkferengi, Martin Greening, cassie and adam, Rosanne Girton, Megan Lewis, Scott Kohtz, Chad Bowden, jjmcgaffey, Richard Parker, Axisor and Firestar, Elaine Tindill-Rohr, Khinasidog, Wolf SilverOak, Beth Morris Tanner, RJ Hopkinson, John H. Bookwalter Jr., Duncan Shields, Teri J. Babcock, The Mystic Bob, Elektra, Brad L. Kicklighter, Lark Cunningham, Jason Palmatier, Christa Bowdish, Ryan Power, Krystal Bohannan, L.C., Ellie Yee, Anthony R. Cardno, Nick W, Carman C. Curton, Jonathan Adams, Anne Burner, Leane Verhulst, Eleanor Grey, Todd Stephens, Aurora Nelson, GMarkC, Patti Short, Ellen Garner Crawford, Stabby the Unicorn, Alison Sky Richards, Michael Murphy-Burton, Margaret St. John, Sam Stilwell, William Leisner, Nancy M Tice, William Rivera, Jeanne Talbourdet, Megan Miller, Ginevra Marner, Lavinia C, SwordFirey, Jeff Conner, DARIN KENNEDY, Karen Fonville, Ichabod Ebenezer, David DiCarlo, Nathan Turner, Jesse Klein, Jennifer Crow, Kathryn Smith, Robert Gilson, Gotherella Biovenom, Emily Randolph-Epstein, Millie Calistri-Yeh, LetoTheTooth, David Holden, Cathy Green, Chris Huning, EM, Sentath, Michael Axe, Taia Hartman, V Hartman DiSanto, Becky Boyer, Colleen R., Steven Peiper, Nora-Adrienne Deret, Craig "Stevo" Stephenson, Sheryl R. Hayes, Lexie Carver, Jo!, Judith Waidlich, Malcolm & Parker Curtis, Katy Manck – BooksYALove, Tom B., Nancy Holzner, Steve Arensberg, AJ Hartson, Todd Ehrenfels & The Science Fiction Society of Northern NJ, Keith E. Hartman, Timothy Pelkowski, Robin Sturgeon Abess, Aysha Rehm, Heather Fleming, Bruce Shipman, Kathleen Kennedy, Hoose Family, Fred and Mimi Bailey, Brendan Lonehawk, C. C. S. Ryan, Tony Pope, Denise Tanaka, Su Minamide, Marcel de Jong, J.P. Goodwin, Walter Bryan, Ashley McConnell, Stephen Ballentine, Richard O'Shea, Nicole Wooden, Corey T, Brooks Moses, RKBookman, David Mortman, Carolyn Mulroney, Joshuah Kusnerz, Christopher Wheeling, Tania, Jörg Tremmel, Tina M Noe Good, John Green, Jill Crowther-Peters, Richard Leis, Alex Langer, Lisa Short, Marcia Franklin, Chris Kaiser, Ronald H. Miller, Matt

Celeskey, Stephanie Lucas, NewGuyDave, Janet Piele, Cliff Winnig, Robert Tienken, Annie Agostini, Steven West, Holland Dougherty, Trip Space-Parasite, Wayne Howard, Helen Ellison, Matt Taylor, Amber N. Bryant, Mark Kiraly, Phoebe Barton, Fred Herman, Brian Burgoyne, Michelle Palmer, Kate Malloy, Camille Knepper, Elise Power, R. Hunter, Gary Phillips, Nick Marone, Benjamin Hausman, Britt Hill, Julia Haynie, Carol Van Natta, Jim Willett, Robert J Andrews II, Anna Rudholm, John Winkelman, Sonya Lawson, Katie Hallahan, Brynn, Michael Barbour, Rolf Laun, Curtis Frye, Jen1701D, Robert Balentine, Jr., James Flux, Shaun Kilgore, Mark Newman, Tibs, Caroline Westra, Robert Zoltan, Kari Kilgore, Carla B, Christine Hanolsy, Marty Poling Tool, Rowan Lambelle, Robert Claney, Kelly Lynn Colby, –Insert Name Here–, Mirranda Prowell, Juli, Kat Hodghead, Anonymous Reader, Jamieson Cobleigh, Carol J. Guess, Keith West, Future Potentate of the Solar System, Bárbara y los Víctors, Dina S, Willner, Lawrence M. Schoen, Nancy Glassman, Nancy Pimentel, Dr. Kai Herbertz, Undead Auna, Elyse M Grasso, Kiya Nicoll, Simone Pietro Spinozzi, Jessica Enfante, Michael M. Jones, Andrija Popovic, Howard J. Bampton, Connor Bliss, Debbie Matsuura, Craig Hackl, Terry Williams, David Quist, Corky Bladdernut, Olivia Montoya, Steve Salem, William R.D. Wood, Robin Hill, Michael Fedrowitz, Judy Lunsford, Céline Malgen, Katrina Knight, C.A. Rowland, Xploder, Stephanie Cranford, Dave Hermann, Holly Elliott, VeAnna Poulsen, Rhondi Salsitz, Stephannie Tallent, C.C. Finlay, James Lucas, Wilma Lingle, Charles Boyd, Sci Fi Cadre, Heidi Lambert, Greg Vose, Ryan Harron, Cat Girczyc, Danni Brigante, Leah Webber, Morva& Alan, Marco Cultrera, Paul D. Smith, Jenny and Owen Blacker, Michael Kahan, Cara Murray, Chris Matthews, Dorian Graves, Larisa LaBrant, Connor Whiteley, Carl Dershem, Andy Dibble, Tory Shade, Jen Maher, Alex Shvartman

Made in the USA
Middletown, DE
14 July 2021